A BAG OF

RED ICE

a novel

by

JAMES NAIDEN

America Star Books
Frederick, Maryland

Softcover 9781681220659
PUBLISHED BY AMERICA STAR BOOKS, LLLP
www.americastarbooks.com
Frederick, Maryland

Also by James Naiden
Summer Poems
Scuttlebone
Crystals
The Chafings of Mortals

Don't worry about dying. Worry about how you live. Go from there.

—*Russian proverb*

Chapter One

Frustration

The grand jury room in the Hennepin County Government Center was high up on the twelfth floor. Police Lieutenant Benjamin Walking Cloud sat next door, waiting to testify in a murder case. The call came from the bailiff and the Lieutenant strode into the room. He took an oath to tell the truth and sat down facing the twenty-one grand jurors.

"Lieutenant Walking Cloud," began Daniel Threebolt, the assistant county attorney, "how long have you been a Minneapolis police officer?"

"Twenty-three years."

"And in that time, you've had extensive training and considerable experience in gathering evidence, interviewing witnesses and suspects in murder cases?"

"Yes, I have."

"How long have you been a detective in the Homicide division?"

"Fourteen years."

"And how long as a Lieutenant?"

"Six and a half years."

"Are you acquainted with the defendant in this case, Walter Germain, also known as Fingers Germain, accused by the people of stabbing to death one John Breamington the third on Sunday evening, the tenth of September, at Rudy's, a restaurant in the near south side located at the northeast corner of Lyndale South and West Franklin?"

"I know Mister Germain, yes."

"Objection!" interrupted Spiggoli, the defense counsel.

"Overruled," said Judge Roberta Jackson quickly. "Continue, Mister Threebolt."

But Spiggoli was adamant.

"Your honor, I—"

"Approach, gentlemen," said the judge, raising her eyebrows in a marked show of impatience. A trim black woman of middle years, she peered intently at them.

"Your honor, the defendant's prior history is *not* relevant here," opined Spiggoli within hearing of Walking Cloud.

"I'm sticking with the Breamington murder, your honor," replied Threebolt. "We cross into that territory only if the defense opens the door."

"And he hasn't yet," said the judge dryly, turning to Threebolt. "So keep it there, counselor. Replacing a grand jury is very expensive."

"Agreed, your honor."

"Continue, Mister Threebolt."

There followed an examination of Walking Cloud's knowledge of the state's case against Fingers Germain.

"So, Lieutenant, the partial thumbprint, the d-n-a test and motive are all present here?"

"Essentially, yes, they are significant enough to convince us that Mr. Germain was the killer."

"Thank you, Lieutenant."

Threebolt sat down. Spiggoli rose and walked slowly past the grand jury members, staring at Walking Cloud.

"Lieutenant Walking Cloud, you say you have a partial thumbprint which bears certain similarities to grooves in the defendant's right thumb, as displayed in the state's exhibition chart here. Is that correct?"

"That is correct."

"But it's not a perfect match, is it? In fact, that partial thumbprint could fit about twenty-thousand other people in the city of Minneapolis alone, couldn't it?"

"I don't know what the statistics are, but yes, it's only a partial."

"So, it's not conclusive, is it?"

"Not by itself. No."

"The thumbprint was also contaminated, wasn't it? Caked in the deceased's blood from his mouth and in contact with extraneous fibers?"

"Yes, unfortunately."

After Walking Cloud's testimony, a police laboratory specialist in fingerprints took the witness chair.

"So, Mr. Miles, in your nine years as a fingerprint analyst, first as an employee at the Federal Bureau of Investigation and now with the Minneapolis Police Department, using the AFIS computer system which can track a fingerprint or thumbprint within a matter of seconds, what are the odds that this print taken from the deceased's forehead is that of Walter Germain?"

"Honestly, I'd have to say the odds are not much better than fifty-fifty. It's not a certainty. Especially with this high degree of contamination."

"Thank you, Mr. Miles."

Following Miles was Martin J. Krewler, known in his boxing days as Marty "Mad Dog" Krewler, who now earned his living both as a waiter at a fashionable French restaurant downtown and as a trainer of pro fighters. In his last boxing match, he fought Fingers Germain but lost a lopsided ten-round decision. Did he now have a grudge? Is that why he was testifying?

"No, I don't have a grudge against him," replied Krewler. "He won that fight fair and square. I retired after that. I'd had enough. I was thirty-three years old. Time for me to quit and do something else."

"I see," said Threebolt. "So what did you see on the night of last September 10th at Rudy's restaurant?"

"I just slipped in there to use the can. Got my hands dirty changin' a tire on my car a short distance away, yuh know. I saw Fingers comin' out-a the john as I was about to go in. I was about to say hello, but he looked very angry as he walked past me. Didn't look my way at all. I went in the can and *there* was this guy bleedin' from the chest, standin' at the mirror, *gaspin'*! He moved toward me. I shoved him back at the shoulders. I was just blown away! I opened the door for him and he staggered out to the lobby. I washed my hands. When I left the john, there was a lot of screamin' and yellin'. People were gawkin' at him. He was on the floor. And then he *died*! Right there on the floor! I got out-a there."

"Did you at any time see a weapon, a bloody knife, stuck in the deceased or elsewhere on the premises?"

"No."

"I show you People's Exhibit C, a color photograph of the deceased taken by the police crime laboratory photographer after he had expired on the floor of Rudy's restaurant. Is this the same man you just described?"

Threebolt held up a photograph and Krewler nodded.

"Yeah, that's the guy."

"Let the record show that Mr. Krewler has just identified a photograph of the deceased, John Breamington the third."

"So entered," said the judge.

It was Spiggoli's turn at Krewler.

"Just one question, Mr. Krewler. Did you see the defendant, Walter Germain, stab John Breamington the night of Sunday, last September 10th?"

"No, like I said, I just saw him comin' out of the men's room. And that was when I found Breamington standin' there, bleedin', with a wound in the rib cage."

After several more witnesses and lab technicians from both sides, the defendant took the stand.

"No, I didn't like the guy. But I never stabbed him! Never even spoke to him that night."

John Breamington the third was a wealthy, ambitious state senator who had been chairman of the crime task force. The previous spring, he had relentlessly grilled Fingers Germain's boss, Abe Aietovsky, about influence peddling, organized gambling, prostitution, distribution of pornography materials and other alleged rackets. He had made enemies. So when he happened to be in the same restaurant that evening where Aietovsky, Germain and another goon named Sharness were having a late supper, his death was too much of a coincidence to let the accused escape a grand jury hearing. Fingers Germain was charged, but it was up to a county grand jury to indict. The people's team, led by Threebolt and supervised by the senior prosecutor, Reginald McCorkle, had their case summed up in an impassioned closing argument to the grand jury members. Spiggoli deftly argued that circumstantial evidence was not enough for a murder indictment, especially with what he claimed was shoddy police work at the crime scene. By mid-afternoon, the jury forewoman indicated through a note to the judge that a decision had been reached.

Solemnly, Judge Jackson spoke.

"In the matter of the people's request for an indictment of first-degree murder against the defendant, Walter Germain, in the death by stabbing of John Breamington the third, what is the jury's decision, Madam Forewoman?"

"We find the evidence inconclusive, your honor. We issue no indictment."

A collective gasp came from the spectators. Walking Cloud's heart sank. He knew the case was flimsy, but let a jury decide after a trial!

"In the people's request for an indictment of first-degree manslaughter against the defendant, Walter Germain, in the death by stabbing of John Breamington the third, what is the jury's decision?"

"Same result, your honor. We issue no indictment."

Not a flicker crossed the judge's face.

"Very well," she said. "The people's case has failed. The charges against Walter Germain are dismissed without prejudice. The people may try again, of course, but if there is a next time, the evidence had better be a lot stronger. Walter Germain is to be released from custody immediately and his bail money exonerated. The grand jury has concluded its work. I thank you all for your service. Court is adjourned."

In the hallway, reporters and television camera people were waiting. Threebolt and McCorkle slowly pushed past them. Walking Cloud and Detective Sergeant Melvin McDour were right behind them, as was their chief witness, Krewler.

"No comment, no comment!" insisted McCorkle to Rhonda Reele, a reporter for the ABC affiliate.

"Will the state try again to get an indictment against Fingers Germain?"

"We're not finished with Mr. Germain, not by a long shot," blurted Threebolt. "He's still our number one suspect in this case."

McCorkle put his hand on Threebolt's shoulder. The younger man had been told not to say anything to the press, but he already had.

"That's all the comment we have, ladies and gentlemen," insisted McCorkle in an avuncular tone.

The gaggle of news media turned to Walking Cloud, who smiled faintly.

"Lieutenant, is your department pursuing new leads or expecting new leads in this case?" a male reporter asked.

Walking Cloud disliked being confronted by reporters. His misgivings on this point had a long history. But he knew better than to antagonize them.

"It's still an open case," he said neutrally. "It's still on the front burner. The Chief of Police will be holding a press conference later today. Beyond that, I can't tell you anything right now. I'm sorry."

Now the bailiffs who were inside the grand jury room appeared and escorted the five men to an elevator.

"What about *me*, Lieutenant?" wondered Krewler as the elevator started to descend. "They're gonna take a run at me. I *know* they will."

"'Let's go to my office, Mr. Krewler," suggested McCorkle. "We're gonna talk about that right now. We'll take care of you the best we can."

McCorkle saw that Krewler was getting paranoid. Providing a police escort, if only a single cop, might be enough to deter an attempted hit, since the danger of a cop getting wounded or killed was something Aietovsky and his associates surely wanted to avoid. Police "harassment" and retaliation were not what they needed if the County Attorney was determined to nail them. The Feds would be shortly behind, anyway.

"We'll watch your back, Mr. Krewler," agreed Walking Cloud.

Krewler was fidgety and uncertain.

Behind his desk, McCorkle functioned much better. At fifty-eight, he had been a lawyer for twenty years, after a frustrating career as a high-school history teacher. After four years in private practice, he joined the County Attorney's office and prosecuted traffic cases at first, then moved up to misdemeanors and small-time crime. Now he was the senior lawyer in the criminal division. The County Attorney, Mike Quinn, was an ambitious pol. He depended on McCorkle to call the shots in most criminal cases, except those that might put him in a favorable image position. The Breamington case had been sidetracked by the grand jury's refusal to indict. The guilty party had for the moment gone free. There was a nervous star witness who had good reason to fear for his life. Casting him adrift would be tantamount to murder. With Walking Cloud and McDour standing like sentries behind Krewler, McCorkle faced him across his desk.

"You came through for us, Mr. Krewler," said Threebolt, leaning against a bookcase. "We'll protect you. We still need you. Don't worry."

"In other words, we're not through with your services in court yet," joined McCorkle. "We're gonna take another shot at that s.o.b.—*and* at the whole Aietovsky empire! We need the Feds to cooperate. They're interested in Aietovsky because of his back taxes—not reporting income from bookmaking and prostitution rings. So far they've been playing it close to their chests. Haven't shared a goddamn thing with us, except when it's suited their purposes. There were a couple agents from the F.B.I. in the courtroom today. Did you notice?"

Krewler shifted in his chair.

"Yeah, well, so what does that do for *me*?"

"It means—since this is still a case under our jurisdiction, and not yet the Feds—we'll continue to provide you with a bodyguard at all times. Assuming of course that you'll agree to testify again against Fingers Germain."

"Course I will! You think I'm crazy? I'm in too deep now!"

A knock on the door. Four people entered with badges on their jackets. Three men and a woman.

"As usual, we'll have a number of cops working round the clock to be with you, Mr. Krewler," said McCorkle. "Each officer works a six-hour shift. So there'll be a cop with you at all times. Every time you go somewhere, there'll be detectives monitoring your movements, keeping in touch as your constant companion. Now the defense attorney, Spiggoli, convinced the grand jury that what you saw was only circumstantial, but you're the closest thing we got to an eyewitness. So we need you alive and well. And until the Feds take over the case, that's what we're gonna do. You'll continue to work the details of your daily movements with the Lieutenant and his people. We've kept in touch with your boss at the restaurant where you work and he's been fully cooperative. Says you're a good waiter."

"Yeah, well, I work at it. I gotta! I'm the only one payin' my bills."

"Right. Well, good luck. We'll be in touch."

Glumly, Krewler got up to leave with Walking Cloud and his detectives.

"Ben, you gonna take part in that press conference with the Chief of Police?" asked McCorkle.

Walking Cloud smiled ruefully.

"Don't think I can get out of it, Reggie," he said.

McCorkle sighed.

"Right, I know."

After the door closed, Threebolt sat down in front of McCorkle.

"I suppose it was my fault the grand jury didn't buy it. I'm sorry, Reggie."

McCorkle looked surprised.

"Don't be! I thought you did just fine. I'm going to tell that to Quinn, too. There was nothing wrong with how you handled it. The problem was with our evidence. We gotta find something *more*. Don't beat yourself up about it. Tomorrow's another workday. I gotta talk to Quinn. Go home, Dan. Get some rest. You put in a long day."

"Night, Reggie."

Chapter Two

Old Reconnaissance

Meeting his lady was always a pleasure, especially now that they were in domicile together. Daniel Threebolt and Julie Tinkham were an attractive pair. He drove up to the front of her office building. She slid quickly into his BMW.

"Hi, how ya doin'?" she said, leaning over and kissing him on the cheek.

"I'm fine. How are you?"

"Just peachy. Had a good afternoon in deposition. Covered a lot of ground. How's the murder case going?"

"Not so good, I'm afraid. The grand jury didn't buy it. They refused to indict Fingers, so the judge let him go."

"Oh, I'm sorry, Dan."

"Yeah, well, our case wasn't that strong. McCorkle seemed to take it in stride. Now he wants to find more evidence and try again. Quinn's pushing to get an indictment, no matter what. Says the Aietovsky empire's gotta be brought down. Fingers Germain seems like the best road to doing that, they think. Of course, it'll make Quinn look good for the next rung up the political ladder."

They turned a corner and went up a hill.

"You still want to go out to dinner?" she asked.

"Sure, if you're still game."

"I am. Where'll it be?"

"How about Rudy's? That's where Breamington was killed, you know. Maybe I'll get an insight about this case."

"That's fine. Why don't we park the car in the building and walk down?"

"Okay. Good idea, Julie girl."

"I'm not a girl, Danny boy."

He laughed. So did she. Then he touched her knee. She put her hand on his there, squeezing it with the strong hint of pleasure to come. He pulled into the underground entryway of his condominium building. They freshened up in his apartment. She gently resisted his advances at first, suggesting it would be the tastiest of nightcaps. He had only to agree. But then she sank to her knees, and he submitted to the delights of fellatio. Afterwards, they lay on the couch, still dressed, and he asked, "Want to watch the local news? It's almost six."

"All right."

"I'm going to tape it, just for kicks."

The first image on the screen was the darkly handsome image of Benjamin Walking Cloud.

"Jesus, I saw him less than two hours ago!" exclaimed Threebolt.

Walking Cloud stepped aside, and Chief of Police Bellicoast went before the cameras and microphones.

"As the Lieutenant just told you, this will be a full-time, ongoin' investigation. We are proceedin' carefully and will handle this case, going back to square one, in a thoroughly profess'nal manner at all times. "

"What a windbag!" said Julie, laughing.

Threebolt switched channels, but found the same event with a different visual angle. As the scene shifted from the press conference to the studio, the blonde anchorwoman launched into a profile of the deceased:

At the time of his murder, forty-two-old John Breamington the third was serving his fifth term in the Minnesota state senate and had been considered a likely candidate for governor…

With her voice-over, there were still shots alternating with file footage of Breamington, scenes of him shaking hands and hobnobbing with a succession of politicos as well as business people. This was followed by footage from the previous Christmas season when Breamington was at a benefit for the Crippled Children's Fund. In this scene, there was a petite dark-haired woman who looked familiar to Threebolt demurely clutching Breamington's elbow. Threebolt wondered where he'd seen her before.

"Hey, I've seen *her*!" Julie exclaimed.

Now the scene shifted back to the studio and the blonde female anchor began happy talk with a male counterpart.

"You mean the little brunette?"

Threebolt clicked off the VCR.

"Yes!"

"So have I. But I can't place her. Can you?"

He ran the tape back, clicked it on again and pressed the pause button.

"Oh, sure! Wait—I don't remember her name, but I think she was at a reception Matt Safony threw!"

"Who's Matt Safony?"

"A lawyer downtown, with Dayton, Shoals & Safony."

"Oh, yeah, sure."

"Anyway, she was there. It was a reception. I got the impression she had something to do with some money venture Safony's into, but I'm not sure. Their office is in our building. I wasn't introduced to her, but she didn't stay long. I've also seen her in the skyway or somewhere. I just can't—"

"Think you could ask around discreetly and check on it for me? It may be nothing, but knowing who she is might help. Strange, isn't it? How you can overlook something important in preparing a case?"

Two miles away, in an apartment on the West Bank, Jenny Schell was watching the same program with footage of herself standing next to Breamington. Her new lover—actually an old boyfriend from years before, a blond, aging Bohemian by the name of Greggie Fitzie—was in her bed. In the other bedroom was her twelve-year-old daughter, Laura, supposedly doing her homework but more likely watching MTV videos.

"Hey, there you are!" said Fitzie. "Were you fucking that guy, Jenny? I knew you mixed in some high circles in your business contacts, but where'd ya meet him?"

Jenny smiled forlornly.

"He was a client. I handled his portfolio. I just couldn't handle him very well. So I ended it. But he kept his account with us. Which was a surprise. Say, let's not talk about the past."

Fitzie had a boozy smirk. He was on his third rum-and-coke. He put his drink on the night table.

"Naw, let's not. You're right. Come here, babe. Let's get down to business."

"You've got to watch your drinking," she said. "You're already drunk, aren't you?"

She flicked off the t.v. and climbed on top of him.

His performance at the press conference had been adequate, Walking Cloud thought. Probably better than his testimony on the witness stand. He didn't like the media, but Chief Bellicoast insisted only because the Mayor was pressuring them. Breamington's death could not be relegated to the "case unsolved" files and then forgotten. Walking Cloud always felt unclean after dealing with reporters. He knew it was an irrational reaction. Nonetheless, he wanted to go home and take a shower before deciding what to do about supper. He managed to escape to the underground parking garage as soon as the press conference was over. The temperature outside, a balmy 55 degrees for late October, was perfect for running. But he decided to put that off till morning. Every other day, usually in the early mornings before work, he jogged around Lake of the Isles, only three blocks from his condo in Kenwood. After showering, he impulsively decided to dine at the scene of Breamington's death five months earlier. Perhaps something he hadn't seen before might occur and help nail down the case against Fingers Germain. It didn't seem to him that others might have the same idea.

"I haven't been here for a long time," said Julie after she and Threebolt were led to a table next to the window with an unremarkable view of Lyndale Avenue.

"Nor have I," said Threebolt. "Maybe it's the location, the busy corner. Anyway, here we are."

He admired his lady sitting across from him. Oh, she was beautiful—with her curly brown hair around a face that mirrored perfection. Pert, ultimately feminine lips within a delicately fair complexion, a slightly upturned nose, blue eyes that registered the most compressed but singular beauty he'd ever seen. She reached across the table suddenly and touched his face. He took her hand, kissing it briefly. She smiled and pulled his hand to her mouth, licking and kissing it.

"I've wanted you ever since I first saw you, Julie," he said. "Now we're together—but—"

"Don't," she said softly. "Why but? Your caveats, Daniel! Don't you respect the here and now? I'm not quicksilver. Don't worry."

"Yes, I know. But—answer me a question."

"Answer you a question?" she replied, looking worried. "Your locutions are a wonder, Daniel. I'll answer your question, as long as it's not about marriage."

He was dismayed. He did not like this restriction. He did not like being teased or straitjacketed or held back. He loved her, period.

"Why?" he asked. "Why can't I ask you to marry me? I have a profession, one we have in common. I have a good salary. I'm stable. No offensive habits. You've never complained of any, anyway. I get along fine with your parents. They seem to like me. What else is there? I'm ready, Julie. I—"

"Daniel Threebolt! Again! How marvelous!"

A familiar voice again. Threebolt thought he might be hallucinating. Looking up, he saw the plaintive, inquisitive mug of Walking Cloud.

"Lieutenant! How are you?"

"Fine, just fine. What a coincidence, Daniel! Don't you agree?"

"I don't—know. I mean, I don't know if it's really that much of a coincidence. We just saw you on t.v.!"

He introduced Julie to the Lieutenant, and invited him to join them. Not surprisingly, Walking Cloud demurred, uttering a little white lie. The white lie, not really a lie, was that he needed to contemplate the scene of the six-week-old crime on his own. But he added that perhaps they might talk again a bit later. Socially, he seemed to imply.

"That would be great, Lieutenant," said Threebolt.

"All right!" exclaimed Julie.

Threebolt was surprised. *Such a radiant young white thing! This boy does not deserve such goodness from his own kind*, Threebolt guessed of Walking Cloud's subtly amused reaction to Julie and her exclamation. The detective nodded politely and the hostess led him to a table across the room. Walking Cloud's veneer was nearly inscrutable, much to Threebolt's submerged annoyance. Threebolt wanted to be agreeable in Julie's presence.

"He's very attractive, Daniel," she said. "Even more so in person. How long have you known him?"

"About two years. I've been dealing with him on the Breamington case and a couple other matters before that. He testified before the grand jury today. Spiggoli got him to admit that the partial thumbprint wasn't conclusive evidence."

A waiter appeared at their table. Julie ordered a light seafood plate, Threebolt spaghetti and sausage. Small dinner salads were served first. He was still smarting from her refusal to discuss marriage. But he had to pretend otherwise, and he did. Moodiness was something he'd had to learn to control, subdue, and banish from his demeanor. Nothing was more alienating to one's lover than pouting or irritability.

Julie suddenly looked toward the doorway.

"Oh, my! Look behind you, Daniel."

A television crew had just arrived.

"Oh, Jesus!" Threebolt muttered.

Across the room, Walking Cloud also frowned when he saw Rhonda Reele and her cameraman talking to the hostess. They were approached by a well-dressed man, who might be the restaurant manager. Rhonda Reele raised her hands and smiled with that ingratiating paste-on expression that t.v. news people like to display when nothing else works. When the waitress came to take his order, Walking Cloud asked her what the t.v. crew wanted. The waitress was about fifty, short dark red hair, and waspishly thin. Probably smoked cigarettes, he guessed. She had what a good novelist once described as Smoker's Face.

"Oh, they wanted to shoot footage of the area where that politician was stabbed to death a few weeks ago. They saw you sitting here, too. That female reporter said you're a policeman? I'd never have guessed it. Well, the manager told them not to bother customers while they're eating. Management's always a little nervous, anyway. It's not like we really need more publicity about that guy's gettin' killed, ya know."

"Right."

"But they can't stop them from doing their thing outside on the sidewalk. Guess they have their orders, too."

"Were *you* here that night? Did the police interview you? I don't remember if—"

"Oh, yeah! My name's Helen Wister. I gave 'em a statement. Just once, though. They never came back. Never asked me to testify. Just as well. Everybody else talked to 'em, too. Told 'em what I saw, which was the guy staggering from the Men's Room, the pay phone area over there, and he falls on the floor! Well, hey, Mister, I don't wanna spoil your appetite. Do you need a few minutes to look at the menu?"

"Yes, that'd be nice. Thank you."

He remembered her name from the reports. The details were all too familiar. He watched Rhonda Reele, and then Ronn Mason, a reporter from a competing station, take a look around. Walking Cloud had already done the press conference with Bellicoast, supposedly his final task of the day. In the Lieutenant's view, reporters instinctively went for sensationalism instead of substance or factual accuracy. Over the years, he'd had brief encounters with them in murder cases, but usually managed to avoid getting burned. Had they spotted Threebolt, sitting with his back to them as he ate and talking with his girlfriend? Did it occur to them that the young assistant prosecutor would be a much more likely news source? Threebolt and his colleagues at the HCA's office would ultimately be responsible for putting away Breamington's murderer. It was his job to make sure an indictable defendant was delivered.

"Are you ready to order now, sir?" asked the waitress.

He ordered a steak sandwich with all the trimmings and a glass of one-percent milk. This was a small luxury he intended to enjoy fully before figuring out how he would evade the t.v. reporters.

"Daniel, things will work out if you take your time and not rush it," said Julie. "We needn't hurry into anything. When the time comes, I'll know. Be patient. Will you? We're together, and being together means finding out about each other, seeing how it might work if—"

"If what?" he probed.

She smiled, lifting her right index finger over her fork.

"If we decide to go permanent. Notice I didn't use the 'M' word."

"I noticed. Do I sound crazy? Insecure? Don't answer that. I get your drift. Well, how's your meal? Mine's delicious."

Julie had a sublime expression, as if pushing her lover back, if only a tiny bit, was what she needed in order to breathe. Threebolt knew this, too. They ate in silence for a minute or two. Then she said, "Come up with any ideas yet on what happened here when Breamington was—stabbed?"

"No, I've been paying attention to you, my dear, and intermittently to Walking Cloud over there—and now these reporters."

Julie's eyes diverted over to Rhonda Reele and her cameraman, who was sitting at a table not far from Walking Cloud.

"Rhonda Reele's after a story here. Wonder if she's noticed you here yet."

"I'm sure she will. You've got the best seat, my dear. You get to look at everyone here and I just get to look at you. Which normally would more than be enough, but—"

"Come and sit by me," she said laughingly. "That way you can touch *and* see. Come on."

Threebolt got up and slid beside her, his right hand immediately landing on her thigh. With a grin, she gently removed it.

"People may get the right idea about your intentions, Daniel. First look at the view—and Rhonda Reele."

What Threebolt noticed first were the variously subtle expressions of Walking Cloud, who was observing discreetly the news reporter and her cameraman.

"Daniel," said Julie, "now you can put your hand in my lap."

"Dessert?"

"A form of dessert."

He put his hand in her lap, then on her thigh.

"Not too obvious," she said.

Threebolt peered again at Walking Cloud. The detective, he suspected, was furtively looking back at him. Walking Cloud was eating a meat sandwich with a fork.

"That policeman looks over here," Julie said. "He's not obvious, but he steals a glance every so often."

"Yes, I know. He admires your beauty."

Julie laughed.

"*Tosh*! He may have noticed me, but he's thinking. He's thinking—and not necessarily about women. He's thinking about business. He'd never have looked at me twice if I weren't with you, Daniel."

"*Tosh*, Julie! *Tosh*!"

She laughed.

"Let's not spend too much longer here," she said. "I want you to take me back up to the apartment so—"

"So we can dine on each other? We will. Everything in due course."

"You've never missed course yet."

Anticipation was almost as pleasurable as the act itself. Threebolt pondered the sweep of love as he and Julie had known it. They had first met a party. Didn't lawyers almost always meet at parties, if not in the course of their daily work amongst each other? Of course, she had been with someone else. Threebolt came alone. It didn't take him long. Two days later, a Monday morning, he called her at her firm and asked her to lunch the following day. She accepted, and the rest flowed naturally. Since then, neither had spent time with anyone else. Not that the opportunities weren't there. Threebolt, for one, was focused—and grateful, even a bit stunned, to know that she was happy with him.

As he ate, Walking Cloud was aware that Rhonda Reele would soon approach him. He tried to ignore her. He contemplated the particulars of the Breamington case and what he thought was the probable guilt of Fingers Germain. His thoughts were interrupted by a sudden exclamation from Rhonda Reele.

"Excuse me," she said to her cameraman, who had put his machine on a chair and was studying the menu. "Won't hurt to try, will it?"

She got up from her seat and went over to him, treading lightly.

"Pardon me, Lieutenant. Rhonda Reele, Channel Five news? May I talk with you for a second?"

Walking Cloud looked up at her. There were lightly etched crows' feet around her eyes, an excessive tinge of eyeliner and turquoise mascara with a dyed tint of yellow and auburn in her thick hair, the original color somewhere deep in her roots. She had firm white teeth, although two or three in her lower front jaw were uneven. The large orange-bead necklace was garish against her white blouse and gray jacket and skirt. There was a small mole on her left cheek. Her body looked trim. Walking Cloud appreciated trimness.

"Sure, ask away. But I'm here on my own time, not the city's."

"I understand. Here's my card. We're here to do a follow-up about—"

"The Breamington case and the grand jury's refusal to indict Germain. Right?"

"Yes. But I didn't expect to see *you* here, of all people. You know, at the press conference, I couldn't tell what was going on. *Does* the police department still regard Fingers as a suspect? Could someone else have been involved and *not* him?"

"Off the record? I'll be glad to talk to you, but off the record only, Rhonda."

"Fine. Off the record, then."

"You may as well sit down. Okay, Fingers Germain had motive as one of Aietovsky's goons and he had opportunity. He's suspected in at least four other killings here and elsewhere across the country since he quit boxing four years ago, but no one's been able to nail him for any of those crimes. It's always possible he's not guilty of this one, of course. His lawyer drove home that point by convincing the grand jury. Hence, reasonable doubt. No indictment. What more can I say? It remains an active case, of course. It's back to the beginning. Fingers is a prime suspect, but we're going to look in other areas, too. I can't tell you anything more."

Rhonda Reele's manner seemed tentative now. He knew she must think he was going to be difficult. She turned on her smile.

"Do you have another suspect in mind?"

"Can't comment on that. Sorry."

"Even off the record?"

"Even off the record."

"Okay, how do you plan to proceed now in this case?"

"Digging, plain and simple. Going over the crime lab reports again, the m.e.'s report. Forensics can tell us a lot. Maybe we overlooked something. Checking out witnesses one more time for corroboration, consistency. One thing leads to another. We may get a break. Maybe not. But we keep at it. That's how murder cases are usually solved."

He leaned back in his chair, took a sip of milk.

"Don't look now. But the young couple seated in the booth in the far corner over there may be of more interest to you than I could possibly be."

He nodded vaguely in their direction.

"That's Dan Threebolt, the assistant county prosecutor who tried to get the indictment against Fingers. He's with his girlfriend, Julie. I think she's also a lawyer, but in private practice. Dan and his bosses at the HCA's office are eager to get an indictable suspect. Why don't you talk to him?"

Rhonda Reele quickly glanced at Threebolt and his companion.

"Yes, I saw him at the courthouse. I got him to speak before an older guy cut him off. Just a minute. You're not leaving right away, are you?"

"I'll be here for a little bit."

She traipsed away, looking like a hawk about to strike.

"That's weird," observed Threebolt. "You see that?"

"Rhonda talking to Walking Cloud?" said Julie. "Couldn't help but notice."

"Now she's coming over here, it looks like."

Rhonda Reele came straight at them.

"Good evening, Mr. Threebolt. Rhonda Reele, Channel Five News?"

"Hello," said Threebolt. "If you want to talk about the Fingers Germain case, I'm sorry. I have no comment. Since I'm on my own time here, I'd rather pass on any other questions."

"Oh, well, I'm just doing my job. I—"

"So am I when I tell you No Comment. Mike Quinn's the one to talk to, if he's available. I'm sorry. I'd rather not."

Having failed to entice him, Rhonda Reele gave him her card and went away.

The Lieutenant wasn't surprised. She had let out a cast fly, but no bite.

"You knew he wouldn't talk," she said almost accusingly as she sat down again across from him.

Walking Cloud kept a straight face.

"I knew he'd have almost nothing to tell you. But it's his call whether to talk to you or not."

"Shit."

Walking Cloud let a small grin cross his face. He knew she wanted to probe, fish, or sift for whatever she could use in a story. Damned if she was doing to use him as a source. Still, she might prove useful. No reason to antagonize her. That wouldn't help.

"If we arrest a credible suspect in this case again—when we do, rather—the news media, including you—will be notified. I suppose Threebolt will still handle the case. What else can I tell you?"

Rhonda Reele got up with an exasperated look.

"Alright. I know when I've been sandbagged. Talk to you later."

She went back to her table. Her cameraman was eating a piece of apple pie with ice cream.

Time to go, Walking Cloud told himself. He decided he would come here again, Breamington's murder and its aftermath notwithstanding. Threebolt and his girlfriend were paying their bill.

"Good night, Lieutenant," said Threebolt. "Probably talk with you again soon, I'm sure."

Walking Cloud nodded with a half-smile.

"Good night," he said.

Walking Cloud paid his bill and handed the waitress a two-dollar tip.

"What-cha got there, Jenny?" mused Greggie Fitzie, sprawled on the king-sized waterbed in his underwear, sipping more hard booze. Was it scotch-on-the-rocks or more rum-and-coke? Jenny didn't care. As long as he behaved himself, she told herself she could put up with the situation. Greggie had his good points, more often when sober. Her own attempt at sobriety after intensive treatment had been successful for almost thirteen years. It led her to conclude that staying sober was a matter of mind over body. Drinking compromised one's success and ability to perform, as well as relationships with others. It was like high finance. Knowing when to hedge a bet, float a security, wait out a downturn on the market.

"You're hungry? No, stay there. I'll get you a little dish. Stay. I'll get it."

She went back to the kitchen and arranged a small plate of the Chinese food she'd bought earlier in the evening and had just warmed up. She served it to him, and then went in the bathroom. When she emerged, Greggie had almost cleaned his plate. He was watching a rerun of *Kojak* on cable.

"Did you enjoy it?" she asked. "I picked it up at Ho Tan's after work. Chinese is just the right thing for a light meal."

"Really," he agreed. "Thanks, Jenny. It was good."

The detective show was over. She took the plate and fork back to the kitchen and rinsed them.

"Gotta pee!" Greggie exclaimed. As she came back into the bedroom to watch the 10 o'clock news, Greggie was slowly hauling himself to his feet. He staggered toward the bathroom. She switched to the Channel 5 News. The lead story was the grand jury's refusal to indict the presumed killer of John Breamington the third. Jenny sat down on the hard wood edge of the waterbed. Her daughter suddenly appeared, leaning on the doorframe.

"I'm not tired yet," she said, "but—can I watch a little more if you're gonna stay up?"

"It's time for you to go to sleep, Laura. School tomorrow. Did you finish your homework? Weren't you supposed to read a geography chapter and do some math problems?"

"Yeah, I did all that," she said, her face now clouded by fatigue and a vestige of stubbornness.

"Alright, go ahead. But get ready for bed. I'll come tuck you in pretty soon. I just want to watch some of the news."

Laura's face brightened as she disappeared.

The newscast began after what seemed like interminable commercials. Finally, there was the lead story, the same as four hours earlier. Behind the anchors were still shots of both Jack Breamington and Fingers Germain, and then a switch to reporter Rhonda Reele who narrated old file footage, beginning with scenes of a Christmas party. On Breamington's left was none other than Jenny herself.

"Jee-sus!" she muttered, suddenly gripped by apprehension. She never really wanted it, of course. Not any of it. It had only been a fleeting relationship. The fact that he had been a client didn't matter. He pursued her, not the other way around. There was Rhonda Reele's voice but now a cutaway scene of an afternoon news conference with Lieutenant Walking Cloud poker-faced before the media. His voice was steady and masculine. Another reporter spoke up:

'Lieutenant, are there any new leads as to who killed John Breamington now that Fingers Germain has been exonerated by the grand jury?"

'He wasn't exonerated by the grand jury. What they said in effect was that the evidence wasn't strong enough to issue an indictment. They did *not* go beyond that. We can bring the case against him again. As for new leads, we'll be looking into that, taking a new look at everything to do with the case. We're asking the public's help in this. If *anyone* has any information about the senator's death last September 10th in Rudy's restaurant, we ask that you please come forward. All names will be kept in strict confidence.'

Now Rhonda Reele asked a question:

'Lieutenant, are you aware of any political enemies of Senator Breamington who might have had motive in this murder?'

'We'll be looking into that again. At this point, we have no conclusive leads other than circumstantial evidence pointing toward Mr. Germain. But we have a lot of ground to go over again and a lot of people to talk to yet. Thank you very much.'

Walking Cloud stepped away from the microphones, and the scene shifted live back to the studio and the blow-dried male anchor.

Jenny now became aware that Greggie Fitzie was retching in her bathroom.

"You slovenly bastard!" she said quietly. He couldn't hear her, of course. Was he puking in the toilet or on the floor? It was pathetic. If she could stay away from the retches, why couldn't he? Why did he have to drink so much? How did he ever get his work done, anyway? His art work, his poems, his miniature cartoon stories that occasionally found their way into print. His disability pension because of wounds in Vietnam freed him from having to work a regular job. So he occasionally went on his little 'toots'— days of uninterrupted boozing without working at all. Jenny remembered this pattern from their earlier time together. The mid-70s. 1975, to be exact. Which was why she moved out and eventually went into treatment. She had to work, be productive, get up in the morning and be presentable in the hustle bustle of nine-to-five. Especially now with a child. Without this discipline, wallowing in self-indulgence, Greggie was paying the price in her bathroom. She sighed and tried to focus on the newscast and the saga of Jack Breamington and his demise.

Chapter Three

The Day After Nothing

The next morning before work, Walking Cloud went jogging around Lake of the Isles. The morning air was delicious. His body rhythms were steady and unhampered by fatigue. He ran easily, gliding almost. He made it a point to run every other morning. Along with a sensible diet, not overeating, he had always managed to stay trim. At six feet, he had never strayed above 185 pounds. At 45, he felt good about his body, his work, and his life. His romantic life, however, was missing an essential ingredient. Since his wife's death six years earlier during childbirth and then losing the child as well, he had stayed free of serious romantic involvement. Her death hadn't lost any of its poignancy. Every woman he dated after a year of grieving passed he inevitably compared to his late wife. He knew this, too, was irrational. He had never gone to a shrink, not even to grief counseling. When his annual talk with the police psychologist came up, he avoided talking about it. But he did talk about his loss the first couple years with a close friend in the Native community, Robert Tall Bear, who had lost his first wife some years earlier and had remarried after four years alone. More recently, however, Walking Cloud and Tall Bear discussed grief less and less, preferring the joys of hunting with bow and arrow in the northern reaches of Minnesota or camping and fishing in the Boundary Waters Canoe Area. As he neared the end of his run, turning off the lake path toward his home, Walking Cloud made a mental note to contact his friend again about another hunting trip this winter. Tall Bear, a social worker for the county specializing in the Native community in Minneapolis, could be counted on for good companionship when Walking Cloud wasn't traveling elsewhere.

Across the city, Jenny Schell was angry with Greggie Fitzie. She drove him to a coffeehouse at 13th and Hennepin. Before he got out, she informed him that if he wanted to see her again, he had to stop drinking. Penitential but unconvincing, Greggie said he'd call her in a day or two.

"Don't bother to call," she warned him, "unless you're really serious about what I said, Greg. I mean it."

When he got out of her car, he seemed to have heard her. But she wasn't sure. She waited for the light to change and watched him enter the coffeehouse. She also knew her own weaknesses. Although it had been thirteen years since she'd had any alcohol, just being around a drinker could weaken her resolve. While it had been three years since she'd stopped going to AA meetings, she knew temptation might suck her back into an alcoholic's life style. She was both revolted and strangely captivated by Greggie Fitzie. Now as she drove to work in the heart of downtown Minneapolis, she wondered fleetingly about an evening without an intimate visitor.

Up early and vibrant were Daniel Threebolt and Julie Tinkham. Since today was his birthday, she had made plans to take him to dinner at the Loring Pasta Bar. Normally she would have met him for an evening run around Lake of the Isles, but instead she wanted to do some shopping and maybe get her run in after that. He would go to his health club. Then they would meet at the Loring at 8 o'clock. He dropped her off at her residence where she kept her car. She kissed him good-bye and wished him Happy Birthday.

At his office in the Hennepin County Attorney's suite, Threebolt prepared to negotiate a plea agreement with the public defender about the Hobart case, involving a Thugs gang leader who was accused of participating in the gang rape and savage beating of a fifteen-year-old girl. Just the kind of case that made him sick when he first began work at the HCA's office, but now it was fairly routine. Plea bargaining had become daily fare. After reviewing the Hobart case again, there was a court appearance at 10:30, lunch with an old law school buddy who was meeting him in the cafeteria downstairs, then back to the grind.

In the old courthouse across the street from the Hennepin County Government Center, Walking Cloud had just entered his office. First to approach was Sergeant Joshua Mygosh.

"Joshua, come on in. What's doing this early in the morning?"

Mygosh, a trim man in his early forties, had twenty-two years in as a cop. Instead of going to law school as he'd once planned after putting in his twenty, Mygosh decided to stay on. His respect for lawyers waned because he'd seen too many culprits go free after a lawyer's courtroom finagling which had nothing to do with guilt or innocence.

"Am I one of the lucky cops who gets to spend time with Krewler? I'm not really looking forward to it, Ben."

"I'm afraid so, my friend. If it makes you feel better, I may even put in a shift myself from time to time."

"Good. You can jog with him then. He told us last night after you left that he wants to take up running again. Wants to get back in shape."

"Not for a return to the ring, I hope."

"Naw, said he just needs to toughen up. Maybe it'll help his nerves, he thinks. You're a jogger, so…"

"Well, that's an angle, isn't it? Yes, I'm up for that. Krewler doesn't seem like such a bad sort, anyway."

A knock on the open door. It was Detective Bill Rails, Mygosh's partner.

"Morning, Lieutenant. I got a chalkboard up for the Krewler detail. Yuh know he wants to take up joggin' again?"

"So I heard."

"Hey, I'm no jogger," said Mygosh. "I play tennis. I eat light. And my wife lets me have a couple beers a week."

"Don't look at me," said Rails. "I play squash, a little golf. That's it."

"And both you guys are middle-aged like me. Running's great! Why don't you try it?"

"Hey, Beth Winchell jogs," offered Rails. "So does Martridge. There yuh go."

The three men went into the day room. A couple perps were handcuffed to chairs while detectives were doing paper work on them. The phone rang. Mygosh answered. Rails and Walking Cloud stared at the chalkboard.

"Krewler wants to go runnin' tomorrow, he says," Rails observed. "Hey, it's his life! What can we do?"

"We stick with him," said the Lieutenant. "He agreed to stay in the jurisdiction as a material witness. His safekeeping is our responsibility, like it or not."

"I don't care," said Mygosh, now off the phone. "But I don't want to go sauntering around Lake Harriet with him."

"I've already had my run this morning," said Walking Cloud. "I see Winchell's paired up with him tomorrow afternoon. That'll work. Just make sure there's a squad in the vicinity."

"We got that covered, too," Mygosh said.

Walking Cloud nodded approvingly.

"Okay. What's the deal on that shooting at King Park this morning?"

The workday progressed. Windup for lunch. And after an hour or so, back to it. The afternoon, and a visit to the morgue where a new homicide victim had just been autopsied. Then a rereading of interviews with witnesses at the scene of Breamington's murder. Walking Cloud knew better than to be obsessed with any case, but the killing of a prominent politician only six weeks earlier was still hot. If not Fingers Germain, then who? He kept reading, his notepad handy. Something had to turn up.

The phone rang. It was Threebolt at the HCA's office.

"Lieutenant, I saw something on t.v. last night that got me thinking. There was one person I don't think we ever interviewed.

I don't know her name, but she was standing next to Breamington at a party last Christmas season. My girlfriend, Julie, whom you met last night, recognized her. Said she works or has something to do with Matt Safony in the Norwest Building. But she doesn't know her name or just where she works. I'm faxing you a black-and-white picture from my VCR tape of last night's newscast. It may be nothing, but she might know something."

"Sure, Dan, send it over. I'll let you know. Can you hang on to the tape? We may need to see that, too."

"You bet. If you need it, I'll send it by messenger."

At this point, Walking Cloud would take what he could get. He looked out his office door. The fax machine was right across the room. After a few seconds, it started to move. A black-and-white pix of the deceased with a clear image of a petite younger woman, clutching his arm and looking up at him with a smile. Mygosh joined him.

"Whatcha got there?"

"Recognize her, Joshua?"

Mygosh frowned.

"Can't say I do. But Bill might. Hey, Rails! Over here!"

Rails took a look and grinned.

"Hey, yeah, that's Jenny Schell! When I was in vice about three years back, she was a witness in a trial. A lawyer named Matt Safony was up on a charge of defrauding his client for a lotta bucks. But he got off. Jenny Schell testified for the defense, I remember. Isn't that Breamington with her? Where'd yuh get this?"

"Threebolt got it off the Channel Five news last night. He couldn't place her, but his lady friend recognized her. Said she works in an office high up somewhere in the Norwest Building."

Walking Cloud picked up the phone.

"Dan, Walking Cloud here. Send over that tape. That lady's name is Jenny Schell, an associate of Matt Safony, a high-stakes lawyer on trial for fraud a while back. He got off, and she testified for him. We're interested in her. She might know something."

"Right-o, Lieutenant. Tape's on its way."

Jenny Schell finished her workday an hour early and left for some errands before picking up her daughter. She stepped into the elevator and was met by the smiling, polite face of a beautiful younger woman who looked familiar. But Jenny couldn't place her, unless this person was merely one of many nameless faces she saw downtown every day. The younger woman's oval-shaped features within light brown hair, her trim figure at just over five-four, her quick smile—all were qualities of the well groomed and successful. In fact, the younger woman was Julie Tinkham, who had in turn recognized Jenny but was careful not to show it other than the demure smile mask she always wore in public.

"God, I'm glad these elevators are fast," said Jenny, impulsively turning to the other.

"Yes, I am, too," said Julie. "Do you—work in the building? I'm sure I've seen you before."

It seemed like an innocent remark. Jenny returned the smile.

"Yes, at Schell and Broad Securities. Thirty-third floor. And you?"

"On the thirty-sixth. I'm with Benson, Shoals and Crisp."

The two women continued talking in a manner reflective of their professional statures, although it was Jenny, her only job training after high school a series of business courses leading to her broker's license, who experienced a sudden terror of inadequacy, belying her calm demeanor. Here was a younger woman, genuinely beautiful, much better educated, speaking with her as if they were equals. No telling how much better read and traveled she was. But then Julie didn't know about Jenny's background. In the first floor lobby, they exchanged business cards. There was an implied acquaintanceship that might go further. They also discovered they were headed to the same underground parking lot. That morning, accommodating Greggie Fitzie, Jenny had taken her car to work. Otherwise, she preferred the short bus ride from her West Bank neighborhood.

"You're a lawyer? What kind of law do you practice?"

"Corporate, mostly. Insurance. Municipal bonds. Pretty dry stuff. But it's a steady practice. I'm enjoying it. And you? You're in investments?"

"Yes, securities. Market speculations. Capital ventures."

The way to the underground parking lot was through a long corridor, then another elevator down to the three ramp levels. Now into the elevator came three more people: a slightly overweight, well-dressed man with gray hair, carrying an attaché case, a tallish middle-aged woman with an olive complexion who carried a near-overflowing shopping bag, and a pale-skinned young man with a pitted face and cropped dishwater blond hair under a black cap. While Julie paid no particular attention to any of them, Jenny noted especially the pale-skinned young man. There was a wild look to his pockmarked face that unnerved her, but also made her feel a kinship with her new acquaintance, a bond of mutual comforting. At level A, the gray-haired man departed.

Julie smiled at Jenny.

"What level are you parked on?" she asked.

"On C. How about you?"

"C, too. I'm at the far end. I usually get a ride with my boyfriend or just take the bus. But I drove today because it's his birthday, so I'm taking him out to dinner. I've got to get him a present first."

She looked on matter-of-factly as the olive-complexioned woman put down her shopping bag and looked briefly in her purse. Now Jenny saw the pitted-faced man's gloved hands. Perhaps they were scarred or otherwise disfigured, she thought. It happens sometimes.

A level C, the pale young man with the pitted face seemed to wait for the others to leave. Jenny looked at the middle-aged woman, who smiled at her for an instant with a curved mouth and big teeth. After everyone else departed, the pitted-faced young man left, too.

"I'll walk with you to your car, Julie," said Jenny. "This is a scary place to go through alone. That guy in the elevator was creepy."

Julie laughed.

"Oh, he looked harmless enough. I appreciate it, but I'll be fine. Really! Don't bother. Say, why don't we have lunch? I know a little Greek place near here that has the most exquisite soups and breads. Are you free tomorrow? Why don't I call you?"

Jenny looked around. The pale man with the pitted face had vanished. Perhaps her sudden anxiety was groundless. He wasn't anywhere in view, so he couldn't be a stalker. Her new friend's confidence was infectious.

"Lunch tomorrow?" said Jenny as they stopped next to her old yellow Cadillac. "Uh, sure. I don't normally go for lunch, but why don't we? That'd be good."

Julie smiled again and offered her hand.

"Great, Jenny. I'll call you, say, about quarter of twelve?"

"Alright, talk to you then."

With that, Julie smiled and waved good-bye, then walked down the half-lit row of cars. Jenny watched her for a few seconds. Without looking around again, she unlocked her car door, got in quickly and locked the door. Inside the big vehicle, she felt more secure. A Cadillac, even one more than a decade old, was a mark of esteem, if not security. Jenny drove up the ramp to the street level.

Julie reached her car and unlocked it. She heard a sound behind like footsteps and started to turn around, but a gloved hand came around and over her mouth. She was spun around. A fist struck her in the jaw. She was thrown on her back on her car seat. She was conscious enough to realize her pantyhose were being pulled off and her skirt lifted. Suddenly, she was choking, desperate for breath. She was being pulled forward again. Something struck the back of her head and she lost consciousness.

On the street, Jenny turned on her car radio. The bass-voiced announcer was guardedly upbeat. "And you gotta wonder, folks in Viking land, how the one-time purple people eaters of the '70s are gonna do in their next game. Can Tom Moss lead 'em to the playoffs? We think so. You're tuned to W-C-C-O! Keep it right here!" Next was the theme of band music and barking dogs. Jenny waited till she got to a red light and switched the radio off. She wondered about Julie and where the young man with the pitted face and gloved hands had gone to. But Julie was probably just fine. No need to worry. Jenny thought of Greggie Fitzie. How could she help him? She couldn't. She could only keep him away if he became a problem. There was her daughter to consider. She turned the radio back on, but there was only static from one station to the next. She turned into a service station and switched off the engine. She had to put some air in her right front tire.

In his office, Daniel Threebolt was enjoying himself. While the Breamington case was on hold, there was a likely guilty plea from a previously stalwart suspect in an aggravated assault case. Today was also his birthday. His lady was taking him out to dinner. They were to meet at eight o'clock for a late supper. First, he would go to his club for a workout, which he'd devised himself, a medley of pulling and pushing on various nautilus machines followed by a three-mile jog around the inside track.

"You got a minute, Dan?"

It was McCorkle in the doorway.

"Sure, Reggie. What's up?"

"How long will it take you to run down the possible pleas we can accept on the Hobart case?"

It was just the case Threebolt had been thinking about. The victim was still in the hospital. McCorkle and Threebolt had originally been assigned to work it together, but since McCorkle had a conflict, it turned out to be Threebolt's ball to carry. Because McCorkle might have to appear at the next stage of the proceedings, they had to juggle the levers of what the state was willing to offer as justice.

"I took it in court last Thursday through preliminary. His public defender—Bob McNee—told me he wants a deal. I told him we'd need the names of the other gang members who were with him that day and Hobart's willingness to testify against them. It's two counts of first-degree sexual assault if he refuses."

"Agreed," said McCorkle.

"And there's false imprisonment, aggravated assault, one count each of deviant sexual conduct and aggravated theft. If he cooperates, we might reduce it to a single count of second-degree assault but a minimum of seven years. He's got a five-year juvenile record. Whaddya think?"

"Sounds good to me."

"Will the judge buy it?"

McCorkle shrugged.

"How long has the victim been in the hospital?"

"Ten days. Detective Blumus says she's just too scared to name anyone more than Hobart, and she did that only when her mother coaxed her. Then she just clammed up."

"Scared. She probably got threats," suggested McCorkle. "Let's keep a daily tab on it. All right. Oh, I hear Happy Birthday's in order! How old are you?"

"Thirty-two. Julie's taking me out to dinner."

"She is? Well, good! She's a pretty lady, Dan. Gonna marry her? I would, if I were you. She's radiant."

"Thanks. I agree. She really is. I'm trying, believe me! It takes time with her. She won't be rushed. She'll come around."

"I'm sure she will. Well, have a good time. See you tomorrow."

"Goodnight, Reggie. Thanks."

Suddenly, Threebolt liked McCorkle much better. He had never discussed his personal life with him before. That the older man was sympathetic to his most intimate desire was mildly surprising. At the club, he started slowly on a succession of nautilus machines with weights and pulleys. He did stretching exercises and walked half a lap before starting his run. As he ran, more a trotting jog than running, he felt his system on high, his legs flowing naturally. Now the small hubbub of the others moving around him in the gym was part of his rhythm, the sweat and flow of muscles and energy.

Mike Quinn left the Hennepin County Attorney's suite of offices precisely at five o'clock. With him was McCorkle. They walked together slowly down the hall and across the high overhead walkway to the elevators.

"Didn't hear from Threebolt today," said Quinn. "Any word from Walking Cloud about what more he's finding in the Breamington case?"

"No, not yet. I just talked with Dan. He didn't mention it. We talked about pleading the Hobart case if he turns state's evidence. The victim's clammed up, but she did identify Hobart in a mug book."

"Yeah? Is she still in the hospital?"

"Yep, been ten days now. McNee in the P.D.'s office says Hobart might go for a deal. State's evidence in exchange for one count of second degree sexual assault and seven years. We'll see."

"Sounds good. Remind me. Who's the judge?"

McCorkle made a dubious face.

"Rapstone."

"Jesus Christ, Reggie! She's on a bender in that area. You gotta make sure we get our share!"

"Easier said than done. But we'll try. Dan took it through preliminary last Thursday. McNee's such a goddamn bleeding heart."

Quinn chuckled grimly.

"Yeah, I know," he said. "And all these grandstanding black community leaders scream bloody murder! The thing is if the victim had been *black*—well, shit. Keep me informed, Reggie."

"You got it."

"I'm just worried—"

The elevator stopped at a middle floor. Two women with civil service in their eyes entered. Quinn spoke in a very low voice, almost a whisper.

"We just can't let him off with very much, if we can help it."

McCorkle nodded sternly. The elevators opened on the first floor. Quinn and McCorkle walked through the lobby and took the escalator to the underground parking lot.

"Today's Dan Threebolt's birthday," said McCorkle.

"I know. I signed the card for him. How's he doing?"

"Fine. Pays better attention to these high profile cases, the details, than the smaller ones. Knows how to negotiate pretty well. He's also in love. Have you seen his girl?"

"You mean Julie?"

"Yeah, she's a beauty. God, how did that sonovabitch luck out!"

"She's with—"

"Benson, Shoals and Crisp. Yale Law. Very sharp, I hear. Nice little buns, too. But don't quote me."

Quinn threw his head back and laughed as they entered the underground parking lot.

Chapter Four

Death for a Birthday

Walking Cloud stood up and stretched, suppressing a yawn. It was the end of his shift. He was in the mood for a hot dog with mustard and potato salad on a bed of lettuce, one of his favorite meals, with ketchup close by, of course. He had received word only moments earlier that Detectives Richard Peterson and Carol Blumus were going to meet at a little café up the street from Rudy's. Peterson was taking over from Blumus as Marty Krewler's bodyguard. Then at midnight, a detective from vice would take over from Peterson. Homicide and vice both had an interest in protecting Krewler from harm, since bringing down the Aietovsky empire was a common goal. The place was the Red Feather Café, where Krewler had chosen to have supper. It was owned by a Native woman, Mary White Eagle, and her husband, a white man from Maine. Walking Cloud knew them. Their cafe had a distinctly American cuisine with some Native dishes on the menu. Walking Cloud decided to go there, then home for a light nap before venturing out to the Loring Pasta Bar and the music of Cornbread Harris and his combo. The Lieutenant locked up his desk and departed.

The atmosphere was friendly enough. Mary Light Eagle greeted him with a hint of surprise. He sat at the counter and studied the menu, which was varied, including several maize dishes. No sign of Blumus and Krewler. Peterson hadn't arrived yet, either. Walking Cloud ordered his hot dog with potato salad. Mary grinned.

"That's a white person's meal, Ben," she smiled. "Indians gotta eat better than that."

Walking Cloud appreciated her banter.

"I knew you'd say something like that. Don't you remember my fondness for hot dogs? I love 'em!"

"I remember. I was hopin' you'd grow out of that before you die. But we got hot dogs and potato salad. Anything to drink?"

"Glass of one-percent milk."

Walking Cloud picked up a newspaper on the counter and skimmed a feature article about the Breamington murder case. Presumably, he thought, this will be in the police clip file. The writer surveyed significant accomplishments of the dead man's career in politics and included a quote from County Attorney Mike Quinn: "Jack Breamington was a go-getter. I knew that about him when we were both in law school together twenty years ago. He would have been successful in politics at a higher level if he'd lived. His absence will be keenly felt in next year's political races. We'll find his killer, despite this setback, and that person will be punished to the fullest extent of the law." An ironic statement, thought Walking Cloud, from the one person most likely to benefit politically from Breamington's death. Walking Cloud put the newspaper down. The cafe was moderately full. New customers were entering—among them Krewler and Carol Blumus. They both smiled when they saw Walking Cloud. They sat down across the counter. Mary Light Eagle put glasses of water and menus before them. Krewler looked much more upbeat than he had the previous day.

"Lieutenant, yuh got some good people workin' for yuh."

Detective Blumus grinned.

"Oh, you mean Carol?" said the Lieutenant.

"Yeah, she's a nice lady. I suppose she's a pretty good cop, too. Right, Carol?"

"I try to be," said Blumus, still grinning, her face tanned, her blue eyes alert.

"You're getting along well, then?" said Walking Cloud. "Good. One of these days I'll be taking a shift with you myself, Mr. Krewler. I'm a jogger, you know. I've been told you've decided to take that up again."

"Yeah, I gotta get back in shape. I feel heavy. What's the word you used, Carol? Leth—?"

"Lethargic."

"Yeah, lethargic," affirmed Krewler. "I've been havin' trouble keepin' up my energy level."

"You're scheduled to be with Detective Winchell tomorrow afternoon," said Walking Cloud. "She's a jogger and will keep up with you, I'm sure."

Mary Light Eagle came to take their orders. Detective Peterson arrived and sat down next to Blumus. A minute later, Mary brought Walking Cloud's meal with the milk and glass of water. Walking Cloud acknowledged Peterson.

"Dick, you get to enjoy Mr. Krewler's charm the next few hours, I assume?"

Peterson smiled wanly. Blumus grinned nonchalantly, her dark locks bristling against the light in the room.

"Lieutenant," said Krewler, "you know, I'm kinda surprised to see you here. Use-ly this place attracts everyone *other* than the police."

"Well, I'm not here on business, Mr. Krewler. Just came in for something to eat."

"All due respect, but every cop I've ever known, including Carol here and Detective Peterson—I mean, you guys are *always* on duty, whether you're pullin' a shift or not."

"Well, we had a good time together, didn't we, Marty?" kidded Blumus.

She smiled in such a way that Walking Cloud wondered fleetingly what it meant, if anything. He decided it didn't matter.

"Yeah," said Krewler, turning to Blumus. "Like I said before, you're nice to be around."

Blumus nearly blushed. Walking Cloud observed that Peterson noticed this, too.

"I mean, if you guys aren't piecin' together somethin' for a case, you're checkin' somethin' else out. Like a chess game. Isn't that what it's all about?"

Krewler's grin was almost cruel, thought Walking Cloud. He was also chatty, even garrulous. Walking Cloud did not want to get into a verbal sparring match. Peterson and Blumus began to chat low-key with each other. Walking Cloud looked back at Krewler. His hot dog and potato salad were still untouched.

"As I said, I'm just here to have a meal."

"Yeah, I'm sorry, Lieutenant. Hey, what you got there is about as American a meal as you can get. Looks good."

Walking Cloud put a trace of mustard on the hot dog and lifted it to his mouth. Everything he wanted at this moment was in the tartness of the hot dog. He remembered his first hot dog as a boy no more than five. His father had taken him and his sister to the county fair in Bemidji. When they stopped at a concession stand, his father explained what a hot dog was. The fat red-haired woman behind the counter smiled with a mouthful of bad teeth. It was the first time Benjamin could remember seeing a white person with bad teeth. He went slowly with his father and sister down the fairway while they ate their hot dogs. Benjamin had mustard on his cheeks. His father laughed and bent down to wipe the mustard off his face with a napkin. Benjamin remembered this was the kindest face he had ever seen. They continued down the fairway. A few stares, but "don't stare back," said his father.

Walking Cloud looked on as Mary Light Eagle took food orders from Krewler, Blumus and Peterson. Then Krewler reached over and took out the sports section of the newspaper. He began reading while Blumus and Peterson resumed their conversation, Peterson suddenly laughing.

"You a sports fan, Lieutenant?" Krewler asked.

"Yes, I am. Baseball. Ice hockey. Basketball. Hunting with bow and arrow. Boxing."

"Boxing?" replied Krewler.

"Yes, I was an amateur pug on Indian teams up north before I came down here to attend the University. It's been a long time now."

"Really! I didn't know that. Yuh know, I had a pretty long amateur record myself. Six years' worth. Then I turned pro but somehow my incentive didn't last. Toward the end I didn't train as I should have. Maybe it was my divorce that took it away. I don't know."

"Let's see. You had a pro record of twenty-six and five, sixteen knockouts. Your last fight was a ten-round loss to Fingers Germain back in oh-eight. That was *his* last fight, too, by the way. And his record wasn't as good as yours. Longer, but he lost a lot of fights toward the end."

Krewler's expression was agape. Then he frowned.

"How did you know—all that?"

Walking Cloud took a bite of his potato salad. He said, "I make it my business to know if I might need to know, Mr. Krewler. I pulled your sheet when you came forward as a witness. Nothing on it so serious you haven't recovered from it. Fingers Germain is a much different story. But that's neither here nor there. Man, this potato salad's good!"

Krewler looked puzzled. Mary Light Eagle brought his omelet.

"Think you and Ben can share that ketchup bottle?" she asked.

"Sure we can," said Walking Cloud, who put the ketchup bottle near Krewler's plate. "Don't have ketchup normally with a hot dog, but it's nice to have as a backup. Relax, Mr. Krewler. Enjoy your supper."

Now Mary brought Blumus a maize dish with corn on the cob. Krewler stared at his omelet and picked up his knife and fork. Disconcerted, he was still hungry. He began to eat.

Walking Cloud finished his meal. Mary gave him his bill. He settled up with her and left a dollar bill next to his plate. He turned to Krewler.

"I'll be seeing you again in a day or so. Don't try to do too much with your jogging right off. Do a mile or so, then walk. You haven't run in quite a while, I'll bet."

"You've got that right," said Krewler. "I need to take some pounds off. That's why I'm doing it."

"Right. Carol, Dick, check in with me on my beeper if you need to. Any time."

Both detectives acknowledged this with nods of the head. Walking Cloud waved good-bye to Mary. He was looking forward to a short nap.

Threebolt completed his three-mile jog and walked a lap. He surmised that Julie was doing the same thing around Lake of the Isles. As he showered, he washed his hair. Minutes later, he left the health club refreshed and looking forward to the evening with Julie. His birthday. Thirty-two. He felt like twenty-two. Unlike ten years ago, he was now in a good profession and was finally seeing a woman he wanted to marry. Life couldn't be better. Before meeting Julie, however, he decided to go home and check his mail. What he found were phone messages from his parents and brother wishing him Happy Birthday. There were a handful of birthday cards, a bill, and some junk mail. He looked in the bedroom mirror, then went into the bathroom and reached for his electric shaver.

Walking Cloud lay on his bed, trying to induce sleep. He reviewed the Breamington case as he knew it so far. According to the forensics report, the partial thumbprint in blood taken from Breamington's face was similar to Germain's print taken at the time of his first arrest for shoplifting thirty years earlier. But the blood-caked partial was smudged, so the resultant configuration led only to a probability instead of a conclusive result. No match on the AFIS network. No discernible DNA strands were evident, either. No murder weapon was ever found. Might Krewler be a factor, too? Unlike Germain, he had no motive. And unlike Germain, his sheet had only two misdemeanor offenses. Krewler was a material witness. Walking Cloud's mind wandered. Sleep was closing in. His father's face came before him. Gone six years now. Walking Cloud looked back to the summer of 1978. He was eight years old. His father, a police officer on the Reservation, had come home in mid-afternoon and found him practicing for a tribal archery contest. Behind them, their small gray house glistened amidst a chorus of pines, maples and spruce. Benjamin turned back on the target and aimed the arrow carefully, pulling the string back in the manner his father had taught him. He released the arrow, which landed in the outermost ring. His father said something about the positioning of his feet. Benjamin adjusted his stance. "Now try it again," his father said. Benjamin took another arrow, pulled the string back and released the arrow. It hit within the bull's eye. "Excellent!" his father said calmly. Their relationship, always affectionate when he was growing up, grew into mutual respect as he matured. Walking Cloud's memories drifted into the fog of sleep.

An hour and a half later, he suddenly awoke with a feeling of doom. He couldn't identify it. Perhaps it was only a slight depression, a sensation he'd had before upon waking. He knew enough not to confide this to the police psychologist whom he saw once a year. His anxiety and depression subsided when he washed his face, another ritual discovered many years ago. Washing one's face or bathing, showering, the mere act of cleansing oneself, has a spiritual as well as a physical dimension. Without this knowledge, there was a strong possibility he would never have made it through the police academy, much less won promotions in the two decades since. To the Loring Pasta Bar now and the music of Cornbread Harris with Fred Jackson on bass fiddle. Walking Cloud was looking forward to a mellow evening of blues, a part of American culture Native peoples had never embraced that much. They had their own versions of the blues.

It was nearly eight o'clock. Threebolt drove across town to the Loring. When he entered, he inquired about the reservations. He discovered they had been made in Julie's name, not his. It was her treat for him.

"Your table will be ready in a moment, sir," said the slender blonde hostess in a slight Gallic accent. "If you like, you may have a drink at the bar. I'll let you know."

Threebolt approached the bar. The other patrons were well-dressed younger people. Threebolt had never been here before, although he'd heard about the Loring. Movie and stage actors, writers and film people were known to frequent the place. Cornbread Harris was performing tonight, he overheard the bartender tell the man next to him. Who was Cornbread Harris?

"A blues piano player," said the bartender, a small dark-haired woman, perhaps in her early thirties. She had a near-Grecian face resembling a youthful image of Barbara Stanwyck. She smiled at Threebolt when he ordered a scotch-on-the-rocks and a glass of ice water. A drink before dinner wasn't a habit, but this was a special occasion. He turned around and looked across at the large windows. It was past twilight. He sipped his drink. It was now eight-fifteen. It was unlike Julie to be late. He wondered what could be holding her up. The hostess came over to him.

"Your table is ready, sir. You may bring your drink, if you like."

Threebolt followed her to a table next to the window. The University of Minnesota was a block away. In less than a minute, a sandy-haired young waitress appeared. Threebolt explained that he was still waiting for someone. She handed him a pair of menus and indicated she'd return shortly. Then it occurred to Threebolt that Julie might have gone somewhere else. But where? Dinkytown wasn't that big. He got up and went into the bar where a series of tables were put together. Two men were playing chess at a corner table. He turned to see a familiar face enter the premises. It was Benjamin Walking Cloud.

"Lieutenant, what brings you here? Not business, surely?"

A wry grin crossed the Lieutenant's face.

"Mr. Threebolt, such an unexpected pleasure! No, I just came here on my own to hear Cornbread Harris and his group. His bass fiddle player is a friend of mine."

"Well, they're playing now. Julie's treating me to dinner for my birthday. But she's not here yet. Why don't you join me for a few minutes while we both wait?"

"I'll be glad to keep you company. Happy Birthday!"

They shook hands. Walking Cloud emitted a rare cordial smile. They went back to Threebolt's table near the window. The waitress came up to them.

"Is this your other party, sir?" she asked.

"No, he's just visiting for a few minutes. Lieutenant, can I buy you a drink?"

"Well, since you're offering, I'll have a light tap beer."

"Right away, sir," said the waitress.

Threebolt looked at his watch. It was past eight-thirty.

"She's more than half an hour late. This isn't like her at all. She's always so punctual."

Walking Cloud recognized the signs of worry in the younger man.

"She'll turn up," he said. "Don't you know it's a woman's privilege to be fashionably late? It's the way they are sometimes."

Threebolt looked mollified. They engaged in small talk at first, but then more serious matters came up. Threebolt was clearly distracted by Julie's tardiness, although he managed to keep a train of thought otherwise.

"Are you going to question the woman in the picture I faxed you? What was her name again?"

"Jenny Schell. Yes, we'll contact her and see what she knows. It's a long shot."

"Could Aietovsky be the killer, you think?"

Walking Cloud frowned. Aietovsky was a consummate sleazeball, but actually murdering an enemy himself would be an act of incredible stupidity. Unlikely, but not impossible.

"We covered that before we went to the grand jury. Remember? I don't think so. Both he and Sharness are under surveillance. We want to see where they lead us. Also, of course, vice has an interest in them."

Threebolt looked at his watch again. It was now almost eight-forty-five.

"Where *is* she?" he wondered out loud.

The tinny sounds of piano music were heard from the stage. Cornbread Harris was starting up again after a break. The waitress came to the table again.

"Sir, would you like to order some food while you wait?"

Threebolt ordered another scotch and a dinner salad.

"Think I'll catch some of the music over in the bar," Walking Cloud said. "I can't stay out too late. Do you have Julie's license number and the make of her car handy, Dan?"

Threebolt frowned. He ran his fingers back through his hair and swallowed hard.

"Jesus!" he said. "Yes, I do. Do you need it now?"

"Let's wait a while yet. It may be nothing to worry about if she suddenly walks in here. Have you tried her cell phone?"

"Yep, no answer."

Threebolt invited the detective to stay at his table. The musicians had gathered on the small stage across the room. The waitress served Threebolt a steak dinner with several kinds of vegetables, sprinkles of something white around the edges of the plate, along with another scotch. It was now nine exactly. Walking Cloud's hot dog with potato salad had fortified him plenty. On stage, an older black man played the piano with three sidemen, including Fred Jackson who alternated on trumpet. Walking Cloud recognized "All Blues" from Miles Davis. The music rose to a crescendo and up through a flourish to the finale. The audience clapped sporadically. Now came a pause. A trim young white woman in a black leather skirt and yellow blouse approached the stage and handed Cornbread a small piece of paper.

Threebolt slowly ate his meal. While his appetite was low because of his increased anxiety, he had downed more than half his second scotch. Julie had not yet appeared. He took out his cell and tried her home number again, but her roommate didn't know anything. He called her cell number again and left a message. Then he dialed her law firm. Her voice-mail message came on and he left another message. He was very worried.

Walking Cloud's attention was riveted to the stage. Julie's face, her mellifluous voice, came to Threebolt above the hubbub. He sighed, knowing something was terribly wrong. Julie had still not appeared. Walking Cloud admired Cornbread's rapid-fire piano soliloquies in "Muskrat Ramble"—where he inserted a few notes of "Happy Birthday To You" within the main melody. An ironic twist. Then it was on with the trills, the drums and cymbals, the percussionist tapping and brushing with perfect timing. Walking Cloud finished his beer. When the waitress came to their table, he ordered another. His third, he noted. He looked at Threebolt, who looked beside himself. The movement of the bar-restaurant life around him was oddly soothing. He felt free, if only for a short while, from the pressures of his job. Threebolt had left the table and gone into the bar, he noticed. Cornbread started another number and began singing in a richly melodious voice:

When the shadows of the night are fall-ing,
How the winds are call-ing…

Now a soft melody with more sweet-toothed lyrics:

I tell you that I love you.
What more can I say…

All with a brisk tempo, more cooing words, the piano trills up, then up again, and the repeat of "fall-ing, call-ing"—ending on a crescendo with a soft drum roll. Applause was stronger this time. Cornbread announced another short break after which they would play "Cherry Red" and other requests. The musicians left the stage. Walking Cloud knew this should definitely be his last beer. Better not stay for the next set. It was already nine-fifteen.

"Good evenin'," came a familiar voice.

It was Fred Jackson, who stuck out his hand. Walking Cloud grasped it.

"Enjoy your music, Fred!"

Jackson nodded with a grin, then turned to Cornbread Harris behind him.

"Cornbread, meet my friend Benjamin Walking Cloud. He came for the music."

Cornbread and Walking Cloud shook hands. The piano player looked curious.

"Howdy, your name is—"

"Walking Cloud. Benjamin Walking Cloud. I just told Fred I'm enjoying the music. Glad I came down."

"Well, thank you," replied Cornbread. The waitress handed him a greenish web-shaped glass of liquid. "The four juices. No booze in this drink."

"That's smart," said Fred Jackson.

Cornbread inquired about Walking Cloud's line of work. Walking Cloud told him. Cornbread's eyes bulged very slightly.

"We need good policemen," he said, half-nodding once. "I been readin' 'bout that senator who got murdered at Rudy's—and that thug who got off. I spoze your people are still workin' that one real hard now."

"Yes, it's an active case. No suspect in custody. You know, it's a relief to come in here and just listen to good music. It's very relaxing."

"Well, I'm glad you like it," said Cornbread. "We do what we can and we appreciate our audience. We workin' musicians *need* good audiences. We got a two-night gig here this week."

Laughter nearby. Someone greeted someone else. Cornbread laughed at something a red-haired woman said. Walking Cloud checked his watch. Nearly nine-thirty. Just then, Threebolt came back from the bar. His expression was blank, even stark. He sat down at the table, nodding politely at the musicians sitting with Walking Cloud.

"Lieutenant," he said intensely, "she's now two hours late. I've called every place she might be. Even a couple lawyers at her firm. No one knows anything, except that she left her office about 4:30."

Walking Cloud looked at Cornbread Harris and Fred Jackson.

"Gentlemen, something's come up. You'll excuse me?"

"Sure thing," said Fred Jackson.

Walking Cloud turned to the distraught Threebolt.

"Come with me."

In the bar, Walking Cloud took out a cell phone and pressed buttons.

"Give me her name, what she looks like, height, weight, what she was wearing when you last saw her, her car license number and auto make."

Walking Cloud conveyed this information to Rails in the Homicide squad room.

"Check the hospitals, the morgue," he told Rails. "If you don't find her, put out an a.p.b. She was supposed to have gone jogging around Lake of the Isles. Start at her law firm in the Norwest Building on the thirty-sixth floor. Then see if her car, a 2010 Buick Skylark, is still in ramp C."

"Lieutenant," said Rails, "are you thinkin'-a comin' in on this one? If it's bad news—"

"Call me. Start at her law firm and go from there. She's not the sort to disappear whimsically."

"Will do, Lieutenant."

Walking Cloud looked at Threebolt.

"Anyone you should notify about this? Her family?"

Threebolt sighed again.

"Her parents. They might like to know."

Threebolt made a call on his phone. Julie's father answered. Threebolt told him Julie was missing.

"I don't want to alarm you, George, but this isn't like her at all."

"No, it isn't," said the voice on the other end. "We haven't talked to her since when—well, Sunday, wasn't it, Jean?"

Julie's mother came on the extension, her melodic voice not unlike her daughter's.

"Daniel, how late is she?"

"More than two hours. I've called everywhere I can think of. Left messages. No one has seen her since she left work at 4:30."

"Oh, my god! Oh, Julie!"

Threebolt suggested they talk to Walking Cloud, standing beside him.

"Lieutenant, what division of the police are you in?" asked Julie's father.

Walking Cloud took a deep breath.

"I'm head of Homicide, Mr. Tinkham. Which is why I know Dan Threebolt. We've worked on a few cases together. He and I just happened to run into each other tonight when I came here off-duty. He's very worried."

Walking Cloud tried to fill up a stunned silence on the other end by giving them the police department's number and his own cell number. Then he said, "We'll let you know as soon as we know anything. We'll find her."

He ended the conversation as best he could. Awkwardly, he looked at Threebolt.

"That's the worst kind of call to make, especially when we don't know what's happened to her."

The Lieutenant then convinced Threebolt to go home and wait for his call. There was nothing else to do. Walking Cloud knew Threebolt had every right to go downtown and start looking for his girlfriend just as the police were doing. Threebolt looked very tired. He went back into the café to pay his bill. Walking Cloud returned to the table to finish his beer. Cornbread Harris and his musicians were back on stage.

Mygosh and Rails were pulling the evening shift on top of their regular day hours. Walking Cloud had put limits on the overtime his officers could work. Now he called in with a missing persons report. Not only that, but the person had been missing for only four hours. Hardly earthshaking. That she was Threebolt's girlfriend was different. Even so, it wasn't something the homicide squad would handle. Let's go, shrugged Mygosh. The Norwest Building was the last place she was seen.

At the Norwest Building, the detectives found a cleaning service inside the law firm's offices. A cleaning woman pointed to an open door halfway down the hall. On Julie Tinkham's desk were some legal documents and correspondence in two stacks. Pink message slips were near the landline phone.

"Nothin' here to indicate much of anything," said Rails. "Looks like she left expecting to return in the morning. Next place is the parking ramp."

With the help of building security, the detectives found parking ramp C, and very shortly the 2010 Buick. Walking Cloud's beeper was a vibrator in his pocket. He called in and was patched to Mygosh's cell phone.

"Ben, we found the young lady's car in ramp C," said Mygosh. "You better come down here. We also found a woman's shoe outside the driver's door. The vehicle is locked. What now?"

"I'll be right down. Cordon off the area. Call in the crime lab. We'll need to sift it."

A basic question faced Walking Cloud. Should he call Threebolt? To do so would mean Threebolt's immediate appearance at the Norwest parking ramp. Not to do so would probably damage a good working relationship with the Hennepin County Attorney's office, at least in the short run. The last thing he needed.

"Dan, we've located Julie's car. It's at Norwest ramp C where she left it this morning. It appears not to have been moved."

"I'll meet you there."

Walking Cloud wanted to get there ahead of Threebolt. He attempted to speed it up by using his flashing light and siren. Light rain sprinkles came as he raced out of Dinkytown to the

Third Avenue Bridge and then into downtown. He got to ramp C just ahead of the crime lab technicians. The area was already cordoned off by yellow tape. The technicians wanted to go to work, but Walking Cloud asked them to wait. Within a few minutes, Threebolt sped up in his BMW. He jumped out and rushed over to the Lieutenant, who gestured to the shoe left on the escarpment.

"Is this Julie's?" he asked.

Threebolt's eyes widened. Then a look of horror overcame him.

"Julie!" he shouted. "My god! *Yes, it's hers! Where is she*, Lieutenant?"

"I don't know," said Walking Cloud. "Dan, listen to me carefully. We're going to let the crime lab people go to work here. We're going to pick the door lock and then the trunk. Unless you have an extra set of keys for her car. Do you?"

"No. No, I don't."

Walking Cloud gestured to Rails, who inserted a shimmy rod and the car door was opened. With plastic gloves on his hands, Walking Cloud looked inside. Then he withdrew, holding a set of keys.

"Are these Julie's keys, Dan? They were on the floorboard."

"Jesus, yes! That's her key chain!"

Walking Cloud nodded to the technicians, who began dusting the vehicle. With a key from Julie's ring, Walking Cloud opened the trunk.

"*Julie!*" screamed Threebolt. "*Julie!*"

Mygosh and a uniformed police officer held him back. Curled up and twisted inside was the partially disrobed corpse of Julie Tinkham, her eyes and mouth open, a bruise on her left cheek, blood caked around her nose, her skirt raised to her upper thighs, her blouse torn away with her right breast exposed. Walking Cloud's nausea was barely controlled. He turned away, and then looked at Threebolt.

"Julie! Let go of me, goddammit, you bastards!"

Walking Cloud nodded to Mygosh and the blue. Gripped firmly, Threebolt was allowed to view the remains of the woman he loved. Then he was coaxed away, weeping and shuddering.

The sights of death's aftermath: the photographing of the corpse as found, the combing of the crime scene for clues, hairs, and DNA strains, then the removal of the body into a dark plastic bag, and the towing of the death vehicle to the police impound laboratory. Above all, the picture taking. The persistent snapping of photographs.

Chapter Five

Wondering Why

Walking Cloud felt great compassion for Threebolt, who had been robbed of the woman he loved in the most brutal way imaginable. Nonetheless, he had to get a statement from him. In the Lieutenant's office along with Threebolt were McCorkle, who had been called in, Mygosh, Rails, and a stenographer. Threebolt had taken a sedative and was coherent, his face splotched with emotion. His answers were slow, as if a trance had been induced. He told them when he last saw Julie alive. Did she have any jealous ex-boyfriends lurking about or had anyone been stalking her? Threebolt knew of no one in either category. Beyond this, it became clear he had no other useful information.

"Lieutenant," said the grieving man. "I better—call her parents. They—".

"We've already done that," said Mygosh. "The Tinkhams are coming in to make formal identification."

"A psycho's on the loose," said McCorkle. "Julie—just—happened to cross his path."

"We'll catch this creep!" affirmed Rails.

Walking Cloud stood up. He said, "We should have the forensics report by noon. The coroner's report will take a little longer."

The desk phone rang. Walking Cloud answered it. It was Rhonda from Channel Five News.

"Lieutenant, the word's out that a woman was murdered in the Norwest parking ramp. Can you confirm this?"

Walking Cloud put his hand over the receiver.

"The media! Rhonda Reele's on to this already! My God, doesn't she ever sleep?"

"Next of kin's been notified," Mygosh offered somberly. "No reason not to tell them."

McCorkle shrugged. Another phone lit up.

"That's affirmative, Rhonda," said Walking Cloud. "Her parents in Roseville have been notified. Her name was Julie Marcia Tinkham."

As Walking Cloud gave information to Channel Five News, Rails asked the wire service reporter on another line to give him a number for a return call. A reporter from Channel Four was put on hold. McCorkle sensed the beginnings of a circus. He was about to ask Threebolt if he needed a ride home. Suddenly, McCorkle remembered he had to return Mike Quinn's earlier call. When Quinn came on the line, McCorkle was matter-of-fact.

"Tell him to take a few days off, Reggie," Quinn replied. "No, Christ, maybe I better tell him myself. He must feel—well, put him on."

McCorkle handed the phone to Threebolt and looked at his watch. It was nearly midnight. The door opened. In waddled Chief of Police Tony Bellicoast, dressed in casual attire. Walking Cloud ended his phone conversation. He looked at the Chief.

"Tony, we may need a press conference on this one."

"Yeah, I was gonna say," replied Bellicoast wearily as he looked around at the people in the room. Walking Cloud motioned him out of his office and shut the door behind them.

"Tony, the young man on the phone—"

"He's Dan Threebolt. Yeah, I know. He's the boyfriend of the murdered girl. He works for Quinn. Right? Give me some credit, Walking Cloud. Not all white people are stupid, yuh know."

Bellicoast had a crude side, Walking Cloud was reminded, despite his keen intelligence.

"What's the deal here?" Bellicoast went on. "What happened? Jus' about to hit the hay and I get a call about a parking ramp murder downtown. Wasn't this ramp secured? Obviously not, huh?"

"No, and apparently it never was. The body was cold. Looks as though she'd been dead several hours. The young woman had left her office about 4:30. Probably happened shortly after that."

"No leads or witnesses, I suppose?"

"Not yet. Give me some slack here, Tony. We can't solve every murder in five minutes."

Bellicoast threw up his hands and shrugged.

"No, hey, I know that, Ben! Christ, all I need is somethin' to go on. Been a cop for a long time, jus' like you! How do you think I got to be Chief, anyway?"

Walking Cloud grinned ruefully.

"That's another mystery."

Bellicoast laughed morbidly.

"Thanks a lot! With friends like you—Jesus Christ! Alright, when do you want the press conference?"

"I don't, but we're going to need it to stifle the heat."

"Right, I understand! Look, I gotta talk to the mayor. She and that goddamn city council president are like fuckin' press hounds, anyway. Whenever I get a call from one of 'em, I gotta pretend like I'm jumpin'! Why doan we say one o'clock? We better put our heads together—"

"Too early. The forensics report comes at ten a.m., I was promised. Won't have the m.e.'s report till later in the day. Myles Kronfort's always cooperative about these things. But the D-N-A tests will take a few days. How about five o'clock? Let the media stew until then. I've also got the Breamington case to deal with. And that stabbing death in King Park—we've only touched the surface."

Bellicoast sat on a desk halfway. He rubbed his face, as if trying to stay awake.

"Alright, make it four p.m. I'll deal with the mayor. You better make sure that young man gets home safely, considerin' what he's goin' through now. Get someone to drive him home and have Mygosh follow you to take you back."

"Already thought of that."

Tuesday. October 24. As I left work, going down in the elevator, I met a very interesting and beautiful young woman. Her name's Julie Tinkham. She's a lawyer up on the 36th floor. I walked with her as far as my car in the underground ramp. We agreed to have lunch tomorrow. As we got out of the elevator to the ramp, there was a creepy guy with a jagged almost pitted face and blond hair with a black cap, dark jacket, and weirdest of all, gloves on his hands! There was also an odd-looking middle-aged woman. We got out of the elevator, and the guy got out, too, and disappeared somewhere. He looked sinister. Julie didn't seem worried at all. She didn't want me to walk her to her car. I was just glad to get in my old Caddy, lock the door and get out of there.

Now I'm tired, about to turn in, but secure in my West Bank apartment, my daughter asleep in her room. A good day at work. Made some bucks in great ventures. A power and light utility co. in NY, a new stock issue by Bagtay. All big bucks over the securities loop. It's 11 PM. Time for sleep.

Jenny's diary entries were usually made late at night. She wrote in it at least twice a week, not knowing why, except that if her own life were to end suddenly, her daughter would have something more than photographs and money as a legacy. Jenny's success as a securities broker was on the premise that because she lacked a college education, she was determined to acquire quality "things." Not one to shop at K-Mart or Target, she preferred expensive shops where, she reasoned, fine quality inevitably meant paying more. Her new acquaintance, Julie Tinkham, had impressed her immediately as a kindred soul. So it had been a good day. She had also delivered an ultimatum to Greggie Fitzie about his drinking. In the fifteen hours since, he hadn't called. But he would eventually, she told herself. The lure of the flesh was not to be denied.

When she awoke seven hours later, it was with relief after a night of bleak, if nugatory, dreams. She bounded from the waterbed and set about her early morning. When she dressed, she chose deep hues of blue and green for skirt and blouse, with matching jacket, and a solid gold necklace timepiece. These made her feel as if she were Queen of the Mountain, at least in her world of business, of provident single motherhood, in succeeding where she was sure ninety-nine percent of women with her background would have failed. In a quarter hour, she had to wake her daughter and hasten her to get ready for school. She prepared Laura's lunch and made a light breakfast for two. As she did so, she listened to the radio. The local news was about to begin.

Minneapolis Police have confirmed the identity of a woman found murdered in a downtown parking ramp. The body of twenty-eight-year old Julie Marcia Tinkham of Minneapolis was discovered in the trunk of her car parked in the Norwest ramp. Her boyfriend had reported her missing after she failed to show up for a dinner date. Homicide Lieutenant Benjamin Walking Cloud said Julie Tinkham's murder appears to have been a random killing...

Jenny sat down on a stool. She let out a shriek.

"Oh, *my god! My god!* That *man!* Oh, *no! Julie!*"

She thought immediately of calling the police to tell them what she knew, that she may well have been the last person to see Julie alive before—

"Mom! What's wrong? Why are you—"

It was Laura, who had rushed out of her bedroom. Jenny put her arms around her child and pressed her close.

"Mom! You're shaking! What—"

Jenny sucked in her breath. She felt her heart palpitating fiercely.

"Laura, something—very—very horrible happened last night to someone I just—met. A woman was killed last night! Listen to me carefully. You mustn't talk about this at school or with anyone else. *No one*, Laura! Do you understand me? Please, just keep it to yourself! *Don't say anything*! Okay?"

Laura looked at her mother and touched her cheek.

"Your face is wet, Mom. I'll dry it off."

Laura took a Kleenex and dabbed her mother's cheekbones and around her eyes.

"I won't say anything. I promise. But will you tell me about it later?"

Jenny realized the man with the pitted face and blond hair was unlikely to know who she was or where she lived, except that she had also parked in the ramp—if he noticed anything else in his single-minded preying on Julie. Jenny turned off the radio and kissed her daughter on the forehead.

"I'm sorry. I didn't mean to wake you early. You could have had a few more minutes sleep, Laura. Maybe you can—"

"I'm ready to get up," said the girl, smiling, backing away toward the bathroom.

Jenny looked instinctively at the front door. It was locked, of course. And there was a security system with a uniformed guard on duty day and night. She had never seen a murderer in the flesh before. A shudder ran through her. She clasped herself on the arms.

"Oh, my god!" she whispered, now almost out of breath. "My god, what do I do?"

Walking Cloud's sleep had been compromised by the murder of Julie Tinkham, if not by his nap the previous evening. Nevertheless, four and a half hours were better than none. As he parked in the underground police ramp, he mused about the randomness of murder. What prevented *him* from being attacked? Not that he hadn't made enemies, but cops were high-profile targets. Mug or murder an ordinary citizen and the official wrath of society might vary. But attack a cop, kill a cop, and the brethren (as they had been known) would mount all manner of devices to catch the perp. Chief Bellicoast liked to say: what should be the people get from their silly servants if not faithful duty and hard work? The elevators opened and the familiar profiles of Mygosh and Rails strode past.

"Gentlemen," said the Lieutenant, "did you sleep well?"

"Hey," replied a startled Mygosh, "did we sleep well? I didn't, really. That girl dyin' like that."

"It's a homicide," said Rails. "I slept like a log, but I had some bad dreams. How 'bout you, Lieutenant?"

"Not that much. But we've got a busy day ahead. We have about fifteen, sixteen open cases now just in the last three months. The murder rate is going to the moon! How're you doing on the Jennings case? You two are the primaries on it."

"Yeah, we are," said Mygosh as they entered the squad room. "The trail's cold, Ben. We put it on the back burner 'cause-a the Breamington case. We've checked out everything we know on it."

Karen Jennings was a young white woman found raped and murdered two months earlier along the East Bank of the Mississippi River. A sometime student at the University of Minnesota, she had been estranged from her husband, a bookstore clerk who was first thought to be the prime suspect but not arrested for lack of evidence. In fact, the DNA strands were quite cold. The fingerprints and semen traces were too old and disfigured to be conclusive. Aside from their estrangement, her husband had no motive, nor did he have any history of violence or brushes with the law. Mygosh and Rails had been on the case from the start, believing it was part of a serial killer's preying on local Indian women. Indeed, Karen Jennings looked Indian, though in fact she was not. Could there be any tie to the Tinkham murder?

"Soon as the m.e. and forensics give us something, we'll check for similarities," said Mygosh glumly. "But Karen Jennings and the other victims—Ben, their bodies were all found outside. This time it's a body in a trunk, like out-a some mystery novel. Also, Julie Tinkham was in a different economic class than the other victims. Much different."

"Well, there may be nothing there," acknowledged Walking Cloud. "But check on it anyway."

Upon waking, Threebolt was severely depressed. He had barely slept. Finally, after several hours of dozing on and off, he got out of bed at half past seven. Only twenty-four hours earlier, Julie had shared his bed. Some of her clothes, shoes and other belongings were in his apartment. He couldn't bear to look at them, but he did. He couldn't control his grief. He was about to go into the bathroom when the phone rang. It was George Tinkham.

"Daniel, I know you're hurting as much as we are."

"She was so beautiful, George. I don't know why this should have to happen. I don't understand it at all."

"Neither do we, Daniel. I—well, let me say something. Jean and I went downtown and identified her."

"Yes, they said you were coming down."

"I signed something for the autopsy, which they're doing this morning, apparently. I know it's difficult, Daniel, but would you like to help us make the funeral arrangements? Jean and Gretchen and I feel it's only right that you should be a part of it since you both loved each other. We knew, Daniel. We saw it in Julie's face every time she came home. She always talked about you. You made her very happy. Would you like to come over here for lunch—say, about twelve or so?"

"Thank you, George. Thank you for saying that. Yes, I can come at noon. I'm taking some time off from my job. Oh, George?"

"Yes?"

"Be careful in dealing with the media. Any reporters. They'll call you, wanting interviews. They can be—very intrusive."

Threebolt thought he heard quiet sobbing in the background. Julie's mother and younger sister, he guessed.

"Yes, I understand, Daniel. Noon, then?"

"Right, George. I'll come at noon. Thanks."

Walking Cloud's phone rang while he was reading the forensics report of the Tinkham murder. It was 10:15. The voice on the other end was Myles Kronfort, the county medical examiner.

"Ben, you wanna come down? We can give you the unofficial results of the Tinkham autopsy. Written report I can give you by half past two or so."

"Alright, Myles. Mind if I bring a few detectives with me?"

"Not at all. The more the merrier."

Walking Cloud took McDour, Mygosh, Rails, Martridge and Winchell with him down and over to the autopsy room where the remains of Julie Tinkham had been examined.

"See here," said Kronfort in his dry voice, pointing to the turned head of the dead woman, "the probable cause of death. A deep edema at the back of the head, probably caused by a brick or portion of a brick. Reddish sediment found in the wound, deep enough to cause major hematoma, deep as the brain tissue—dried clay identical to material used in the making of bricks. She was also strangled, but the probable cause was the head wound. The killer may have strangled her just to be sure, but he almost broke her neck. She was also raped. Traces of semen in the uterine track, bruises near and around the entrance to the vagina—not uncommonly the result of sudden, forced entry. The rape occurred before she was dead, most likely. Pubic hairs not hers in the vaginal area indicate some i.d. here. Won't know for sure till we run some tests, but probably a Caucasian male, thirty to forty years old. Bruises on her thighs—see here on the inside?—indicate he was probably light in weight, say no more than 160 pounds. There was, still is, some smudging on the face to indicate the assailant wore some sort of make-up, a light cream, along with rouge on his mouth. Quite possibly lipstick. It's the same kind a stage actor might wear. Very unusual. Also, the cartilage in the victim's nose is bruised, even separated right here on the bridge—*see?*—indicating a blow to her face. There were also some fabric remnants in her mouth. Look here on the tray. These are consistent with tears in her pantyhose. The killer likely put his hand over her mouth to quiet her, then smashed her in the face with a gloved fist, rendering her defenseless. Then he hit her on the back of the head with a stick or something very much like it, causing her to lose consciousness."

Walking Cloud opened the forensics file he had brought along.

"Says here there were no other markings or dirt other than blood on her clothes, so she was probably assaulted as she opened her car door, then was shoved inside where the rape took place. Semen traces were found on the car seat."

"Makes sense with what we found," suggested Kronfort. "No bruises on her back or the buttocks or the backs of her legs. So—"

"You're saying she was unconscious while being raped in her car?" probed Winchell. "Then the pantyhose was partially in her mouth and she was strangled with it while—"

"All the while," interrupted Kronfort, "she was hemorrhaging from the back head wound. She was certainly unconscious."

"Then after the rape and strangulation inside the car, she was stuffed into the trunk," said Walking Cloud.

"Her purse was also in the trunk," Mygosh added. "Credit cards, drivers license, checkbook. Fifty-five dollars and twenty cents in her wallet."

"Right," said Kronfort with a small sigh. "All I can tell you is how she died. Laceration causing severe hematoma, then strangulation. Death from either or both, most probably."

"Was the blow on the back of her head enough to kill her by itself?" asked Rails.

"Yes, but not instantly. She was hemorrhaging. Without medical attention, she had no chance. The pantyhose in her mouth made it impossible to breathe properly. And while he was penetrating her, the killer was probably strangling her all the while she was bleeding from her head wound."

"My god!" exclaimed Winchell, a hand to her mouth.

"I'll have the written report to you by two-thirty, Ben," said Kronfort. "You say the press conference is at four?"

"Yep. Thanks again, Myles. Appreciate it. You can release the body to her family. Advise them. No cremation."

A quarter of an hour later, the six detectives passed through the squad room to the Lieutenant's inner office. Walking Cloud spoke first.

"One question is, how did her car keys wind up in the front floorboard on the passenger's side? Remember the ignition key was bent. According to forensics, it was bent in the door latch, then yanked out, probably by the assailant."

"It means," suggested Winchell, both hands in front of her like a conductor, "that after putting her in the trunk, the killer got back in the front seat, but couldn't get the key into the ignition properly. So he threw the keys on the floorboard in frustration, taking precaution, however, to lock the driver's door before leaving."

"But he forgot the shoe on the cement ramp beside the car," added Mygosh.

"Which means he may not have noticed it in his haste or simply disregarded it," observed Martridge, jabbing a toothpick between his lips.

"A Caucasian male," said Rails, "probably between thirty to forty, trim, no more than 160 pounds, grease on his face. Acne?"

"Doesn't say," answered Walking Cloud, handing Rails the forensics file as the desk phone rang. "Homicide, Walking Cloud."

The voice on the other end was McCorkle's.

"Ben, how'd the autopsy on Julie Tinkham go? Quinn wants to know."

"We just came from the morgue. Right now, we're brainstorming. Did I understand you're representing the HCA's office at the four p.m. press conference?"

"You got it. Normally, Quinn does the press conferences on these things, but on a grisly one like this, it doesn't matter till there's a suspect or unless the killer strikes again. Can you give me some idea what Kronfort told you?"

"Come on over here, Reggie. Might be better."

"Alright. See you in a bit."

When he looked up, Walking Cloud saw Winchell wave good-bye. She had Krewler guard duty.

Chapter Six

What To Do?

Krewler had come to resent police intrusion into his life. Until the Breamington murder, he'd had a fairly quiet existence. The tips at his waiter's job were adequate. Work at Poggie's Gym training fighters had just begun, too. So far it had only been one session. Another one tomorrow night. This afternoon he would have a lady cop with him for his first run around Lake Harriet. He'd met her once before, the day Fingers was let off the by grand jury. Not a bad looking dame, he thought. Young, pretty (he liked dishwater blondes), but—unlike Carol Blumus—this one seemed all business. No hanky panky. What the hell? Maybe she'll soften up. She's due at noon, Krewler reminded himself as he played chess in his living room with a young vice detective named McCoy. Anyway, he would jog with Winchell and then come back here to get ready for his evening wait shift. The doorbell rang. Five minutes to noon. Must be Winchell already.

Half an hour later, Krewler and Winchell were at Lake Harriet. He was in a T-shirt, shorts and tennis shoes. She was also dressed for running and wore her shield from a chain around her neck. He did limbering-up exercises first. Then it was her turn. As he jogged in place, he noticed the marked squad car hovering nearby. They started out on the path clockwise around the lake. He was taking a chance, but he felt good for the first quarter mile or so. He saw that Winchell ran easily. She even smiled at one point. The stone face is cracking, he thought. Then he began to feel winded. He hadn't done any roadwork since before his last fight back in '08. That was a disaster, up against Fingers Germain, whose ugly face still haunted him. Dammit, he tried to be a good fighter, but he was never that diligent about training. Only ran three miles when he should have been doing five or more six days a week. Now as he jogged again after all this time, he was more and more winded, and weaker. His legs were heavy. His heart was pounding harder and harder. But he kept on, Winchell right behind him, the marked squad car somewhere not far behind. He knew this was the test, even for a fighter out of training for several years. His heart was pounding like a sledgehammer. He felt like throwing up. His legs started to weaken more as if there were no controlling them. Suddenly he felt light and airy. The lake and the trees and the blacktop path beneath him tumbled.

Her morning had gone smoothly, despite glitches here and there caused by nervousness. Jenny Schell hadn't called the police about what she knew. As lunchtime neared, she was at the end of a teleconference with Richard Schickdolzher and Matt Safony, her business partners, and three brokers in the East. From a box, a female colleague's voice from New York warbled, "Okay, that's what we thought, too. We can go down half a point on the Rexon blue chips if you can bid higher by that much this Friday, Jenny. Can you do it?"

Jenny hesitated, and felt a nudge on her elbow.

"Jenny," Safony said, "she's talking to you."

Jenny realized she hadn't been paying attention. She nodded and tried to speak.

"I think she said Yes," said Schickdolzher in a puckish tone. "Go ahead, Irma. We can handle it if you're absolutely sure there's no conflict."

"We're sure if you're sure," came Irma's flat New York twang. "Anything else from Minneapolis today? We've covered some good ground."

Schickdolzher and Safony exchanged winks. Jenny had been caught not paying full attention. She disliked their male smugness.

"I think we're okay," answered Schickdolzher. "Talk to you Friday, Irma. Jed? Mac? Anything else?"

"Philly's okay," came a fast-clipped male voice through the box.

"So's Atlanta," came another in a lower register.

Afterwards, Safony said, ""First time I've ever seen you diverted, Jenny. Care to unload any big secrets?"

Again, Jenny distractedness was brought around. She knew she'd been winging it all morning and couldn't afford to let her colleagues take serious notice. But they had already. She was supposed to be on top, but she hadn't so far today.

"I'm sorry," she offered lamely. "I've had a lot on my mind."

"We've been noticing, Jenny," said Safony with a grin. "You wanna talk about it? Is it business-related?"

Schickdolzher snickered. Jenny knew that beneath this artifice of cordial teasing, they were reappraising her. She didn't like it, although she regarded neither as a threat to her professional status. They were her partners. Her financial expertise and broker's license combined with the money of one and the legal expertise and money of the other to set up the business.

Suddenly, as if out of nowhere, Safony wondered, "Either of you know that woman who was found murdered in her car trunk last night?"

"No, but I knew who she was," said Schickdolzher. "I'd see her in the elevators occasionally. Her law firm's three floors up."

Jenny sucked in her breath.

"I did," she blurted. "That's what's been on my mind all morning. I'm sure I was the last person to see her alive—in the parking ramp."

Safony and Schickdolzher looked at her in amazement.

"I also—saw the man who killed her," she continued. "I'm frightened to death, and I don't know what to do about it."

"So that's it!" said Safony. "Why didn't you tell us? We'll protect your confidentiality. Legally, there's no problem. You'll have to tell the police what you saw. Have you—talked to the police?"

Jenny ignored the question. Instead she told them what occurred during her conversation with Julie Tinkham. She let it pour forth, particularly her description of the pitted-faced blond man with gloved hands.

"You're sure he was the killer?" asked Safony.

Jenny was startled. She frowned at the lawyer.

"I didn't see him do it," she said slowly. "But he looked like—"

"A killer?" Safony parried. "Circumstantial evidence. Not even that, really. But the police will certainly be interested in hearing a description to see if it matches their forensics report."

"I—I don't want to talk to the police, Matt. That's the problem."

"You don't have any choice, Jenny. You're a witness. Albeit a material witness. The man you saw, if he's the killer, may well strike again. You realize that? But whoever the killer is, he may know who you are."

Of course she knew this. She also knew discretion in dealing with her colleagues here and now was very important. Having told them, she realized she had put them in the position of forcing her hand. If she had to talk about Julie Tinkham, the police might also ask about Jack Breamington. And she didn't want to talk about that. It would be damaging to her professional reputation.

"Maybe you don't understand, Jenny. Withholding evidence in a criminal investigation is against the law. As a lawyer, I'm also an officer of the court—"

"I know! I know that, Matt," she protested, her hands up defensively. "But if this gets out to the press—"

She stopped short and put up her hands.

"Never mind," she said. "Will I need a lawyer if I talk to the police?"

Safony assured her she did not need a lawyer if that was all there was to her story. She assured him it was. Schickdolzher lightheartedly suggested they all go out to lunch. There was an awkward silence. Safony agreed it might be a good idea.

Sometimes, he intimated, the best decisions are made on a full stomach.

They found a Chinese restaurant, buffet-style, just off the skyway. Jenny chose chicken soup with an appetizer that looked like a skinny burrito and hot tea. She ate pensively while Safony and Schickdolzher discussed her options. They concluded again she had none except to tell what she saw. Grimly, she nodded.

"Jenny, you want to call that Indian homicide detective who's always on the news?" asked Safony. "What's his name?"

"Walking Cloud," offered Schickdolzher.

Jenny found Safony's pushiness tiresome. But she couldn't avoid the inevitable. They were both looking at her expectantly.

"No, I can do that myself, Matt," she said. "I'll call him when we get back to the office. You can listen in, give me hand signals."

Safony chuckled awkwardly.

"It's the right thing to do, Jenny. Believe me."

She smiled stiffly. She didn't want to discuss it further.

A small crowd had gathered around Marty Krewler's stricken form. Detective Winchell tried at first to get them to stand back, but they still hovered. The marked squad unit was slow to assess the situation. Finally, the two blues came over. One of them had already called for an ambulance. A stocky young red-haired woman in a blue smock with a stethoscope in her hand rushed toward them.

"I'm a medical student!" she yelled. "Let me see what's wrong with this man! Please, *make way*! I'm a *medical student*!"

The police officers, including Winchell, stood aside while the red-haired medical student knelt over Krewler, who was gasping. She put her stethoscope over his heart.

"Is he dying?" an elderly woman in sunglasses inquired casually. "It's so beautiful out here today. Not a bad day to die if your time is up."

"I don't know," said the red-haired woman with the stethoscope. "Please, hold your voices down! Please!"

The three police officers began to disperse the small gathering, some reluctant to go away. A silence descended as the wind whipped over the lake on this mid-autumn day, only to be broken by the distant sounds of a dog barking, the high-pitched giddy laughter of children, the soft lapping of water against a wooden dock, and geese and ducks wandering into and out of the water a few yards away. Groans came from the prostrate man.

"Please, sir, don't try to move," said the medical student. "An ambulance has been called for you. Please, no, please don't try to get up!"

Krewler did try to raise himself, only to look into the red-haired woman's face. She had a jaw like Mussolini's. Then he saw Winchell right beside her, looking down at him intensely.

"Lie still, Mr. Krewler," Winchell said reassuringly. "Please, do as she says."

"Your heart may be overworked," said the medical student.

"Please let me get up," he stammered. But he sank back down, his eyes rolling, the square reddish face above him kindly, beseeching. He closed his eyes, barely hearing the sounds around him.

"I think you'll be alright, sir, but you should be checked out."

Minutes later, Krewler was loaded into the orange-&-white Hennepin County ambulance. Winchell sat on a stool, her hand on his shoulder. There were others present, too.

"Sir," said a young female voice, "can you tell us your name? Sir, please! Open your eyes! Tell us your name!"

"Please, let him be," said Winchell. "Let's just get him to the hospital!"

"I'm just doing my job," retorted the young female voice. "Are you his wife, girlfriend, whatever? Just let us proceed, please!"

"I'm a *police officer*!" declared Winchell with mild irritation. "*Back off*! He's under a great deal of stress as it is."

"I'm just following procedure here—officer," said the other female voice. "I'll try not to upset him. Do you mind letting me do my job?"

"All right, but lighten up," Winchell told her.

"Sir," said the other female voice, "can you tell us your name? Sir, please! Open your eyes! Tell us your name!"

"Sir, can you open your eyes?" demanded a male voice. More words. Krewler could barely understand them. He was too exhausted. He heard Winchell's voice now, arguing with the medics. His chest was still pounding.

"I'm going to put an oxygen mask on you, sir," said the male voice. "It will help you breathe easier. Here goes."

They took him to Hennepin County Medical Center. In the Emergency Room, a determination was made that he might have had a heart attack. A middle-aged nurse with a clipboard used a softer tone to ask if he had any insurance. Luckily, he did. She asked if there were any people he wanted called. Yes, Benno the maitre d' at Le Café Francais.

"I'll call him," said Winchell, standing nearby. She identified herself to the nurse.

"I see," said the nurse. "Is he under arrest or something?"

"No, but we're looking out for him. He's a material witness in a very important criminal case."

Winchell looked at him again.

"Mr. Krewler, I'll call your employer at the restaurant right now. I'll be right back. I won't be far away now."

Krewler lay on a cot in the emergency ward for what seemed like at least half an hour before they transported him two floors up. Winchell stayed with him all the while. A quiet, beautiful guard, he thought. In the cardiac ward, he was dressed in hospital garb and put into a bed. An IV unit was attached to his arm, the plastic bag hanging with its pellucid fluid like a surrealist's beehive. He felt very tired. At last, he was told he could sleep. Then a young dark-haired nurse brought a phone into his partially curtained cubicle and plugged it into the wall.

"A call for you, Mr. Krewler," she said pleasantly. "Would you like to take it now—before you sleep?"

The voice on the other end was familiar.

"Mr. Krewler, this is Walking Cloud. Beth told me about your mishap. I'm sorry to hear about it."

Winchell stood silently nearby, watching him on and off.

"I guess—I ran out-a steam tryin' to keep up with her," he said. "Joggin' wasn't as easy as I thought. It's been a while."

Winchell had a faint smile now. She folded her arms and looked down at the floor.

"Well, few of us can keep up with Beth," replied Walking Cloud. "She's a go-getter. Listen, take it easy over there. Do what they tell you. I'll call you again, probably tonight, and see how you're doing, Mr. Krewler. Beth will stay with you till six. Then someone else will take over. Probably a uniform since you're going to be in one place."

"Alright, Lieutenant. Talk to yuh."

Walking Cloud clicked off. Krewler now remembered another call to be made. He dialed the number of Poggie's Boxing Gym and left a message on the tape. Then he lay back in the undulative folds on the white sheets. Within seconds, he was fast asleep.

A few blocks away in his office, Walking Cloud made a note in his daybook to call the cardiac unit again before he went home. Krewler sounded upbeat, but also weak.

"Krewler have a heart attack?" asked McDour.

"They don't know yet. They're keeping him there for observation. Beth is on duty with him. They were jogging around Lake Harriet when he collapsed."

"Line two for you, Ben," said Mygosh. "It's a female."

"That witness in the Breamington case? Sarah Steeples?" wondered Walking Cloud.

"I don't think so. Not sure."

On the other end was the becalmed voice of Jenny Schell, whose name he recognized instantly.

"I have some information about Julie Tinkham," she told him.

"Go on. I'm listening. Did you know Ms. Tinkham?"

"I only knew her in what were probably the last fifteen minutes of her life."

Walking Cloud asked if she would rather tell him the details in person.

"I can come to see you, if you like, Lieutenant," she said.

Chapter Seven

Looking For A Needle

An hour later, Jenny was sitting in Walking Cloud's office. The procedure for interviewing witnesses was standard, but flexible. He interviewed her with McDour, Blumus, a tape recorder going, and a stenographer present. She told them how she met Julie Tinkham and what they talked about, and then about the three people in the elevator. She was emphatic about the blond man with the pitted face.

"He looked absolutely evil!" she declared.

"Looking evil is not a chargeable offense," said Walking Cloud. "Did he say or do anything suspicious or unusual?"

"He wore gloves. Gloves in October when it's not cold?"

"Did the others in the elevator wear gloves?"

"I—I don't know. I didn't see that."

"Alright. What about the rest of the blond man's clothing? What was he wearing?"

"He had on a leather jacket, I think, black leather—was it?—and gray pants. He was wearing a beret. No, it was a cap. One of those workingmen's caps."

Jenny was asked to describe the woman with the shopping bag again.

"I didn't watch her closely," Jenny admitted. "She was probably about my age, maybe older. I'm 41. I'm almost five-four. She must have been five-eight or even taller. She was solidly built, but slender. She wore a green raincoat and was carrying a red-and-white plastic Target's shopping bag. She had strong features. A darker complexion."

"Would you recognize her if you saw her again?"

"Yes, I'm sure I would."

"And you'd recognize the blond man with the pitted face?"

"Yes, definitely."

"His face," Walking Cloud said, "would you describe it as pitted or craggy? Were there any other unusual features, like scars, that you saw?"

"His face was pitted. Acne scars, it looked like. No other scars, but I didn't look at him for too long. I thought he might look back, so—"

"After you got off the elevator at ramp C, what happened?"

Jenny recounted how the woman with the shopping bag turned to go the opposite way, how the blond man seemed to be watching them, that he was nowhere to be seen a few seconds later, how she offered to walk with Julie to her car, that she declined with a smile but suggested they have lunch and that she said she'd call her the next day, how she walked away so nonchalantly, how Jenny herself quickly got in her Cadillac, locked the door and drove out of the ramp.

"Did you see where Julie had her car parked?" asked McDour.

"No, I didn't. As I drove out, I caught a glimpse of her—still walking. Can you tell me, was she attacked in her car?"

"Yes, we think the killer probably got to her as soon as she opened her car door," said Walking Cloud, "before she had a chance to get inside and close the door."

"Oh, my god!"

"Ms. Schell, the man you saw *may* be the one who did this. We won't know anything for sure until we have more information. We would like you to talk to our police sketch artist who'll work with you to create a likeness of him. But first we need you to look at some photographs. Mug shots. It's possible the man you saw has a history of attacks against women and you'll recognize him."

"If you'll come with me," Blumus said, "I'll get the mug books. If you don't find him there, we'll have you work with our sketch artist. Is that okay with you?"

"Yes," said Jenny. "Anything!"

"I have a few things," said McDour, who had been writing in his notepad. "Did the blond man have any make-up or other substance on his face that you saw?"

"No, I don't think so. And I don't remember any scent, either. I was standing only a foot or so away from him. He looked so creepy."

"How tall was he?"

"About five-ten, maybe five-eleven. Not quite as tall as the Lieutenant here."

"I'm six feet," said Walking Cloud. "What about the woman with the shopping bag? Did she have any make-up on?"

"Yes, I'm sure she did. But—I wasn't concentrating on her so much. She had kind of an olive complexion. And big teeth."

"Big teeth?" wondered McDour.

"Yeah," Jenny shrugged. "She had big teeth. She smiled, I remember. I think she did, anyway. It just seemed she had big teeth."

"Thanks," said McDour, flipping his notepad shut.

Blumus escorted her out the door.

"You didn't ask about Breamington," said McDour.

"No, better to take it one at a time," Walking Cloud said. "She's high-strung."

"Well, what forensics said and what Myles Kronfort said converge on one thing," observed McDour. "The killer had some sort of facial make-up."

"Right," agreed Walking Cloud. "Which means our blond man was wearing make-up and she didn't detect it—or he's not the killer."

Jenny was seated at a table in the next room and was presented with a floppy mug book.

"Just go from page to page," Blumus told her. "If you find a likeness of the man you were describing—uh—"

"Jenny. Call me Jenny. That's my name."

"Alright, I'm Carol, by the way."

"Hi. With men we have to be so formal. Professionalism, they call it. But it just creates a lot of distance."

"Yes, I agree," said the detective, grinning. "I think they need it for their own self-esteem. Anyway, make a note of any likely face with the page number on this pad here. All these men have been arrested and convicted in the last fifteen years for any number of crimes. In this first book, they're a gamut—murder, assault, rape, armed robbery, burglary, domestic violence, selling or facilitating the sale of illegal drugs. All felonies. Take your time, Jenny. I'll be back in a few minutes."

Jenny began scanning the rows of male faces. Here and there she saw a face that bore similarities to the blond man with the pitted face. But none did conclusively. She persisted, face after face after face, page after page. Toward the end of the book, she saw a face that looked remarkably like the man she saw. But this one was younger and had dark hair. Did the man in the elevator have dyed hair? Why hadn't she noticed that? No acne scars were evident in the picture. Below was the name: Johnson, Marlin Anders. The date was June, 2000. Jenny made a note of him. She kept on, finishing the first book and taking up the next. Blumus reappeared. Jenny told her of the mug shot that looked possible.

"Take a look at this guy," Jenny said. "There, that man. He looks like him, but his coloring is darker. I remember being afraid to look at him more than a second or two."

Blumus looked at the mug shot.

"You're sure?"

"I'm sure there's a similarity. No acne scars here, but the nose and the mouth and eyes look the same."

"I'll run this by the Lieutenant, Jenny. Keep looking."

Walking Cloud was reading the m.e.'s report on Julie Tinkham's death when Blumus tapped on his open door.

"Jenny Schell's picked a possible. A June-two-thousand shot of Marlin Anders Johnson. Got his sheet here. Convicted for battery against his ex-wife, then the same year pled no contest to grand theft auto in Saint Paul. Says here he took part in a chop shop operation over there. Twenty-six months in Stillwater, another three years probation. Been clean since."

"Any priors before then?"

"Yeah, a couple drunk-and-disorderlies. '98, '99. Arrested in '01 by the Secret Service for attempting to pass counterfeit money, but the charge was dismissed because of prosecutorial misconduct. Born 6-8-69, Moose Jaw, Saskatchewan. Came to Minnesota in 1990 after two years in the U.S. Merchant Marine. Has U.S. citizenship. His parents were U.S. citizens, missionaries for a Pentecostal sect up there, so he's got dual citizenship. Can't be deported."

"Live here now?"

"Apparently. As of November-oh-six, his last known address is 3208 Lyndale South. Here's his sheet."

Walking Cloud perused the file. McDour and Martridge appeared in the doorway.

"Anything more you need for the press conference, Ben?" asked McDour.

"The chief's coming here at 4:45," Walking Cloud said, looking at his watch. "We'll need a final copy of the press release and forty copies for reporters. We may have a possible pickup. What do you think, Carol? Jenny Schell still here?"

"Still going through the mug books. Just that one so far."

Walking Cloud stood up, handing the Johnson file back to Blumus.

"Stick with her, Carol. We may have to put this guy in a line-up if we can find him. Ethan, check out Marlin Anders Johnson's current address. He's no longer on probation."

Martridge nodded and disappeared.

"Bill called in a few minutes ago," McDour said. "No leads at the victim's law firm. She hadn't been involved with anyone there or anywhere, apparently. Just her boyfriend at the HCA's office. From all accounts, she was very happy with him."

"Yes, I saw them together the other night. They looked happy."

"I don't know any more," said Jenny after the third mug book. "All these faces. Oh, my God!"

"Nothing?" said Blumus.

Jenny stood up and stretched. She looked at her timepiece hanging from her neck by a gold chain.

"Well, here's one more, Jenny."

Blumus plunked down another floppy book. Jenny looked at the first page with dread. Again, it was face after face, row after row. She tried to recall once more the details of the blond man's face in the elevator. Then she remembered other things. The woman who left with them at ramp C, and her round lips and big teeth. Her strange smile when their eyes met. Jenny remembered glancing again at the blond man's pitted face. He never looked at her, not even sideways as far as she could tell. She sighed and put her hands up to her face.

"Jenny, are you feeling okay?" asked Blumus.

Jenny put her hands down and blinked her eyes.

"I'm—I'm fine," she said, standing up. "I think I just need to wash my face. I'll be right back."

As she made her way to the bathroom, she passed several people in the hallway, among them a tall, slender man with close-cropped brown hair and a pitted face. He wore a blue sports coat with a badge i.d., identifying him as a police officer. The blond man's face in the elevator was very similar, she thought. The detective with the pitted face went on his way down the hall without, it seemed, having noticed her. She shuddered and went into the Women's Room. Minutes later, as she dried her face with a paper towel, she tried to compare the two faces. It couldn't possibly be, she told herself. No, it's ridiculous. Just as similarity of faces. She reapplied a dab of make-up to her eyes and apprised that her good looks at forty-one were better than many women her age. She tried to reassure herself that while she wasn't earning her keep being here, she was being a good citizen. She returned to the mugshot room where Blumus was waiting.

"You know something?" said Jenny. "I—saw—a police officer—in plain clothes—in the hallway a few minutes ago. He was wearing a badge on his coat. He looked more like the man I saw in the elevator than the face I picked out earlier."

"Really?" said Blumus, surprised.

"Really! I mean, we were in an *elevator*, Carol! It wasn't across a room or down a hallway. He was no more than a foot away!"

"And the cop you just saw? Was he the same height or taller or—"

"Taller. Oh, it's so crazy! And their coloring is different. It's not the same person. No. I'm sorry."

"I think I know who you just saw," said Blumus. "Captain Blatsky. He handles mostly administrative matters in homicide and robbery for the downtown precinct. One rank above the Lieutenant. I don't think he's a likely prospect, Jenny."

"No, I realize that. He's not. You're right. It's just that—every time now—I see a man with a ruddy face—"

"I know. Listen, we have only two of these big books left. If you haven't found another possible after these, I'm going to have you look at several men in a line-up. All right?"

Jenny swallowed hard and wiped her brow.

"Okay."

Mygosh and Rails were in Walking Cloud's office.

"Here's the file on Marlin Anders Johnson," said the Lieutenant. "We need him to cooperate. If we need to, we'll get a warrant. All Jenny Schell said was that his mug shot had similarities to the man she saw in the elevator before Julie Tinkham's death. When was this taken? Six-three-two-thousand. Not enough for a probable here. So you need to lean on this guy. He's been clean as a whistle since his parole ended in '01. In fact, he was a model prisoner at Stillwater. No infractions. No parole violations. Been clean a long time, in fact. Go to it, gents."

Minutes later, Mygosh and Rails were driving on Lyndale Avenue South. They found Johnson's address and buzzed his apartment. A voice came through the speaker.

"Yes, may I help you?"

"Yeah," said Rails. "Detectives Rails and Mygosh, Minneapolis Police, here to talk to Mr. Marlin Anders Johnson. Is he in?"

A pause, then: "Yes, I'm Marlin. What do you want?"

"It's police business, Mr. Johnson. We need to talk to you. Can you let us in, please?"

Another pause, then the buzzer. After they stepped inside, Mygosh opened his manila file and nudged his partner.

"Remember, this is what he looked like in two-thousand. It's been a while."

When they found the right apartment, Rails stood to the side while Mygosh rang the doorbell. The door opened. A gaunt, thin man stood before them.

"Marlin Anders Johnson?" said Mygosh.

"Yes, that's me," the gaunt man said. "You said you were police detectives?"

The detectives produced their shield i.d.'s. Johnson looked at them starkly.

"All right, I believe you are who you say you are. What can I do for you?"

"May we come inside, Mr. Johnson?" asked Mygosh. "It'd be more appropriate than standin' out here in the hallway."

"I guess so."

Johnson stood to the side as the detectives entered his apartment. The first thing they saw was another man standing in front of the long maroon sofa in a simply furnished apartment, clean and uncluttered. A large photograph of Robert Mapplethorpe was on the wide wall behind the sofa. Johnson's guest was also thin, with close-cropped hair and a carefully trimmed, reddish mustache. He wore a white shirt, a thin brown tie and baggy trousers.

"It's fortuitous, I trust," said Johnson, "that you should be paying me a visit at the same time my attorney is here. This is Tim Guise. He's drawing up my will."

"How do you do?" said Guise with a half smile, shaking hands with the detectives.

"He's doing your will?" wondered Rails.

"Yes, my will," said Johnson crisply. "I have AIDS. I just got out of the hospital this morning. I don't know how much longer I have to live, and Tim is serving as my attorney. We were discussing my will when you rang."

An awkward pause. Mygosh and Rails were speechless, but it was Guise who spoke up.

"You gentlemen are obviously here in an official capacity?"

"Yes, we are," said Mygosh, turning to Johnson. "We're investigating a murder, Mr. Johnson. Can you tell us where you were yesterday between 4:30 and 10:30 PM?"

"Is this about the parking ramp murder downtown?" Johnson asked. "Well, I was in University Hospital, hooked up to an I-V machine. I was released this morning, as I just told you."

"I can vouch for that," said Guise. "The hospital staff and the records will confirm it. Marlin has been losing strength very gradually. He's very prone to infection now. He hardly has the strength for conversation for very long, much less to assault and kill anyone."

"We're not making accusations," said Mygosh. "All we're asking are simple questions. We're just doing our jobs. We're not interested in anything else."

"Oh, I believe you, Detective," rejoined Guise. "But Marlin is *not* the parking ramp murderer. How on earth did you come to think he might be?"

"We're checking out any lead we get in this case, Mr. Guise," said Mygosh. "This is one of them. Do you mind?"

"No, not at all under ordinary circumstances. But my client is obviously *not* the person you're looking for! Why do you persist?"

"As I said, we're here because of a lead. We have to track it down. Mr. Johnson, in this case it looks false, but we have to be sure. We have two requests of you. First, we'll need the references on your stay at the hospital, and second, we need you to come downtown today and appear in a line-up. If you can do these two things, we can eliminate you as a possible suspect."

Over the protest of his lawyer, Johnson agreed to both requests.

Jenny Schell had not been able to identify another face in the remaining mug books. She stood behind a one-way window while six men, including Marlin Anders Johnson, mounted a platform and stood before her.

"Take your time, Jenny," said Blumus.

Jenny nodded nervously. What she did not know was that three of the men, including Johnson, were ex-convicts. Two were police officers.

"If I could see them from the side," said Jenny.

Rails spoke into a microphone and asked the six men to turn one way, then the other. Jenny stared at them some more. Number Two, whom she didn't recognize, was Captain Blatsky with a blond wig. Number Five was Marlin Anders Johnson. Other than a splotch on his upper right cheek, Johnson's complexion was clear.

"I'm sorry," she said, shaking her head. "The man I saw doesn't look like any of them."

She turned to Blumus, who asked, "You're sure?"

"Well, yes, Number Five is too thin and too short, and his complexion isn't the same. Number Two is too tall and his hair is too long. The others, not at all."

"Okay," said Winchell, who tapped on the glass.

They went through the Squad Room into Walking Cloud's office.

"Maybe if you found that man I saw in that earlier book of pictures," Jenny suggested.

"We did find him, Ms. Schell," said Rails. "He was Number Five, who you just said was too thin and too short and had the wrong complexion. Marlin Anders Johnson."

"He looked very different from the picture in your book," Jenny said.

"Yeah, well, that was taken back in—two-thousand," explained Rails. "And since then, he's gotten AIDS, which has probably made him lose weight. A lead is a lead, though. Gotta check 'em out."

"AIDS!" exclaimed Jenny, now seeing Johnson enter the waiting area. "Oh, my God! That poor man!"

Walking Cloud knew that Guise wanted to speak to him. When he opened the door, Jenny Schell suddenly went past him.

"Jenny!" urged Blumus. "Don't—"

Marlin Anders Johnson and his lawyer were conversing with each other intensely. Guise looked angry, but Johnson's demeanor was of resignation. Jenny stared as she slowly walked toward them. Behind her, Walking Cloud and the other detectives could only watch. Johnson and Guise did not pay attention to them at first. Guise suddenly turned to his right and spotted Walking Cloud, not noticing the small dark-haired woman coming toward them.

Jenny saw Marlin Anders Johnson closer and closer. The man with him was looking past her with consternation in his face. Then suddenly he looked down at her. Johnson now saw her, too.

"I'm sorry," she said to him. "I saw your picture in—in a book they showed me. I—I said it looked something like the man I saw in the elevator—just before Julie was killed. I didn't know anything about you—or that you've been so ill. I didn't mean to cause more—more *pain*—in your life. I'm very sorry."

She reached out and took his hand, holding it in hers.

"The man I saw looked nothing like you," she said. "Please forgive me."

She released his hand, then turned and left the room, her eyes welling. Blumus followed her out the door.

Walking Cloud noticed how the expressions on Johnson and his lawyer changed from depression and anger to disbelief.

"It's good what she said," Johnson said slowly. "It was nice to hear someone apologize."

The two men looked at Walking Cloud.

"Go in peace," said the Lieutenant. "We're sorry to have bothered you."

"Take care," offered Mygosh.

"Thank you," replied Johnson, his face looking gaunter than before. He took Guise by the arm, and they turned to leave.

Blumus followed Jenny down the hallway.

"Jenny, please! May I talk to you?"

Jenny turned the corner and stopped. They didn't say anything, but walked down the hall and then some steps into the underground walkway to the basement-level cafeteria and the Government Center.

"It's after four-thirty," said Blumus. "I'm supposed to be off-duty now. Do you need a ride home?"

Jenny remembered that her mother was picking up Laura at her school and would bring her home by five o'clock.

"That poor man! I—I don't know if I broke some sort of etiquette, but I felt I owed him an apology."

"No, no. I understand. That's fine, Jenny. You did the right thing."

"Did I? I guess I didn't care. My god, he has AIDS!"

"Yes, we discovered that just before he came in. But our procedure is to eliminate any doubt. That's why we asked him to come down and stand in the line-up."

"I suppose now you want me to talk to your sketch artist, right?"

"You're the closest thing we have to a witness. Tomorrow morning at nine, if you can."

Jenny took in a slow deep breath.

"I thought so. Is your offer of a ride still good?"

"Chief Bellicoast, what does it say about the climate of this city when there's a murder here almost every day?"

The reporter was Kevin McTigue, whom both Walking Cloud and the Chief distrusted.

"What does it say?" Bellicoast replied with a heavy sigh. "The answer lies in your own question. This is a fair-sized city, yuh know. It's not some idyllic fairyland where nothin' bad ever happens. I mean, where are you livin', anyway? The police have done a conscientious job here. So what are we doin' about the murder of this young woman? I'll tell yuh. Our profile of the killer is bein' worked up as we speak. For that, I'll turn yuh over to Lieutenant Walking Cloud. Ben?"

"Our concern now," said Walking Cloud, "is not to create a climate of fear. Julie Tinkham was assaulted and murdered, we believe, by someone who did not know her. So far we know of no one she knew who had any motive to commit this crime. Forensic evidence leads us to believe that this was a random killing. The perpetrator, we think, was a male between the ages of thirty to forty-five—"

"Lieutenant," interrupted a tall black male reporter wearing horn-rimmed glasses, "does this mean you intend to go into the African-American community looking for the perp?"

"Not if the perp is white or of some other ethnic background," interjected Bellicoast, leaning past Walking Cloud into the microphones. "We have never targeted any group on account-a race. We go where the evidence leads us. *Period!*"

"And where does your evidence lead you now?" asked a thin blonde woman reporter standing under a boom mike.

"We're still assessing the evidence," said Walking Cloud. "At this point, we believe the killer was most likely Caucasian, between thirty and forty-five, as I said, and no heavier than 160 pounds. Probably five-eight to five-ten. When we have more information, something specific, about his identity and if it's appropriate, we'll make it public. We want to find this killer before he strikes again."

"Lieutenant!" shouted a male voice over the others. "Are you saying this is the beginning of a serial killer's rampage?"

"No, I'm not saying that," Walking Cloud answered quickly, then slowing his delivery to a non-contentious tone. "It'd be far preferable if all the parking ramps in the Twin Cities were secure enough so that all our citizens, especially women, could come and go without risk. But that's not the case. Safety precautions by our citizens have to be taken. In this instance, we believe this killer is capable of striking again. We want to apprehend him as soon as possible."

More heated questions. Walking Cloud stuck it out for a bit longer and finally glanced at his wristwatch.

"We have to go back to work."

"Thank you," Bellicoast said. "We'll make every effort to keep you all informed of developments in this case."

"Sometimes I hate reporters," said Walking Cloud as they walked back through a hallway. "When I was very young, I actually wanted to be a news reporter."

"No kiddin'," said Bellicoast. "I wanted to be a surgeon. Then I realized it meant seein' blood and guts every day. I changed my mind."

"And you haven't seen blood and guts as a cop?"

"Oh, I've seen my share. *More'n* my share! But—the way I think about it, hey, I could-a been a butcher, too. Like my father. I remember he'd carve our Christmas ham just like a surgeon. Gotta have the knack for it, I guess. Well, what's next? How's Krewler doin'?"

"Okay as far as I know. I'm monitoring the situation."

Krewler lay in his hospital bed, his IV unit adjusted by a nurse.

"Try and rest now, Mr. Krewler," she said. "The doctor will come see you in about half an hour and discuss your symptoms with you."

"Do you know what my symptoms are?" he asked weakly.

"The doctor will talk with you. We're taking good care of you."

The nurse slipped past the curtain. He was in a state of total inertia, drained by a continuous state of drowsiness.

"Mr. Krewler," a female voice shot through his fog of sleep. "Mr. Krewler, please open your eyes. I'm Doctor Simpson."

Before him was a blonde woman, lumpishly pretty, probably in her late twenties, a clipboard in hand, her white coat immaculate, her ponytail in a ring at the back of her head, her status confirmed by three other sets of eyes, two of them male and in white coats, one with a mustache and goatee, the other clean-shaven and praetorian. The third was the nurse of a short while ago. The young doctor, her manner empathetic, explained that he had not suffered a heart attack. Instead, he had had a "coronary incident" of relatively little consequence over all. The doctor talked about taking up vigorous exercise in a "calibrated schedule," not diving into it suddenly.

He listened as she asked questions. "Did you eat anything just prior to this incident?" and "Do you have any history of heart problems?" and "When was the last time you boxed and were hit in the head?" He replied with the shortest answers possible. The doctor then conferred with her colleagues, each taking a turn looking at him as though he were a specimen. Involuntary flashes suddenly passed through his brain. It was a later round of his fight with Fingers Germain. His hands up, his legs moving as if on automatic pilot, he saw the hate on his opponent's blotchy face. He felt again the relentless pounding of the jab and combinations thrusting at him, his breathing, sapping his ability, even his desire, to respond effectively.

"Oh, *no!*" he exclaimed. "*No!*"

The faces with white coats looked startled.

"Mr. Krewler, what's the matter?" asked the nurse. "Do you feel pain? What's the matter?"

What Krewler saw was Fingers's determined face coming in and out, his left jab pummeling. Krewler heard garbled voices. Quickly, his arms were restrained. Something was clamped over his nose and mouth, and he was breathing deeply. Within seconds, he was out.

Chapter Eight

A Psycho's Glee

As the final chore of his work shift, Walking Cloud put in a call to the coronary unit at Hennepin County General Hospital.

"He had a paranoiac incident, Lieutenant," said a nurse. "Probably hallucinatory, as far as we can tell. We had to restrain and etherize him. We expect him to sleep for another hour or so. His condition has been upgraded to stable. We'll give him supper and if he needs it, a sleeping pill to get him through the night. Barring complications, he could be released sometime tomorrow."

"An hour or so, you say? When are visiting hours?"

"Eleven a.m. to nine-thirty p.m."

Walking Cloud's workday was now officially at an end. Of his detectives from the day shift, only Martridge remained, sitting at his desk nearby, having just finished a phone conversation. Two detectives working the evening shift came in the squad room.

"Lieutenant," said Martridge when Walking Cloud stepped out of his office, "there are some things about this Tinkham case that don't add up."

"You noticed that? Both forensics and the m.e. said a make-up with a cream base was on the victim's face, likely from the perp's face while he was raping her in the front seat of her car. But Jenny Schell didn't see any make-up on the blond man in the elevator. Myles said it was the kind of substance that actors wear, the kind sold to theater companies."

"That shrink over at the University you asked to work up a profile?"

"Yeah?"

"He faxed it while you were doin' the press conference. I been readin' it. Look, he says here that the killer is most likely a loner, a single man livin' alone with extreme misogynist tendencies. Or why would he rape and then kill a woman he didn't know? This just isn't a garden-variety serial rapist. Here's a quote: 'The fury of his attack on the victim may indicate long-held resentment of women because of previous rejections and/or feelings of sexual inadequacy, possibly including unresolved issues with his mother or a maternal figure from the past.' Hey, now, I've known cats like that. They take it out on the women they know in their lives to get back at Mama."

"Look at this," observed Walking Cloud, reading over Martridge's shoulder, "'the killer may well strike again soon.' Well, I figured that much! I'm wondering whether we're supposed to be looking for a perp with a sheet or not."

Martridge nodded, and looked at the fax.

"The shrink says—what does he say here?—yeah, look at this, Lieutenant! He says, 'Not necessarily a previous offender, but one whose anger has finally reached a need for consummation after a long period of dormancy. Quite possibly, this individual has worked successfully in a creative profession for some time, but has never fully integrated his personality with the opposite sex in a particular or general instance.' I suppose that means he don't get laid that often. Right?"

"Could be," said Walking Cloud with a grim smile. "But if this psychologist is right, it means that our perp's anger *has* reached the breaking point. He can't get satisfaction any other way. But first he has to humiliate his victim. Then he kills her. Julie Tinkham was also very pretty. Could be he picks out only good-looking younger women."

"We got a lotta good-lookin' women in this town. I'm married with two little kids, but I still look, yuh know."

"Keep your fingers on the piccolo! You going home now? I'll walk with you to the parking ramp."

In Kenwood, not far from Walking Cloud's condominium, a young woman was leaving her parents' home after supper. She laughed and hugged them at the door. She was heading back to an apartment she shared with two other students near the University of Minnesota. She carried a bundle of clean laundry down the steps. Her father toted a package of food that her mother had fixed for her.

"Be careful, honey," said her father as he bussed her on the cheek. "Call us tomorrow."

"I'm always careful, Pop. Tell Mother thanks again for the care package. I can always use the stuff. I'll call you tomorrow. After my biology exam."

"Drive safely! Good luck on your test."

The young woman got in her VW rabbit station wagon and rolled the window down, smiling up at her father.

"Talk to you later," she said. Then waving to her mother, she yelled, "Bye, Mama!"

Her parents both smiled and waved as she drove slowly away. It was early evening.

On parade three blocks away was Arthur Boyood, who had just stepped out of this third-floor apartment in women's clothing, something he had done before, each time with a different ensemble. He didn't have a name for his female persona, although he wanted one. More important, he thought, to refine what he, now she, looked like. Nothing garish. Nothing ostentatious. Indeed, Boyood wanted to be noticed only as a woman. His whole being changed and changed again when he was in women's clothing, "on parade" as he thought of it. There was the most extreme bliss, then at other times anger and violent rages that only he, now she, could fashion into a statement. A statement by doing something, taking action! He had practiced to make his voice, normally a somewhat high for a male, into what he thought was acceptably female. Slightly deeper than average for a woman, but very feminine, he hoped. Still, preciousness was something to avoid. So was coquettishness. This was serious business, not play-acting. He knew he had a woman's soul inside his male body, though emboldened on occasion with masculine anger at past injustices, especially. Now he, at this moment she, had left the apartment on Lincoln Avenue. It was starting to rain slightly. Only a few sprinkles, but enough to worry Boyood. Would his, her, make-up run? Would his, her, mood turn from elation, as it now was, into depression, even rage? There was no way of knowing just yet. Something like rain, however, might complicate things considerably. Boyood walked north down Hennepin Avenue across from the Methodist church. A car came around the corner and was about to turn into the short frontage street parallel to Hennepin. Impulsively, he turned and thumbed a ride. Surprisingly, the vehicle stopped. Inside was an attractive brown-haired young woman—a "pretty girl" as Boyood called such creatures. She smiled and yelled through her open passenger window.

"Need a ride? I'm going down to Oak Grove Avenue and turning right toward downtown. I can take you that far. Is that okay?"

Boyood smiled at the young woman and got in her car.

"Thank you. I'm not going far, really."

Waiting first in line at the stoplight the opposite direction, Walking Cloud was going home. He intended to fix himself a light supper, take a nap, and perhaps watch the 10 o'clock news, where he might find himself and the Chief of Police featured. He also remembered Cornbread Harris was playing the second of a two-night gig at the Loring Pasta Bar. No, that's Friday. Tonight was a French-Canadian *chanteuse*. Possibly that, too, although late-night hours were not his habit on week nights. He didn't notice the dark blue VW rabbit station wagon stop to pick up a hitchhiker. Nor did he take any note of the vehicle as it turned and went past him turning left onto Hennepin. Instead, he wondered how Krewler was doing at the hospital. A "paranoiac incident?" What was that, exactly? The nurse didn't say, nor did he ask her what the former boxer had done to get restrained and etherized.

At the next intersection, the young woman turned right onto Grove Avenue. Less than ten seconds later, Boyood let out an exclamation and asked her to stop the car immediately. Puzzled, she slowed to a stop. As soon as she did, Boyood pulled a knife and stuck it to the side of her throat.

"Alright, honey, now turn this pile of shit around and park behind that truck! See there? Make one funny move and I'll carve your neck into a fountain of *gore*!"

"What is this?" the young woman cried. "You're not a—*a woman*! What do you want from me? I give you a ride because it's raining and you pull a *knife* on me! Please, just get out of my car! *Get out*!"

Boyood pricked the side of the young woman's neck and it bled into a trickle. Now frightened, she did as she was told. She couldn't believe this was really happening.

"My neck, it's bleeding!" she cried, looking at the blood on her fingers and on Boyood's knife, which he held up to her eyes. "What are you—"

But her question was stopped when Boyood slammed a fist into her mouth and then repeatedly hit her till she lost consciousness.

In his apartment, Walking Cloud fixed a meal of green beans and broiled steak, with a glass of light beer. He ate and listened to one of his favorite recordings, Erik Satie's *Trois Gymnopédies* and *Je te veux*, with Anne Queffélec on piano. Then he read the newspaper, which occupied him for nearly an hour until a nap beckoned. He set the alarm radio for ten o'clock. Then he changed his pillowcase. He was asleep within seconds.

Jenny Schell decided to call Will Alsted at his home. Alsted, a lawyer who was handling the probate of Jack Breamington's will, including his investment portfolio, had called her at work concerning the account. Because of the aftermath of Julie Tinkham's death, Jenny hadn't returned his call right away. She had met him briefly for the first time at Breamington's wake at the family home in Kenwood. She sensed immediately that he fancied her, but would keep within bounds no matter what happened. He would be easy to turn down, if need be, but then she wondered if it might not be such a bad idea. He was surprised by her call, but cordial. Predictably, he suggested they have a preliminary discussion of the Breamington portfolio over dinner at the Black Forest Inn. Fine, she said. Good, he replied, how about six o'clock? He would pick her up at her place. She accepted. She'd have a dinner date with a reasonably handsome, eligible bachelor who had the power to yank or let her keep a lucrative account. Did he know about her affair with Breamington? She decided not to worry about it. It was, she told herself, a business dinner date, sort of. Then she thought of the next morning, when she would spend time with the police sketch artist. She resolved to leave by 11:30 whether the cops liked it or not and spend the afternoon at her job, making money.

When his radio alarm sounded at ten, Walking Cloud got up and washed his face. He turned on the news and there he was, explaining to an insistent reporter about the forensics report and the police department's profile, albeit his own based on years of experience, of Julie Tinkham's killer. The shrink's profile he didn't see until afterward. When the weathercast came on, he suddenly remembered to call about Krewler again in the cardiac ward. He knew that uniforms were assigned to guard him during the evening and graveyard shifts. He decided to go to the bar and possibly then go check on Krewler in person.

Walking Cloud arrived at the Loring Pasta Bar and was surprised by the crowd, which was dense and beery. A space opened up at the bar and Walking Cloud ordered a mineral water with lime. Alcohol he'd had earlier, if only a single light beer with his supper. Since he intended to visit Krewler at the cardiac ward, he didn't need booze on his breath. Someone touched his arm. It was Anna, the bartender who had served him the night before. She was taking a break, it appeared.

"Good evening," he said.

"This is a different crowd than the ones who came to hear Cornbread," she said. "We could probably use a cop here. Interested?"

Walking Cloud smiled.

"I'm off-duty now," he mused. "Never work outside the department. Made that decision a long time ago. That's for uniforms, anyway. I live within my means."

"I kind-a thought so," she said. "I heard you were a policeman. I was surprised."

"I'm a homicide detective. Lots on the plate these days."

"I hear the murder rate's going down so far this year."

She didn't dwell about his job, sensing—he thought—that he couldn't talk about it except in generalities. On stage was Francine Roche, the French-Canadian chanteuse, with a fast-paced song in French. The dance floor was crowded as she sang Piaf ballads, slower and quite danceable. Walking Cloud asked Anna to dance when Roche began "Je ne regrette rien." They kept on for "La Vie en Rose." There was a soft, exquisite lull in the room, compared to the frenetic pace of the fiercer songs.

"You're talking a break from work?" he asked.

"No, I was off at ten," she said. "I started at noon, worked all day, so here I am, just hanging out before I go home."

"You're tired, I'll bet."

"A little bit."

They retired from the floor when Roche began singing another fast song. Now Walking Cloud felt fatigue, as well.

"You're going home?" she asked.

"Well, not directly. I have to visit someone in the hospital first. Gotta get up at six-thirty. Tomorrow's my day to run before work."

Anna pressed his hand and said she'd be right back. She returned with her purse and coat. Walking Cloud offered her a ride home.

"Sure it's not out of your way?" she asked. "I live northeast."

"It is, in fact, but no problem."

"Thank you. Ready to go?"

As they were about to leave the room, a man selling roses in a bucket appeared. Walking Cloud bought a red rose and gave it to Anna, who did not seem surprised. When they left the Loring Pasta Bar, rain was falling in sprinkles. It continued lightly while they drove on Fourth Street, Bob Dylan's very own, toward Hennepin and up into "nordeast Minneapolis."

"So what should I call you? By your name or rank or what?"

"How about Ben? Friends, colleagues, call me that."

"Ben. That sounds nice. I have to work tomorrow night. Cornbread will be playing again."

"Yes, I know. If I can, I'll come down. Right now at work, we're on the track of a vicious murderer—"

"That woman in the parking ramp?"

"Yes," said Walking Cloud, surprised.

"I pay some attention to the news," she said. "I also volunteer at a women's shelter a few hours a week. That really got our attention over there."

"Yes, I can imagine."

When they reached her place, she invited him in to see her apartment. He looked at his watch. It was eleven-thirty. He accepted her invitation. Then his car phone rang.

"Yes?"

"Lieutenant Walking Cloud?"

"Yes, this is."

It was Detective Peterson.

"Captain Blatsky said to call you right away, sir. A young woman's been found unconscious, beaten, possibly raped, strangulation marks on her throat—"

"Where'd they find her?" cut in Walking Cloud. "Where?"

"In a car parked on Oak Grove Avenue alongside Loring Park. She was discovered by a passing jogger and taken to Hennepin County General. Forensics is at the scene now."

"Get me a full report by morning. I have to go to the hospital, anyway. Who are the primaries? You and Hyslip?"

"Depends on what you decide, Lieutenant. The name of the victim is Lori Ruth Mueller. M-U-E-L-L-E-R."

"Got it. I'll check on her. Emergency room?"

"Affirmative, sir."

"I'll meet you at the crime scene in ten, fifteen."

Anna put her hand to her mouth.

"It's the same—"

"Same m.o. as the young woman in the parking ramp?" said Walking Cloud. "Well, not quite, but it could be. She's still alive. Let me walk you to your door. I'll have to take a rain check on—"

"Oh, that's okay. I understand."

When they got to her door, Anna turned and kissed Walking Cloud on the cheek. She took his hand.

"Thanks, Ben. I'll see you tomorrow. Despite this, I hope you're able to get some sleep tonight."

"Put that rose in water now. I'll try to come down tomorrow night."

He waited till she got inside and locked the door, then went back to his car. He drove to the end of the block and put out his flashing light. He phoned Martridge and asked him to come to the crime scene immediately.

The area was heavily trafficked, cut off by a yellow police ribbon. Walking Cloud and Martridge made their way through a small crowd. Detectives Peterson and Hyslip were already there. A blue named MacNeil gestured grimly to the open front door of a small dark blue VW station wagon.

"The victim was found slumped over," MacNeil explained. "She was seated in the passenger side. The vehicle is registered in her name. Lori Ruth Mueller. Here's the workup, Lieutenant. She was barely alive. Indications are she'd been in the car for at least a couple hours. This is Tom Lupe, who found her."

In jogging attire, in his twenties, and wide-eyed, Lupe told how he was running by and happened to see the top of the victim's head slumped inside the locked vehicle. MacNeil added that Lori Ruth Mueller had strangulation marks on her throat, her nose and jaw appeared fractured, and there was blood on her legs.

"Forensics found this piece of paper, Lieutenant," said Peterson, holding up a plastic see-through bag just handed him by a technician. Walking Cloud held it up to the light. Inside was a scrap of brown paper, the kind used in making grocery bags. The letters were in crude black felt pen:

DEAR LT. W.C.

   —NUMBER TWO

FOR <u>U</u>!

   —PANDORA KILLER

Martridge looked over his shoulder.

"Jee-sus *Christ*! That's addressed to *you*!"

Walking Cloud handed the plastic bag back to Peterson.

"Make a copy of this and put it on my desk. It's confidential, Peterson. Don't lose it."

"Yes, sir."

"Lieutenant, we've got visitors," said Martridge.

Looking up, Walking Cloud saw none other than Rhonda Reele, the Channel Five reporter, hurrying from a news van with a cameraman right behind her.

"Peterson, Hyslip, MacNeil!" said Walking Cloud. The younger detectives looked at him in the seconds before Rhonda Reele would be within earshot. "Without exception, refer all questions from reporters to *me*. *All* of them. *Got it?*"

"Yes, sir, Lieutenant," said Peterson. Hyslip and MacNeil both nodded.

A tow truck from the police lab backed up to the blue VW station wagon.

"All we can tell you is the victim of this assault is in the emergency room at Hennepin General," said Walking Cloud. "We're withholding her name till her family's been notified."

"But she's alive, isn't she?" pressed Rhonda Reele.

"Yes, as far as we know. If you'll excuse us, we're headed to the hospital now."

With that, Walking Cloud strode away quickly and got into his car. Martridge kept up with him.

"I'll bet they're going to the hospital, too," Martridge said of the reporters.

"Sure, if I were a reporter, I'd probably do the same. Wouldn't you?"

At the hospital, more reporters awaited them with frenzied insistence. Walking Cloud and Martridge waded through them. A doctor named Jenkins led them to the elevator.

"Prognosis bad?" asked the Lieutenant.

"She's unconscious," said the doctor. "It doesn't look good. There's barely a read on her brain waves. The attempted strangulation cut off the blood supply and oxygen to her brain, and then the fact that she was left to die with no attempt at resuscitation makes it probable that she may never come out of it. She's been moved to Intensive Care, up on the third floor."

The doctor led them into the room where Lori Ruth Mueller was hooked up to machines, with plastic tubing into her throat and nose, an IV needle in her arm.

"To answer your question about her prognosis," said the doctor, "at this point, it's very poor. You see the marks under her chin and down around the tubing going into her throat?"

"Yes."

"Leather marks. Probably assaulted with a pair of soft leather gloves or possibly a belt of some kind. She was also raped vaginally and anally. Bruises around both orifices. I understand she was found in the front seat of her station wagon. I'd guess it was done while she was unconscious in the front seat. Her nose and jaw suffered traumatic insult as well, mostly likely a fist straight on repeatedly. She's a small person. Weight's probably a hundred pounds at most. This kind of beating is like a truck hitting anyone else. You get the picture?"

"Yes," said Walking Cloud. "Were you able to extract the fluids, etcetera, for forensics?"

"Yes, and it'll all be sent over to your lab for analysis."

"Were there any smudges of facial make-up on her face or neck?" asked Martridge.

"Yes, and I understand they were noted by your forensics technician before they were wiped off when we prepared to insert the catheter. We'll need to have a surgeon reconstruct her nasal cartilage once she stabilizes and regains consciousness. *If* she does."

"Lieutenant, the parents of the victim are here," said Peterson. "Just arrived. Do you—want to talk to them?"

Talking with relatives or survivors after a crime was something Walking Cloud always dreaded. He felt least equipped to perform such duty. But never ask a subordinate to do something you won't do yourself.

"Yes, thank you. I'll talk to them."

They were led into a waiting room nearby where three people—a middle-aged man and woman, and a teen-age youth—were waiting. They were Albert and Maya Mueller, and their son, Keith. Walking Cloud expressed condolences and got through the conversation with delicate questions. Does their daughter have a boyfriend? Yes, but he's a student in Milwaukee. What's he like? Nice, a good person, never a complaint of any kind from their daughter. Had she ever talked about other men recently? No, but that might not mean much, said the father. She always had a tendency to be secretive, even as a child. When was the last time they had seen her? Earlier this evening, said the mother.

Lori had come home to do her laundry and have supper with them. And so on.

After leaving the Muellers in their grief, Walking Cloud went to a hospital office and called Blatsky and Bellicoast on conference hookup. They agreed to meet in the Chief's office the next morning. Walking Cloud didn't mention the note the killer had left at the scene of the crime. Hit them with it after a night's rest.

Chapter Nine

Pandora Killer at the Hospital?

When he arrived at Krewler's bedside, the Lieutenant encountered other visitors.

"Poggie Williams," said the older black man. "And this here's Kid Garter. We jus' checkin' up on Marty. Soon as he gets out-a here, we got a fighter tuh ready for a bout at the end-a next month. Marty's helpin' wid the trainin'."

Krewler was awake, though groggy. The physical restraints were gone.

"Mr. Krewler, how're you doing?" asked Walking Cloud.

"Sleepy. Tired. I don't know why."

"We got special permission to come this late from that lady doctor on duty," explained Poggie, "'cause Marty was asleep all evenin' long. We jus' wanted tuh see how he's doin'. They let us come on up here if we doan stay too long."

"I see," said Walking Cloud.

An orderly with a cart of medical supplies puttered about a few feet away. He was a trim, swarthy man with a small mustache and ponytail.

"I understand you might be released tomorrow," Walking Cloud said.

"Uh, huh," mumbled Krewler. "They tell you that?"

"They also said you had a paranoiac incident and had to be restrained."

"Uhm, he don't look too energetic to me," observed Kid Garter. "Good thing ya ain't still puggin', Marty."

Krewler managed a weak grin.

"Yeah," Poggie chimed in, "yuh gotta git your strength back." Then turning to Walking Cloud, he said, "I imagine your visit here's biz-ness, Loo-tenant."

"That's right."

Walking Cloud glanced at the orderly, who seemed to linger nearby and quickly looked away, then pushed his cart toward the swinging door to the right. There was a plastic i.d. hanging from his shirt pocket. The uniformed cop was wandering somewhere in the hallway, taking a break as soon as he saw the Lieutenant enter the ward.

"Excuse me a minute," said Walking Cloud.

"Sure," replied Poggie.

Walking Cloud went over to the nurse's station.

"May I help you?" asked a nurse on duty.

"That orderly who was just here with the cart, have you seen him here before?"

The nurse looked at Walking Cloud blankly and glanced around the ward.

"I didn't notice. Did he have an i.d. badge?"

"Yes, he did. What are his duties? Do you know?"

"Quite possibly any of a hundred different things. Refilling supplies, checking equipment on request, whatever. What's the problem?"

"Thank you."

Walking Cloud went out into the hallway, up and down, looking into rooms. A young uniform sat on a stool, chatting with a young woman in a white jacket. She turned and looked at the Lieutenant. The uniform stood up and tried to look alert.

"Is something wrong, sir?" asked the young woman in the white jacket. She wore her blonde hair in a coiffure. Her nametag read Jill Munson, M.D.

"Who are you?" asked Walking Cloud.

"Dr. Munson," she said, startled. "I'm an intern in cardiology."

"Do you have a picture i.d. list of employees who work in this area?"

"Personnel on the first floor would have that information, but they're closed at this hour."

Walking Cloud described the man he'd seen. Now another male orderly came by pushing a cart with plastic containers, small cardboard boxes and blankets underneath. Walking Cloud stared at his badge i.d.

"Have you seen him before?" he asked the doctor.

"Yes, he's worked here at least as long as I have. Nearly two months now. I'm doing a residency here."

Walking Cloud's instincts in aberrant situations had rarely, if ever, failed him.

"Thanks, Doctor."

He went back to the coronary care ward, just as Poggie Williams and Kid Garter were about to leave.

"We'll check on ya tomorrow, Marty," said Poggie. "Nice meetin' ya, Loo-tenant."

"Yahssir, real nice," affirmed Kid Garter.

Walking Cloud shook hands with them. As he watched the two old fighters leave, he wondered if the uniformed cop in the hallway might be better stationed in the room. A nurse came by, entered Krewler's area, and stared briefly at Walking Cloud.

"You're the police, aren't you?"

"Yes."

"Well, Mr. Krewler has fallen asleep. Visiting hours were over at nine-thirty, sir. This patient needs his rest."

The broadest of hints could not be missed.

"All right. Thanks. I'm going to have the officer on duty stay near his bedside as a security precaution."

"That's fine, as long as he's quiet."

"I'll relay your concern, Nurse."

He decided to check once more on Lori Ruth Mueller. He told the blue to go into the cardiac ward, sit in a chair near Krewler and keep a close eye on anyone who went near him. When the elevator doors opened, Walking Cloud entered. As the doors began to close, he heard a crash, then some yelling.

He immediately thrust his arms out and the doors sprang back, just as a figure dashed past him, knocking the young cop down with what looked like a karate chop. Walking Cloud thought he recognized the back of the man's head. It was the ponytail, the same orderly he'd been suspicious of earlier.

"*Stop!*" he yelled. "*Police! Stop right there!*"

The perp ran to the stairwell exit, turned, picked up a bucket of water and hurled it at Walking Cloud, missing but causing his target to slip and fall. The dark-haired man with the ponytail took a mop handle and hit Walking Cloud in the head as he tried to get up, knocking him down. The young cop tried to get up and was also hit in the head. The perp disappeared down the stairwell. Walking Cloud was seeing double for a few seconds. His forehead was bleeding. He got up slowly. He checked on the cop, who was out cold. Instead of trying to give chase, Walking Cloud got out his phone and headed back to the cardiac ward where he saw bedlam: an overturned desk, a torn curtain where Krewler lay, and two people in white clothes bending over a nurse on the floor. Krewler was attended to by a nurse and Dr. Munson. An oxygen mask had been clamped over his face. Dr. Munson looked up at Walking Cloud.

"We caught someone trying to *smother this patient!*" she said. "He looked like the man you described, Lieutenant."

"How is he?"

"Barely breathing! A close call!" Then to the nurse, she said, "Keep that on his face."

Walking Cloud alerted hospital security and ordered the hospital closed down. No one could leave or enter till further notice. He described the perp and told Peterson and Hyslip to come up to the cardiac ward and bring five cops as well as a forensics unit. He hurried to the exit where the perp had disappeared. He drew his weapon and proceeded into the stairwell. There was no movement. He heard nothing.

On the first floor, Poggie Williams and Kid Garter had left the elevator and were heading toward the 6th Street exit when alarms suddenly went off. Police were running to the exits, stopping and checking those who attempted to leave or enter. Sirens were in the distance, coming closer.

At the 6th Street exit, two cops were talking to each other.

"Walking Cloud said someone was trying to kill a patient!" said one.

"Jesus, Mary, Joseph!" said the other.

"Walking Cloud!" repeated Kid Garter.

"You see Walking Cloud just now?" asked one of the cops.

"Yahssir, we jus' come from up dere," said Kid Garter. "Who was gettin' killed up dere?"

"Not—not Marty, was it?" said Poggie, who had stopped chewing his candy bar.

"He didn't say," said the cop, his senior demeanor matter-of-fact. "I can't let you out during lockdown. Sorry. You fellows have some i.d.?"

"Yahssir," Kid Garter replied.

The cop checked their driver's licenses and then looked at Kid Garter.

"You look familiar," he said. "Edward Garter? Hey, aren't you *Kid Garter*, the fighter?" The cop smiled, baring slightly yellow teeth. "Yeah, I saw you fight on t.v. 'Member when you knocked out Fingers Germain on E-S-P-N! Boy, what a picture perfect left hook! Man! Glad to *meet* yuh! I'm Art Daniels. This is my partner, Sergeant Bill Crouse."

Handshakes. Kid Garter and Poggie were both surprised.

"Thank yuh," said the Kid. "My fightin' days are long behind me. Ah train fighters now. This is Poggie Williams, mah biz-ness partner."

People were collecting on both sides of the glass doors. More cops showed up. Detectives Peterson and Hyslip came out of an elevator.

"Where's Walking Cloud?" yelled Peterson.

"Somewhere between here and the fourth floor, chasing a perp who tried to smother a patient," a blue answered.

The detectives chose five uniformed cops to go with them. Peterson took out his phone: "Lieutenant, this is Peterson. Where are you?"

"The Men's Room. Second floor. Come on up."

On the second floor, Walking Cloud showed them a rubber mask with a likeness of the perp, fibers from a fake mustache and hairpiece, and a slim blue orderly's shirt and pants.

"He's put the slip on us. No telling who he is or what he looks like. But why does he want *Krewler* dead? Krewler's got to know something or have seen something that implicates somebody. More than what he testified to before the grand jury. This is a pretty elaborate costume. Keep the guard on Krewler. I want to know the minute he's discharged. Dust this john and the railings up the stairwell. No one gets in here till it's sifted. How long? Thirty minutes?"

"Yeah, about that," said Peterson. "Alright, guys, you heard the Lieutenant." Then to Walking Cloud: "We got some other bad news, sir. Lori Ruth Mueller died about fifteen minutes ago. According to forensics, the match-ups look the same as the Tinkham case. They're doing DNA tests, but it looks like Number Two for Pandora Killer. Like he said in his note."

Walking Cloud went down to the first floor. When he got to the 6th Street doors, he saw Kid Garter and Poggie Williams.

"These two men can leave," he told the blues. "I know them." He looked at Kid Garter and Poggie Williams. "Someone just tried to smother Marty Krewler. You remember that orderly up there?"

"Yeah, I saw you eyeballin' him," said Poggie. "He had one leg shorter'n the other."

"One leg shorter than the other?" said Walking Cloud, incredulous. "I didn't see that."

"Yeah, one-a his shoes was lifted," said Kid Garter. "I saw that, too. The left one. He was jus' slightly off-balance. You can tell, workin' wid fighters, yuh know. Seein' when someone's balanced, when he's not. The guy's left leg was mebbe quarter inch shorter."

"Hey, Lieutenant!" said Daniels. "This is *Kid Garter*! He k.o.'d Fingers Germain back about twelve, thirteen years ago on E-S-P-N! *Beautiful* left hook!"

"Well, thass all a while ago now," said the Kid effacingly. "Don't think Fingers fights no more. And I don't, a-course. Time catches up."

"You knocked out Fingers?" said Walking Cloud, mildly surprised.

"Yep, he sure did!" chimed in Daniels. "Third round!"

"You don't mind the opinion, Kid?" said Walking Cloud. "You did better against him than the county prosecutors have. Tell me, you guys think you'd recognize the gait and balance of that fake orderly if you saw him again? The reason I ask is he's just changed his appearance."

The two old fighters agreed they might be able to spot the perp and would wait with the police to observe at both street-level exits. The lockdown had ended. A stream of disconcerted people hurried through the doors. Walking Cloud knew the perp would recognize him quickly. He took out a pair of reading glasses, put on an old hat and sat in the waiting room with a full view of the 6th Street exit, where Kid Garter watched with Peterson. Poggie waited on the 7th Street exit with Hyslip. Cops were also posted outside. Walking Cloud suddenly became aware of his own fatigue again. He'd been at a steady pace for nearly nineteen hours. He didn't like working when tired.

He watched people come and go through the doors. He looked at their feet, at their gaits. An elderly black woman, then a middle-aged Asian woman, left the building, passing a tall white man with a beard who came in with a folded newspaper in one hand, a small piece of paper in the other. Next an older balding man with a limp and a cane moved toward the exit. He was shabbily dressed, the lining in his worn sports jacket hanging in tatters from the hem. Then a younger man on crutches with blond hair in a ponytail accompanied by a slender young woman with dark hair in braids down her back. She was talking and gesticulating. Her companion had a cast on his left foot. Walking Cloud stood up, then sat down again.

"Peterson," said Walking Cloud into his finger mike, "check out that blond guy on crutches. Check the girl's i.d., too."

"Right-o," replied Peterson.

Walking Cloud beeped Hyslip. "It's Walking Cloud, Bob. How're you doing?"

"Watching closely, sir. No one remotely so far."

"You know what to do."

"Gotcha, Lieutenant. Over and out."

More people passed by—young, not so young, old, Asian, white, black, some hospital personnel, a myriad of humanity at a big city hospital. Someone looking old in a wheel chair wearing a hat and his lap covered with blankets was being pushed to the exit by a chunky man with a brown ponytail wearing a light blue orderly's outfit. Walking Cloud spoke into his lapel mike again.

"Look at those two carefully, Peterson."

"Old guy looks about seventy-five," said Peterson. "Pretty sickly looking. So why's he being wheeled outside?"

The feet hanging from the chair were ordinary black shoes. Other people passed by, blocking a clear view of the orderly's feet as his ponytail bobbed out the door. Kid Garter was looking at them, too, and he shook his head curiously. Walking Cloud edged forward. Kid Garter looked out the glass doors.

"They still there?" Walking Cloud asked.

The old boxer shrugged.

"Dunno. Disappeared somewhere."

"Jesus!" said the Lieutenant, pushing the door open. Peterson was right behind him. They ran out to the sidewalk and looked one way, then the other.

"Lieutenant, *look*!"

The ponytailed man was pushing the old man into the intersection, forcing two vehicles, then more, to stop in mid-traffic. He turned and spotted the detectives, who had drawn their weapons. He pointed his own at the old man's head and shouted, "Throw down your *guns! Now! Toward me! On the street!* You have *four seconds!* One—two—*three*—"

Just then a police squad car raced into the scene. The ponytailed man ducked behind the wheelchair and shot at the squad car, hitting the front tire. The vehicle lurched, skidded and turned on its side, hitting the curb and a light post. The two detectives jumped for cover as it exploded into flames. The ponytailed man commandeered one of the cars he'd stopped, pulling a middle-aged woman from the passenger side, shoving her to the ground and getting into the car. He put his pistol to the face of the driver, a well-dressed man in his forties.

"Drive, you bastard! *Drive! Now!*"

"Okay! Okay!" said the man behind the wheel. "Please, don't hurt my wife!"

"I'll blow her fucking *brains* out right now where she is if you don't *move!* Now *drive! Go!*"

The gray sedan suddenly lurched forward and sped away just as Walking Cloud and Peterson ran around the burning squad car.

"Holy Mother of Christ!" yelled Peterson.

"Something like that," said Walking Cloud, memorizing the license plate number. "Come on!"

They rushed to the still figure in the wheelchair. At Walking Cloud's touch, it fell forward, a dummy with stuffed clothing.

"Jesus!" moaned Walking Cloud. "It figures."

They ran to Peterson's vehicle half a block away. Right light on top, they went the direction the gray sedan had gone.

"This is Walking Cloud. A.P.B. on Minnesota license A-G-T-4-0-3. A gray Mercedes Benz four-door sedan, late model, heading south on Portland from Sixth Street South. Do not attempt to intercept. Suspect armed and dangerous with a hostage driver."

But no sooner had the Lieutenant said this than the gray sedan seemed to have vanished in the night air.

Two blocks west on 7th Street, the gray sedan was moving through nighttime downtown traffic, flowing through green lights unnoticed and past Nicollet Mall. Holding his pistol low, the ponytailed man commanded his well-dressed hostage: "Don't attract attention! *Slow down!*"

Sirens were in the distant background. The ponytailed man glanced quickly in the rear window. Police vehicles were blocks away, heading in another direction. Now a parking ramp appeared on the left.

"There!" he ordered. "Drive in *there!* Go up the *ramp! Go!*"

"Alright!" the hostage agreed nervously, his head beginning to tremble. "Look, what do you want? Is it money? I can give you *money*. Just don't hurt me! *Please!*"

"You have money?"

"Yes! Yes! I'll give it to you! Just don't—"

"Shut up, you asshole! You're getting on my nerves!"

The gray sedan entered the parking ramp, no attendant visible.

Several blocks away, Walking Cloud and Peterson realized they had lost the perp.

"It's pointless!" the Lieutenant said. "Let's go back!"

From his car phone, he called Captain Blatsky and Chief Bellicoast again at their homes. Both agreed to meet him right away at the hospital. Walking Cloud knew the media was on the story and would not be put off. Lori Ruth Mueller's death, the deaths of the two cops in the burning squad car, preceded by the attempted murder of Krewler and the suspect's escape with a hostage—these marked the chaff of the evening.

"Park over there in the far corner," the ponytailed man ordered his hostage.

The gray sedan slid into the corner slot. The hostage was ordered out of the car and forced to disrobe. Standing in his underwear, he pleaded with his captor once more. But the ponytailed man merely unlocked the trunk latch and ordered the terrified hostage to get into the trunk. Then he clamped a silencer on the muzzle of his weapon and fired two shots. The hostage, dead instantly, slumped forward over the edge of the trunk. The killer shoved the dead man back inside the compartment and slammed the lid shut. Running into the stairwell, he removed a fake nose from his face, then a hairpiece, revealing close-cropped light brown hair. He stopped at the first landing and changed into the impeccably tailored clothes of his newest victim.

"We can tell yuh this," said the Chief of Police into the t.v. lights. "We have three deaths in what we believe are two different cases, two different perpetrators. One of these perps has a hostage at gunpoint somewhere in this city. The hostage is identified as Mr. Louis Bertram, a local attorney who lives in Edina. The squad car carrying the two police officers to their deaths unexpectedly came into a confrontation between police detectives and Mr. Bertram's abductor, whose identity we do not know at this time. The two police officers who died, Peter Johansson and Thomas Runbar, were actin', as far as we can tell, on their own initiative. The other perpetrator, the slayer of both Lori Ruth Mueller and, we believe, Julie Tinkham this past Tuesday evenin', has left us a written message. We won't release the contents, but we can tell yuh that he signed it 'Pandora Killer,' manifestin' a long pent-up hatred of women. This guy is a *predator*. We want him *bad*. And we'll get him and the other suspect the way we've always solved cases in Minneapolis. By solid police work! We'll provide updates on pert'nent information at our next press briefin' sometime tomorrow. Thank you. I'm sorry, but no questions. No questions."

Walking Cloud himself was too exhausted physically and mentally to respond to reporters' questions. To Captain Blatsky, he said, "I'll dictate a report tomorrow morning, Ed. I've got to go home now."

Blatsky nodded grimly and touched him on the arm. Walking Cloud then told him that this had been the worst day of his professional life.

Chapter Ten

A Pol's Dilemma

"We can't move on this until the police do their jobs, perform their end of it," said Mike Quinn into the phone receiver the next morning, trying not to show his exasperation. A copy of *the Star Tribune* was on his desk. He stared at the headlines, the savage black letters:

2ND WOMAN SLAIN BY 'PANDORA KILLER';
2 POLICE ALSO KILLED IN HOSPITAL MELEE!
LOCAL ATTORNEY TAKEN AS HOSTAGE

Quinn was talking to a newspaper reporter, a young woman he didn't trust.

"Yes, I'm *exploring* a run for governor," he told her. "That's no secret. When will I announce? In due time. There's no hurry."

Finally, he was able to end the conversation. He took a deep breath. His phone buzzed again. It was his secretary, Melanie Wisp.

"Rhonda Reele and a cameraman are here, Mike, in the outer reception room. She said she'd like to talk to you about Pandora Killer, among other things. Looks like she's out for blood!"

"I'll bet she is," said Quinn, suspecting a trap. "She didn't call ahead for an appointment?"

"No, they just appeared without warning."

"What goddamn *nerve* these people have! Tell her I'm in a meeting. Then get McCorkle and Finegrad for me, Melanie. Interrupt them, if necessary, unless they're in court. Tell them to meet me in my office right away and to use the inner hallway."

"Will do, Mike."

Quinn stared at the newspaper again. The emergence of a serial killer since Tuesday had eclipsed the Breamington murder.

"Look, tension from this one's already sky-high," suggested Finegrad, the ex-cop.

"I know it's hot, but it's the law we have to worry about," declared Quinn. "We can't just pretend Walking Cloud's gamble paid off, can we? Two cops are dead, the policeman's union's screaming, and we've got a missing hostage. Louis Bertram's not just anybody!"

"He's a Republican lawyer from Edina," said Finegrad. "How the hell did he get in the middle of this, anyway?"

"Wrong place at the wrong time. Listen, we got reporters in the lobby. They're out to get me on this one. *Goddammit!*"

"They know you're running for governor," said McCorkle. "It's an ongoing sport with them, Mike. Work up a boilerplate answer. Call a press conference in half an hour outside the front doors here. Tell 'em you're confident the Minneapolis Police will apprehend suspects in both the Breamington *and* Pandora murders, but it takes time—"

"Tell 'em police work isn't magic," interjected Finegrad. "Tell 'em it's intensive, hard work, and murders aren't solved by waving a wand. I was a cop for twenty years. *I know!* There's a lot of slow, tedious work in solving most murder cases."

McCorkle chucked sardonically. Quinn smiled dourly, then stared at the desktop and worked his mouth in a tense manner. He looked at his two subordinates distractedly.

"Dick, have you talked to Walking Cloud yet this morning?"

"No, but I left him a message to call when he gets in."

"He's got to *produce* for us, dammit! My political career depends on it. My candidacy for governor isn't worth a damn if I've got one hand tied behind my back."

McCorkle and Finegrad looked at their boss with sudden new insight. Morning light streamed into the room.

In the parking ramp a few blocks west, the gray Mercedes-Benz filled the corner like a pouting sentry, its face turned away. Now at 9:45, a young watchman scanned the top floor as he entered from the stairwell. The entire floor was reserved for a law firm. A complaint just received from one of the lawyers was that his parking space was occupied by another vehicle. Please check on it. The young watchman checked the license plate and make, which did not match the vehicle assigned to the space. He took out his phone and was about to report to his dispatcher when he noticed a dried substance, a spot, on the outside of the trunk, then more dried spots on the shiny silver fender and the cement escarpment. He knew what it was. Shaken, he lifted the phone. He called in the make and license plate. Then he said, "There's something here, Jane. I'm pretty sure it's dried blood. Better call in the cops."

Walking Cloud entered the squad room five minutes later. He had slept reasonably well, considering the previous day and evening. He was anxious to resume the hunt. He also had taken his morning run around Lake of the Isles. Martridge and Winchell looked up from their desks. Rails was on the phone. Mygosh was standing at his desk and was about to speak when his desk phone rang. Walking Cloud went into his office, followed by McDour.

"Homicide, Sergeant Mygosh."

Mygosh listened for half a minute and went to Walking Cloud's doorway.

"Ben, a security guard at Miller's Parking Ramp next to Macy's on 7th Street found Louis Bertram's car on the top floor. Dried blood spots at the back of the vehicle."

Walking Cloud sighed.

"Alright, get a forensics team over there, Joshua. Better let Finegrad at the HCA's office know, too. Call Blatsky and the Chief and tell 'em our meeting will have to be later. Meet us there, Joshua."

The scene was bleak, like the skyline. The young watchman was waiting along with a middle-aged supervisor.

"When did you find this vehicle?" asked the Lieutenant.

"About thirty minutes ago, sir. We had a complaint from the regular occupant of the space."

"Mervyn, where's forensics?" demanded Walking Cloud as he pulled a pair of plastic gloves on his hands. Just then, the forensics unit appeared.

"Dust this vehicle and the stairwell and the elevator," Walking Cloud told them. "Look out for the blood spots here. Jesus, whoever was bleeding lost a lot of it!" Then to Rails: "Got your shimmy key?"

Rails inserted the shimmy key into the trunk lid, which sprang open to reveal to the bloodied corpse of Louis Bertram in his underwear.

"*Goddamn*!" said Rails in a low voice.

Walking Cloud had expected as much. From his inner coat pocket, he withdrew a driver's license photocopy with Bertram's likeness.

"Yeah, it's him," said Rails, touching the corpse's hand. "He's cold. Rigor mortis. I recognize him. Cross-examined me once in a trial."

"Alright, let's let forensics get to work," said Walking Cloud. "Call the wagon, Bill. Alert Kronfort."

Walking Cloud's pager buzzed. It was Quinn.

"We just found Louis Bertram," Walking Cloud told him. "Shot twice in the chest and left dead in the trunk of his own car. The killer took his clothes and wallet, too. The body's stripped down to skivvies. It's him, though."

"Thanks for the info, Lieutenant. Keep me informed when you have anything more on his killer. I know you tussled with him last night. We've got a press conference here at eleven. Rhonda Reele and the rest of the media have been camping out in my lobby. I'm told they're going to ask about Pandora Killer.

That's four deaths in the last sixteen hours and they're going to try to ram it to me. You know what that means, don't you?"

Walking Cloud kept up with the newspapers. He knew Quinn intended to run for governor.

"We're mounting a full-scale investigation," he said. "It's top priority. I can't give you any more than that unless I make something up."

"No, don't do that. But please keep me informed, Lieutenant. Will you?"

"Of course. We certainly will."

At eleven o'clock, Quinn appeared at a podium in front of his office suite.

Walking Cloud was back in the squad room. The t.v. was on.

"I'm fully aware," said Quinn, "that my office cannot move until the Minneapolis Police Department completes a thorough investigation of these heinous murders and has suspects in custody. I've received assurances from both Chief Bellicoast and Lieutenant Walking Cloud that the police are treating this latest rash of killings as top priority, including the murder of a university student, Lori Ruth Mueller, and the deaths of two policemen in the line of duty last night—Officers Peter Johansson and Peter Runbar—and the subsequent execution-like murder of Louis Bertram, a respected Minneapolis attorney who was found dead in the trunk of his car at a downtown parking ramp within the last hour. We extend our condolences to the survivors of all these victims…"

Walking Cloud recognized a slick operator when he saw one. Suddenly, the prepared statement was over. Quinn nodded to a reporter.

"Isn't this a critical time for you? You've got several murders and no suspects and yet you're also running for governor. How do you square a round peg?"

"I don't. Look, I'm not saying anything bizarre or presumptuous. It's not my job or within my powers as county attorney to apprehend the suspects in these crimes. That's for the police to do. Once we have a suspect with credible evidence against him, we'll take it to the grand jury. If we get an indictment, we'll have a case to prosecute and we'll do that very aggressively. Jim?"

"You're known to be exploring a race for governor. How can you prepare for a statewide race when you've got a full-time job here with very pressing responsibilities?"

Quinn nodded perfunctorily, but didn't hesitate.

"Well, that's the same question again, isn't it? Let me try to answer it this way. Look, beyond my job and my family, there is some time for other things, believe it or not. I have a complete staff of full-time lawyers. I attend to *my job* very conscientiously. No one's *ever* accused me of not fulfilling my commitments. Okay, I gotta go. Thanks."

He hurried through the reception area to his office.

"It went well," offered Melanie. "You looked good."

"Let's hope the pundits think so, too," he replied. Turning to Finegrad and McCorkle right behind him, he said, "How long does it take for the homicide squad to come up with something, usually, Dick?"

"Depends on the case. We got two murderers here."

"How do you know it's two?" pressed Quinn. "Could it be just one? One killer—who does women for kicks but contract killings on the side? Who was the intended victim in the hospital?"

"Krewler. Don't you remember, Mike? He's the principal witness in the Breamington case. Walking Cloud's had him protected ever since he came forth as a witness against Fingers Germain!"

"Could this be a hit ordered by Aietovsky, you think?"

"We don't know. The guy's a waiter in a French restaurant downtown. Used to be a pro boxer."

"Any underworld connections?"

"We're checking on that now with Detective Martridge doing a cross-reference. Don't know yet."

Quinn sat on the edge of his desk, frowning.

"We can't do the homicide squad's work for them. No disrespect to your former profession, Dick, but unless we can get someone under indictment for those killings—the guilty party, I mean—I wouldn't even stand a good chance for re-election, much less for governor! We've got six—*six!*—high profile murders in this town since Sunday! Not counting all the others. This is gonna eat me alive if something doesn't break soon."

"I'll check with him on the single-killer theory," said Finegrad. "Knowing Walking Cloud, he's already thought of it."

Chapter Eleven

Bits and Pieces

Walking Cloud examined the forensics report on Lori Ruth Mueller's death. The m.o. in this case had similarities to Julie Tinkham's assailant. Both victims had been traumatized in the face before being sexually assaulted. A stage make-up, a light cream base with olive-colored tint, was also found on the faces of both women. In the Twin Cities area, there were a score or more of retail outlets for this substance. The profile of the killer, refined by the university psychiatrist, showed several characteristics. He probably lived alone, had never married, was under 45 and in a creative profession. As he pondered this, the Lieutenant was handed a folder by Martridge. It was the forensics report on the would-be killer of Krewler at the hospital, likely the same perp who murdered Louis Bertram. No fingerprints, as was also true in the deaths of the two women. There were other significant details. Krewler's would-be killer had worn plastic gloves, make-up and a mask with a false hairpiece. While the bullet fired by the ponytailed perp into the squad car's front tire hadn't been recovered yet, the autopsy on Louis Bertram would probably reveal bullets from the same weapon. How many theaters in the area had engaged an actor within the past year whose physical dimensions and age were within the profile's range? And his voice! Yes, he had shouted at Walking Cloud and Peterson—a booming, sonorous voice that might well and probably did sound very different in normal conversation or even on the stage.

Detectives Martridge and Winchell were assigned the duty of assembling and combing through recent personnel lists of theaters in the metro area, a task they began by phone. At one point, Martridge remarked, "Finegrad called me this morning and asked if Krewler's ever had any underworld connections."

"No indication of that," Walking Cloud said. "There's nothing in his sheet to suggest that, as I remember. But you might cross-reference with the F.B.I. He's lived here for years."

"Right. I already did. Just minor stuff! Nothing recent. Shall I tell Finegrad?"

"Go ahead. They're trying to figure it out, too. The question I have is why someone should want to *kill* Krewler? We have a guard on him because his testimony, while circumstantial, is strong enough—the HCA people feel—to put Fingers away for good. Maybe even dent Aietovsky and his sleaze empire. But—"

"But why *are* they trying to kill him? Is that the reason?" said Martridge.

Walking Cloud punched in the numbers of the coronary care ward of the hospital.

"He's doing okay," said the nurse. "He's awake. He's had breakfast. He's able to receive visitors. Nothing heavy, but he can talk."

"When's he scheduled for release?"

"No decision on that yet. Depends on how soon he recovers from last night's trauma."

"Thanks."

Detective Blumus came in with Jenny Schell. They had three drawings by the sketch artist of the blond man with the pitted face. The sketches revealed a thin, almost wizened, face with probable acne scars, and close-cropped blond hair.

"Are these good likenesses of the man you saw?" Walking Cloud asked Jenny.

"Yes, they are," she replied in a tired voice. "As near as we can get them, as I remember him."

There was little, if any, resemblance to Marlin Anders Johnson or to the perp who had assaulted both Walking Cloud and Krewler at the hospital.

"How tall was he? Can you estimate, Ms. Schell?"

Jenny frowned.

"I'm not a good judge of men's heights, but I'd say he was not as tall as you. You're—"

"Six feet even."

"But maybe a shade taller than him," she said, indicating McDour.

"I'm five-ten," said McDour. "So this man was five-eleven, you'd say?"

"I'd say so. I mean, my eyes were at his chest level, so—"

"Really?" wondered the Lieutenant.

The level of her eyes was not quite an accurate indicator, he thought but did not say.

"I told you all this before," she said with a hint of impatience. Then her face reddened a bit. She looked anxious.

"I know you did," said Walking Cloud. "We're just trying to piece things together. A lot has happened in the last forty-eight hours."

His gaze was impassive as he looked at the three sketches in juxtaposition, holding them at arm's length.

"Thank you, Ms. Schell," he said. "We appreciate your time and effort. I know it's tricky remembering details, getting them just right. Sometimes even then you're not sure you're remembering everything."

Jenny looked as if she were being kept after school for an infraction she hadn't intended. She glanced at her watch. It was 11:15.

"Is there anything else?" she asked.

"I'm not sure, Ms. Schell. When we think we have a credible suspect in Julie Tinkham's murder, we'll certainly need you to look at another line-up. You understand?"

"I suppose so."

"You know, there's one thing about both the murders of Julie Tinkham and the young woman who died in the hospital last night—"

"Yes, they found her in her car, too."

"But not in the trunk, oddly. In the front seat, the passenger side. Both victims had a substance smeared on the right side of the face. A light cream-based make-up with an olive tint. From forensics lab analysis and some phone calls, we know it's a substance used most frequently, if not almost exclusively, by stage actors."

Jenny's eyes widened. She looked down as if suddenly realizing something. She looked back up at Walking Cloud.

"Why—do you think—it was there?"

"In the act of intercourse, in this case forcible rape, the assailant has had a habit of positioning himself in that manner on top of his victim's body, his face to her right. In both cases, it was about the same amount of make-up on the right side of the face and neck."

"You're kidding?" Jenny blurted.

"No, I'm not kidding. Why—"

Jenny raised her hand, as if to quiet objection. She pointed to the sketches Walking Cloud held in his hand.

"But that man wasn't wearing any make-up?"

"Not that you could see," said Blumus.

"No, no, I *could* see, Carol. That's just it! He wasn't wearing any make-up. The skin on his face was dry and ruddy. If he did have any make-up, it was clear and must have been put on several hours earlier. I can see him right now!"

"There's no possibility he could have been wearing an olive-tinted substance?" asked McDour.

"No, not on his face."

"You saw both sides of his face?" Walking Cloud inquired.

"Yes, no olive-tinted make-up," Jenny insisted. "Maybe he rubbed it on their faces as he was committing the crimes or afterward."

"What would the motive be?" wondered McDour.

"No motive," said Walking Cloud. "It doesn't add up. Thanks for your time, Ms. Schell. When we need to talk to you again, we'll get in touch."

"You're welcome," Jenny replied.

"Mervyn," said Walking Cloud, handing the sketches back to Blumus, "let's go call on Mr. Krewler, see how he's doing."

McDour nodded to Jenny, and the two senior detectives went out the door. Suddenly Jenny felt depleted, used up, even depressed.

It was just after 11:30 when Walking Cloud and McDour arrived at the coronary care ward. The uniformed police presence at both doors was enough, the Lieutenant hoped, to discourage any more attempts on Krewler's life. A nurse preceded the detectives to his bedside.

"I'll wake him up," she said. "He dozed off after lunch."

After rousing Krewler, the nurse left him alone with his visitors.

"Good afternoon, Mr. Krewler," said Walking Cloud. "How're you doing?"

"Tired. Been sleepin' a lot. Don't know why."

"This is Sergeant McDour of the homicide division. We're here to find out what you know, what you don't know—if you feel up to talking."

"Yeah, I guess."

"There was a man here last night who tried to kill you. Do you remember the incident?"

Krewler frowned for a second. He then relaxed his face. Walking Cloud took a chair near the corner of the bed. McDour sat on a stool, his notepad open. Krewler blinked his eyes.

"I was asleep, I guess. The doctor and nurses told me about it. Is that why you got two cops here all the time?"

"You guessed it," said Walking Cloud. "Why would someone want you dead?"

"I can't tell you. I never did nobody any harm." Then he smacked his lips silently. "Not lately, anyway."

"Is there anything more you know about the death of John Breamington the third that you haven't told us, that didn't come out in the grand jury hearing?" asked McDour.

"I don't think so," said Krewler. "I didn't see who knifed him. Not for sure, anyway. I can't remember! All I saw was him comin' toward me. I hadda keep him off me! He was lookin' wild-eyed, and then I saw the blood?"

"Where was this?" probed McDour. "Where did you see him? Is this Breamington you're talking about—or Fingers Germain?"

"Breamington! I didn't know who the hell he was, except that he looked familiar. Guess I'd seen his picture in the paper or on t.v. I don't know."

"So it was to wash your hands that you went into Rudy's in the first place?" suggested Walking Cloud. "After changing your tire?"

"Yeah."

Krewler sighed and closed his eyes, then opened them again, looking off.

"Why didn't you just wash them in the place where you were playing pool across the street?"

"I don't know, man. I'd been drinkin', you know. Spur-a the moment thing, I guess."

"Okay," said the Lieutenant. "Go on."

"Yeah, where was I?" said Krewler. "Oh, yeah, well, I went into Rudy's. Ritzy joint. It was crowded. I told the hostess I was lookin' for somebody and could I look around? She let me go through. I found the Men's Room. When I pushed the door open, someone rushed right out at me. I recognized him, but I don't think he saw me. I said this in court. He went by me—and I went into the can. There was Breamington bleedin' from the chest, though I didn't know that was his name—"

"We understand," said Walking Cloud. "Go on, Mr. Krewler."

As Krewler talked, Walking Cloud realized his memory was acute and sharp, and that there was no deviation from what he told the grand jury earlier in the week. While there was nothing new in what he said, there was also no clue as to who might want him killed or why. No one other than the Aietovsky crime syndicate, who had a vested interest in keeping Fingers Germain out of jail, if for no other reason than Fingers might prove to be a singing bird when faced with a return to prison. After quarter of an hour, Walking Cloud had heard enough.

"You'll be under police protection until a decision is made about another grand jury attempt to indict Fingers Germain, Mr. Krewler. We also want to find out who tried to kill you, because that person is also responsible for three deaths after coming here last night. Round-the-clock protection, as McCorkle told you before. Now it's even more urgent."

"I looked at the paper this mornin'," said Krewler. "This the same guy who abducted the lawyer?"

"Abducted and *murdered* the lawyer," added Walking Cloud. "He was found a couple hours ago stuffed in the trunk of his car with a bullet in his chest. Yes, we think it's the same perp. We wouldn't keep you in the dark, Mr. Krewler."

Chapter Twelve

Colors Over the Phone

"Lieutenant, we got somethin' from McDougal and Richey tailin' Aietovsky."

It was Detective Rails, handing a printout to Walking Cloud, who asked, "What do I need to know here?"

"Except for fairly routine business, Aietovsky's been makin' calls from a couple cell phones, neither one in his name. He's also got a couple car phones, which aren't billed to him directly. We're monitorin' all-a 'em."

"Is this is leading to anyone significant?"

"We're not sure. Take a look at page four. Included here are transcripts of all his calls, but here's one—very short—of a coded conversation with someone usin' one-a his cell phones and an unknown female party from a pay phone in the entryway at the Black Forest Inn, a German restaurant."

"I know the place."

"Yeah, it's at 26th and Nicollet, which ties into the conversation here. We got the tape, too."

Rails held up a c.d. and pointed to a place on the transcript. He inserted the c.d. disc into a player.

Female Voice: "Yeah/"

Male Voice: "You got red or white?"

Female Voice: "Whaddya want?"

Male Voice: "Red. A bag of red."

Female Voice: "Your deal."

Male Voice: "Tomorrow, twenty-six, oh-seven-hundred."

Female Voice: "Got it. Deal."

Then a couple clicks, and it was over. Walking Cloud looked up at Rails, then at Mygosh who had just appeared.

"When was this?"

"Monday night, the twenty-fourth," said Rails.

"All right, what does it mean, 'red or white'?"

"The female voice supplies either an item or a service," suggested Mygosh. "Or she's representing someone who does, more'n likely. The male voice is the consumer, procurer. The call was initiated from one of Aietovsky's cell phones at 8:02 PM, Monday, the twenty-third."

"The guy doesn't sound like Aietovsky," said Walking Cloud. "His speech is quicker than that."

"It's our pal Fingers Germain," said Mygosh with a sardonic grin. "Just to be sure, we had the voice-print lab run an analysis of this disc and the recording of one of our interrogations of him before his indictment. Perfect match!"

Mygosh produced a sheaf of tabloid newspaper ads with markings in red ink.

"See here, what's checked in red?" he pointed. "Narcotics and the DEA regularly scour all the papers, especially the weeklies, yuh know, the so-called alternative papers. These are from *City Pages*."

"Yeah, I've seen it occasionally," Walking Cloud said. "Not much to it. But they run these ads?"

"Oh, yeah!" said Rails. "And they don't check 'em. Don't verify 'em, either. They're hidden in the personals columns. Take a look at this one from two weeks ago."

Red, white, blue eyes.
Immed. serv.:8-8/15pm/
M-W-F/612-873-8603

"That's the number Fingers called on this tape," Mygosh said. "He called at 8:02 to be exact, Monday night. DEA says 'eyes' is probably a euphemism for 'ice'! And 'ice'—"

"Means either a contract killing or dope," surmised Walking Cloud. "And the colors?"

Mygosh tossed the newspaper on the table.

"Blue eyes or ice—maybe crack or smack—or cocaine. Red means murder for hire. Red eyes. Red ice."

"A bag of red ice," wondered the Lieutenant. "Meaning a victim's been chosen along with the time and place. Got the current issue?"

"Right here," said Rails. "The same ad appears on page 36. I checked it."

"Looks like the same one," Walking Cloud said. "Today's Friday, which means if we call tonight, we might make contact. But the female voice—"

"Gotta be a runner or a go-between," suggested Mygosh.

"Let's set it up for tonight, then," Walking Cloud said. "I know it's Friday night. You're both cleared for overtime. So are Ethan and Carol. Mervyn's gotta go home, of course. Joshua, see if we can get a tap on that cell phone. Will the judge's order cover it?"

"Should, I think, but I'll check."

He arrived at 6 o'clock sharp. Well-dressed in a British-made wool sports jacket, dark slacks, a discrete blue tie against a luminous white shirt, Will Alsted was an attractive man, Jenny thought. And he had a pleasant, if not disarming, manner. They went to the Black Forest Inn. They ordered drinks in the bar while waiting for their table. Alsted ordered beer, while Jenny asked for a glass of white wine. Just one, she thought, would be quite enough. When they were eventually led to their table, it became clear that Alsted was in no hurry to discuss the Breamington profile, which was fine with her.

"How old are you?" she asked him at one point.

"Thirty-seven last month," he said.

"And you're not married?"

To this, he replied that he and his college sweetheart were married the day after graduation, but they gave it up after two years and a baby son because of constant bickering. He saw his son, Charles, now fourteen, on a regular basis. He fed her pieces of his life story, she noticed, but only in response to questions. He wasn't evasive or ambiguous, but at the same time he didn't ask her any leading questions. When she picked a proper context to tell him she was four years older, he smiled blandly and said, "Four years isn't much. We're in the same generation." It was clear they had some things in common: good professions, each with a child from an initial but failed marriage, and a tacitly understood desire for companionship. But common interests? She would know that soon enough.

Their meal together was extraordinary, she thought. Her choice was Hungarian goulash. He ordered a Deutschburger casserole. They ate slowly, talking pleasantly about nothing in particular. She had a second glass of wine, but then switched to coffee. He chose an amaretto with black coffee. Their conversation was livelier than she expected, somehow. After a while, she sensed he was about to bring up the subject of Breamington's will. The waitress went away, and Alsted cleared his throat.

"Jack Breamington left a reasonably good fortune," he said almost casually. "Your office sent a fax about the size of his portfolio under your management. Ten million, eight-hundred and twenty-three thousand dollars, if I remember correctly."

"That sounds about right," she answered. "But it's fluid and spread around quite a bit. It's more than tripled since his initial investment."

"Which was just under three million?"

"Yes."

"Jack's will is peculiar in some ways. Did he ever discuss incentives with you?"

Incentives? Other than going to bed with him on a perpetual basis, swearing fidelity and making a commitment, none of which she wanted, no, Jack hadn't discussed incentives. But that wasn't what Alsted meant, of course. She felt she was on uncertain ground.

"He never mentioned incentives. No."

Alsted pattered on about the fortune left behind by sudden homicide. A net worth of eighty million plus. No wonder the three mil wasn't something Breamington worried about, despite her rejection of him. He must have regarded it as seed money for another fortune, albeit a small one. Could it be that the account itself was an incentive? And now there was also Will Alsted. Jenny permitted herself a small fantasy about where this first date might lead. Suddenly, she realized he had just asked her a question.

"I'm sorry, Will. I didn't catch that."

Alsted grinned and repeated the question.

"Is there any reason you can't continue to manage this portfolio, Jenny?"

She blinked, paused while chewing her food, and said, "No, there's no reason. My partners and I would love to keep the account, naturally."

"Good! The executor of the will is his mother, by the way. Since the cash and other liquidities were for the most part kept in trusts for his children, it's my job as the attorney pushing it through probate and final resolution to make sure all the investment components are in good hands. I'll report to her that you're willing and quite able to handle this portfolio and have done very well with it since—since when?"

"December first, oh-eight."

"December oh-eight. That's right. Mrs. Breamington wanted to know if your firm is willing, so I'll tell her the good news."

Alsted smiled and raised his amaretto, touching it against her wine glass. This is good, she thought, subduing her elation. Earning money is always good, and that was why she was here, presumably. Once the formal business was taken care of, minimal though it was, they talked about their respective children, parents, and other family members, the normal sitting dance of getting acquainted.

The judge agreed that the wiretap order covered the phone numbers listed since they might have been used in the commission of a crime. An unmarked police van with Peterson and a technician monitoring a recording camera was parked across the street. Sitting next to Peterson, Hyslip and another technician were waiting to record conversations from the pay phone. Laser beams aimed could penetrate walls of cement, even steel, if need be. Walking Cloud and Martridge were in another unmarked vehicle with a clear view of the wooden front doors.

Inside the restaurant, Blumus stood close to the inner glass doors and kept an eye on both entrances. Now she noticed Jenny Schell sitting with Will Alsted in the larger dining room. Jenny appeared not to have seen her, or Rails and Mygosh near the bar. Rails stood with a soft drink among a clutch of bibulous customers, his gaze toward the entryway. An arm's length away, Mygosh sipped a glass of ice water further back.

"Alright, try it, Ethan," the Lieutenant told Martridge, who dialed the number. It was 8:03 PM. The pay phone rang.

"There's no one to pick it up," said Blumus into her fist mike.

"Think we scared 'em off?" wondered Martridge.

Just then, Jenny happened to get up from her table. She told Alsted she'd be right back. A visit to the Women's Room, she thought, would be a good idea before they went to a late movie. Then she saw Carol Blumus near the doorway speaking in undertones into her fist. Back at the end of the bar, only a few feet away, were two male detectives Jenny recognized. Better not distract them, she thought, but at least she could say hello to Carol.

"Jenny Schell and Will Alsted are having dinner here," said Blumus into her fist. "She's seen me. Looks like she's coming over."

"Say hello, but send her on her way if you have to," said Walking Cloud. "Got it?"

"Got it."

"Carol, a dark-haired woman—looks Asian and wearing glasses—is entering," he then said.

Jenny smiled as she came toward Blumus, who offered a slight but serious grin in return. As Jenny approached, there was now a presence in the entryway. It was the dark-haired woman, her face obscured.

"I can see you're busy, Carol, but hello anyway," said Jenny as she went past.

"Thanks, Jenny. You're right. I'm busy."

Jenny didn't turn to see what Blumus was observing, but she did notice Mygosh and Rails looking right past her toward the entryway. The dark-haired woman took off her glasses as she turned and looked in her purse. Blumus saw that she was indeed Asian as she tilted her head up and shook her lustrous mane, then looked down and rummaged through her purse.

"She's out of my sight," said Blumus. "Has she left?"

"Not yet," said Walking Cloud.

"An Asian female, about five-five, perhaps thirty or so," said Blumus. "I see her reflection. She's standing next to the west wall of the entryway."

"Stand by," said Walking Cloud. "Winchell and Wyler, you there yet?"

"We're here," said a female voice Walking Cloud recognized, wind-swept sounds in the background. "Kitty-corner, on foot. We'll get to the southeast corner."

Detectives Beth Winchell and John Wyler were experienced night cops. None better, in Walking Cloud's view. He watched as they went across the street. Another detective, Peter Rafaelson, was in an unmarked car, now crossing the intersection and pulling into a space near the drugstore entrance kitty-corner on Nicollet.

Inside the restaurant, a trio of customers had paid their bill and exited past Blumus, talking animatedly.

"Three coming out," said Blumus.

"Two males entering," said Walking Cloud.

"We see 'em," said Rails.

Walking Cloud looked at his watch. It was 8:07.

More people came and went through the Black Forest Inn entrance. Then the pay phone rang. It was 8:09. She lifted the receiver.

Female Voice: "Yes?"

Male Voice: "Got any red?"

Female Voice: "Affirmative."

Male Voice: "Sat, oh-thousand, nineteen, nik, blue top. A bag red eyes."

Female Voice: "Deal. Sat, oh-thousand, nineteen, nik, blue top. A bag red eyes. Deal."

Male Voice: "Deal."

A pair of clicks. The Asian woman hung up.

"When she comes out, follow her, Winchell, Wyler," said Walking Cloud. "And Rafaelson, keep in sight of her."

But the Asian woman didn't leave immediately. She waited.

"She's standing next to the west wall again," said Blumus, noting the door hadn't opened.

"We'll wait for her to move," said Walking Cloud.

At 8:16, the Asian woman pushed the wooden front door open and went outside.

"Winchell, Wyler," said Walking Cloud, "don't turn around yet but she's heading to your corner and now turning left and south down Nicollet Avenue. Now you turn. Keep her in sight. Rafaelson, move into traffic but stay with her. Keep your lights on."

"Roger, Lieutenant."

The Asian woman turned the corner and walked south past the service entrance of the restaurant. Winchell and Wyler were two car lengths behind her.

"Carol and Bill," Walking Cloud said, "cross Nicollet and hurry south. Joshua, join us in the van."

The Asian woman went down the dimly lit sidewalk. Two larger figures, both male, came forward and went by her. Arm-in-arm, Winchell and Wyler followed her. Across the street,

Blumus and Rails watched from a distance. Walking Cloud and Martridge turned the corner and pulled within two car lengths of Rafaelson, who had stopped within paces of the second Black Forest parking lot the Asian woman had entered. Three marked squad car units were alerted, one hovering at the corner behind them.

"Lieutenant, someone's stopping her," said Winchell. "In the parking lot! He's hassling her!"

"Don't intervene yet," said Walking Cloud. "Get as close as you can."

"Look like he's trying to assault her, Lieutenant," Winchell said tightly. "I heard 'gimme that purse.'"

"This is Walking Cloud. A two-thirteen, check 'em out! Quick, the second parking lot on the left!"

The marked squad car was already moving, red lights swirling and bright lights searching as it turned sharply into the lot.

"This is the police! What's the problem here?" came a male voice over a loudspeaker.

The lights from the squad car revealed a tall black man holding the Asian woman by the hair, a knife pointed at her throat. His eyes were wild, Walking Cloud saw through binoculars.

"Don't come any closer!" he screamed. "I'll *kill* the bitch! I'll *kill her*!"

"Request for backup," came a voice from the box. "Hostage situation. A two-thirteen…"

"Jee-sus, that's just great!" said Martridge.

Walking Cloud peered through his binoculars.

"Let's see where it goes," he told his detectives. "Could be anything. The squad units will handle it."

The tall black man yanked the Asian woman's hair again. She shrieked. The police slowly moved in, now half a dozen uniformed officers shining fierce lights and pointing their weapons. Walking Cloud, Martridge and Rafaelson left their vehicles parked on Nicollet Avenue and stayed at the rim, their shields on their breast pockets.

"Don't come no closer, honky pigs!" yelled the tall black man, moving backwards with his terrified hostage. The parking lot was closed behind them by a wire-mesh fence. It was also instructive, Walking Cloud noted, that the uniformed officer talking to the perp was Sergeant Delvin Wilson, also black and a no-nonsense cop with over twenty years experience. He and Walking Cloud had been classmates at the police academy.

"Sir, if you release her and drop your weapon, no harm will come to you!" boomed Wilson into a bullhorn. "But we're not going anywhere until you let the lady go and *throw down that knife*! Let her *go*! *Throw down that knife*!"

Suddenly the perpetrator turned and lurched to his right toward an officer who had come within ten feet of him. The officer drew back and a shot was fired from a marksman's weapon, striking the perp in the right shoulder. Instantly, he fell to the ground, the knife dropping a few feet away. The Asian woman fell to her knees, her hands on the ground. A policewoman went to her. Three uniformed officers surrounded the wounded man, yelling in agony.

"*I bin shot! I bin shot!*" he howled. "You didn't havta do it!"

"Get an ambulance here pronto!" ordered Wilson. "Parsons, search this perp! Hold the sumbitch down like a squashed bug if you have to! Read 'em Miranda!"

Walking Cloud and his detectives went back to their cars. Under Wilson's supervision, the Asian woman routinely would be taken downtown to make a statement. It was Walking Cloud's call. Should he weigh in and attempt to find out where she was heading with her pay phone contact? Or should she merely be questioned about this incident and let go? Was her wounded assailant merely a freak interloper? Walking Cloud considered these questions during the ride downtown.

At the Black Forest Inn, Jenny was surprised that Carol Blumus and her male colleagues were no longer there when she emerged from the Women's Room. As she sat down again, she guessed that Alsted was oblivious. He smiled and suggested dessert. They decided to divide a serving of apple strudel with ice cream. Minutes later, they heard the wail of a siren outside but thought nothing of it.

Half an hour later, they left the Black Forest Inn and walked down Nicollet Avenue to the second parking lot. It was a cool evening. There is a kind of symmetry about things, Jenny thought. Not every time, but tonight everything seemed right.

Blumus read the information from a computer screen and printed it out.

"Susan Lee, age 28, lives in Chicago but is staying in an apartment building leased by the Guthrie for its actors," she told her colleagues. "She said she's working at the Guthrie, which is why she's in town."

"Has she asked for a lawyer yet?" asked Peterson.

"Not yet, but then she's not under arrest," said Walking Cloud. "We just don't have enough yet."

In the observation room, Susan Lee looked edgy, nervous, crossing and uncrossing her legs. She searched in her purse, found a cigarette and lighter, and lit up. She tried to inhale, then coughed. Smoking was not her thing, Walking Cloud observed. But she did have a name, finally.

"She have a record?" he asked.

"Nothing turns up in criminal," Blumus replied, handing the printout to Walking Cloud. "Stopped in March '09 in Chicago for speeding. Paid a fine. Nothing else, before or since."

"Associates?"

"Not known. The Guthrie's personnel office isn't open at this hour. We do have quite a sheet on the guy who assaulted her."

"Did he actually hit her?" wondered Rails.

"No, but he had her by the hair and stuck a knife to her face threatening bodily injury," said Walking Cloud. "Enough for felonious aggravated assault right there. Who is he, Carol? You got his sheet?"

"Albeen McDaniel. Born 6-2-72. No known address. A twenty-two-year history of repeated incarcerations, drug busts, car theft, burgling, assault—you name it—rape, attempted rape. Everything except murder."

"And that's only a step away," said Rails. "What say? We gonna talk to this lady?"

Minutes later, Blumus and Rails entered Interview Room #1 where Susan Lee sat restlessly. She looked up as they went over to the table.

"Ms. Lee, I'm Detective Blumus. This is Detective Rails. We'd like you to tell us what happened tonight, from the beginning. Are you willing to do that?"

Observing on the other side of the one-way glass were Walking Cloud, Mygosh, Martridge, Winchell, Wyler and Peterson, as well as a c. d. recorder.

"This interview is being conducted at 10:02 PM, Friday, October 27," said Blumus. "Alright, Ms. Lee, what happened?"

Susan Lee stared uncomprehendingly for a few seconds, then finally spoke.

"I was going to my car in the parking lot on Nicollet down the block where the Black Forest restaurant is. It—it was the second parking lot. In fact, my car's still there."

"What time was this?"

"I don't know. After eight, I think."

She squirmed and dabbed her cheek, then sighed. Her stress point had been reached, Walking Cloud observed, but she was trying to stay calm.

"I—I was in the restaurant—and was just going back to my car."

"What were you doing there, by the way?" pursued Rails. "I mean, in the Black Forest?"

Susan Lee looked uncomfortable. She swallowed hard, looking at Rails, then at Blumus. Behind the one-way looking glass, Walking Cloud was handed an audio c.d. by Hyslip, who had just come from the voice print lab downstairs.

"Voice analysis says it's identical to the previous conversation," Hyslip said. "One and the same female voice. But not the same male voice. The call tonight originated from a cell phone transmitting from northeast Minneapolis. Up near Central Avenue and 24th."

"Really?"

Walking Cloud wasn't surprised.

"I was—talking on the phone," said Susan Lee. "I thought about having a drink, but changed my mind. It's Friday night and it was busy there. So I left."

"Okay," said Blumus, "you left the restaurant—and then what?"

"I started back to where my car was parked in the lot for Black Forest patrons. Then this tall black guy came out of nowhere. He came right up to me and made a derogatory racial comment."

"What did he say?"

"Something about 'Chinese cunt'! I'm actually of Korean descent. And he *grabbed me*! I tried to get away from him, but he held on to me, tried to take my purse. I screamed. Then he slapped me. And he got hold of my hair and kept *yanking* me! And—thank *God*!—a police car came! Well, you know the rest."

"Yeah, we know the rest," said Rails. "You'll have to sign a formal complaint, Ms. Lee. We already have him for resisting arrest and a couple other charges. Will you do that?"

"Of course!"

"Is there anything else you care to tell us?" Blumus asked.

"I don't think so."

"By the way," said Rails, "if you're an actress at the Guthrie and this is Friday night, how come you're not at the theater?"

Susan Lee didn't blink. She said, "We're in repertory. I'm not in this evening's production, but I am in two others."

Now it was Walking Cloud's turn. He knocked briefly at the door, and then entered.

"Ms. Lee, I'm Lieutenant Walking Cloud of the homicide division. How do you do?"

"*Homicide*?" she said, her voice rising perceptibly.

"Yes," he said, taking a chair next to Blumus. "In fact, you're in the homicide squad room area. Detectives Blumus and Rails are both on the homicide squad."

Susan Lee looked puzzled. Remember, Walking Cloud was reminded, this lady is an actress by trade.

"You see, Ms. Lee, we're all more than a little on edge around here. We've had several murders in Minneapolis this week. We have reason to believe the killer in most of these deaths is skilled in the use of make-up and disguise. Something your profession uses, for example. We're looking for a male, probably under forty, forty-five at most, who's very adept in the art of disguise."

"Yes, I heard about him," she replied. "Pandora Killer? So why are you talking to me about this? I don't fit that description, do I?"

"No, you don't. But let me give you another detail. Our suspected killer has a particular psychopathic hatred of women, but he won't hesitate to kill a totally innocent person, male or female, to get his kicks. One characteristic of the killer—at least in the deaths of the two young women—has been the use of a stage make-up, an olive-tinted substance, on the face. While engaged in the sexual assault each time, the killer's facial make-up rubbed off onto the face of his victim. In both cases, forensics identified the substance and we've checked. The Guthrie Theater, as well as a number of other theater houses around here, orders a certain quantity of it every month. Any actor or actress has access to make-up at your theater. Isn't that right, Ms. Lee?"

Susan Lee drew her breath in a long sigh. She compressed her lips, then stared off for a second or two.

"Look, I was assaulted this evening," she insisted. "I wasn't hurt much, but I'm here to answer questions about *that*, aren't I? You've discovered what I do for a living and now you're telling me that one of my colleagues might be a—a murderer."

"Not just that, Ms. Lee," said Walking Cloud. "A *serial* murderer! We have reason to think five people are dead because of this one person. Two women in their twenties—in your age group—were raped before being killed, two police officers are dead and another innocent bystander was found shot to death in the trunk of his car. Now the connecting incident to all these events was oddly a bungled murder attempt, surprisingly amateurish, against a potential witness to yet another murder."

"That senator stabbed in Rudy's?"

"Yes, in fact," said Rails. "How did you know?"

"I read the papers," she said. "I watched the news about the melee at the hospital. I know about the murdered lawyer. You'd have to be living in a cave not to know. I don't know how I can help you in this. I'd really like a ride back to my car now. Can you give me one?"

How to break her down before she clams up completely or asks for a lawyer? pondered Walking Cloud. The recorded conversations of her phone conversations were the ace in the hole, not to be used except as last resort. Of course, none of it could be proved yet, making it difficult to establish probable cause.

"Yes, in fact I can give you a ride myself," said Walking Cloud. "We'll need you to come down tomorrow morning to sign a statement about the incident with Albeen McDaniel."

"The incident—with whom?"

"Albeen McDaniel," repeated Blumus. "The perp who assaulted you this evening."

"Well, certainly," replied Susan Lee. "I can do that."

The interview was over, for now. Walking Cloud let her wait in the reception area while he conferred with his colleagues. On several computer screens were enlarged composites of fingerprints. Hyslip and Peterson were engrossed with two juxtaposed enlargements.

"This curvature of the inner circle here is identical to this one here, Lieutenant," said Peterson. "This one was on the mop handle you were struck with at the hospital. It matches a print—

several prints—found in both Louis Bertram's car and in Lori Ruth Mueller's vehicle."

"Ah!" exclaimed Walking Cloud.

Now Peterson had a significant expression.

"Wait. The trouble in this print is also an identical match with that of a prisoner now in the Washington State penitentiary at Walla Walla. He was also an inmate at Stillwater, June '97 to March '01. William Allen Lewiston, in prison now for a multiple burglary conviction. Been there since last February. I talked to forensics and the F.B.I. Somewhere our rapist-killer's got hold of Lewiston's prints, had 'em reproduced and printed into a soft, almost tissue-like plastic which can absorb the body heat of the person wearing 'em but leaves the phony prints just like the real thing. The question is—"

"The question is where and how did he get the prints for his plastic tissue gloves?" interrupted Walking Cloud. "Keep at it. Let me know what you come up with. All right, Carol, you're in charge of getting the report done this time. Leave it on my desk. I better not keep Ms. Lee waiting any longer."

Blumus nodded. Peterson handed her a manila file. Walking Cloud told them a conference would be held in his office the next morning at nine, albeit a Saturday. He reminded them of the red ice contact at 10 A.M., 19th and Nicollet. Overtime duty noted for all.

"Sorry to keep you waiting, Ms. Lee," he told her. "Ready to go?"

Susan Lee stood up with a blank expression. As they walked to the underground parking lot, an unmarked police car came around a cement pole up to them slowly and stopped. Walking Cloud recognized Captain Blatsky behind the wheel and immediately asked Susan Lee to wait to the side. Blatksy's window went down.

"Late hours again, Ben? I'm not surprised. Who yuh got there?"

"Potentially a very significant witness. Susan Lee, a Guthrie actress. I'm giving her a lift to her car near the Black Forest.

Carol's getting the report typed up now. We're making slow but incremental progress, Ed. A meeting tomorrow at nine, if you're interested."

"Keep me apprised. I'll need to see the report, but not till Monday. Call me at home if you need to. Overtime for all your crew?"

"Most of them, I'm afraid."

"Figured. All right. See you Monday. Get rid of that woman as quick as you can, Ben. She looks hotter'n a nuclear bomb."

With that, his window went up and he drove away. Susan Lee stood impassively, waiting.

"A cool evening," she said as they drove up the ramp.

"Late October in Minneapolis. Tell me, Ms. Lee, I assume you're going straight home to your apartment on Grove Avenue now?"

"In view of what's happened this evening, I suddenly feel dangerous, Lieutenant. Tired, but dangerous. I may or may not go directly home. I'm not sure."

Walking Cloud decided not to draw out the meaning of this statement. He remembered what Blatsky said. He drove south from the Old Courthouse underground lot up past the Minneapolis Convention Center and down to Nicollet Avenue, where he turned left. The Black Forest parking lot was several blocks south.

"What time are you going downtown to sign your complaint against Albeen McDaniel?" he asked as they passed over the freeway.

"They said nine-thirty tomorrow morning. I'll do it. Don't worry, Lieutenant. I'll show."

At the Black Forest parking lot, he waited till Susan Lee got into her car and drove away. His window down, he inhaled the cool wind of late evening. He drove west to Hennepin Avenue, then waited at the red light and was suddenly tempted by the prospect of a late-night beer.

Jenny Schell and Will Alsted had gone to a movie featuring Robert Redford. They decided to top off the evening by a late drink at the Loring Pasta Bar over in Dinkytown. As they drove south on the Third Avenue bridge over the Mississippi, she noticed a police car at the far end with swirling red lights behind a stationary motorist. She was reminded of the police presence in the restaurant earlier. She asked Alsted if he'd noticed anything unusual. He said he hadn't. Then she told him about the detectives there. Really? he marveled. And to think what might have been going on and he'd missed it entirely. They parked in back of the county library a block from the Loring Pasta Bar. Impulsively, he turned and kissed her on the lips.

"Let's go to the Loring," he said, half smiling.

"Yes, let's," she answered, not displeased.

They entered the Loring through the bar door. It was mildly crowded. Whoever the musicians were, they were on break. Then she saw a very familiar face.

"Oh, my god!" she said. "Look over near the wine bottles."

"I see him," replied Alsted. "Is Walking Cloud a bachelor?"

"I think he must be. Why else would he be here alone?"

"Perhaps just to wind down."

Jenny noticed the dark-haired female bartender talking to Walking Cloud. Suddenly, the bartender laughed at something Walking Cloud said. She had a full-throated laugh, her near-crystalline white teeth breaking up any darkness suggested by the many isolated moods or variances in the room. Jenny also observed the Lieutenant, who now appeared preoccupied, gazing off toward the empty stage. After a few seconds, he turned. Jenny shifted her gaze. The bartender now asked what she and Alsted would have. She asked for a mineral water with lime. Alsted ordered a glass of tap beer. She noticed that Walking Cloud was coming into the bar room.

"Good evening, Ms. Schell," Walking Cloud said. "Mr. Alsted."

Jenny smiled at the detective. The two men shook hands.

"I see you on t.v. more and more, Lieutenant," said Alsted genially. "I admire your dedication, but I don't envy you your job."

Walking Cloud took a sip of his beer and said, "Thank you. It's been quite demanding lately. I just came in here for an after-hours break."

Jenny excused herself and went to the Women's Room. When she emerged minutes later, she noticed a striking Asian woman with thick black hair enter the bar and pass behind Alsted and Walking Cloud. Jenny rejoined them. Alsted was speaking.

"Law enforcement is tough job. When I first started out as a lawyer, I took on my share of pro bono cases. Petty theft. Larceny. Bad checks. Burglary. Cons. Muggers. Prostitutes. Pimps. But when it came to defending drug dealers, I pulled away. I still do pro bono work. I think every lawyer should. Many don't, of course. Remember Robert Bork and why Senator Paul Simon said he voted against him way back in the late eighties? One reason was because he'd never done any pro bono work. A telling statement."

"What about defending an accused murderer?" asked Walking Cloud. "Have you ever been asked to do that for what the state pays you—or pro bono?"

A solemn look overcame Alsted's features.

"No, I haven't," he shrugged. "Murder cases, from what I know of them, take up a lot of time and energy. That's what public defenders are for in our system, if the accused is indigent."

Just then, Walking Cloud noticed Susan Lee talking to several people across the room. He suspected they might be theater colleagues. Susan Lee took off her coat and sat down. A waiter approached her. After a minute or so, she bounded for the stage, just as a man sat down at the piano and a bearded violin player appeared. Microphone in hand, she stood before the filled room and began singing. Walking Cloud understood some of the lyrics:

Get me some money,
Get me some money, honey,

Like some other men do…

Her singing, apprised Walking Cloud, wasn't that bad. She obviously had benefit of voice training. She tossed her head back and successfully reached a high note. Now the rose man came in the room with his long-stemmed flowers in three colors. If she can perform this well, why is she acting as a go-between in a nefarious activity she must know is illegal? Surely not for money, whatever it might be.

Stopping at the actors' table, the rose man made a few transactions, putting small plastic water cylinders at the stem end of each rose he sold. Susan Lee began another song, this time in French. "La Vie en Rose" was a durable staple here, concluded Walking Cloud. The French he could barely make out, despite nearly a year in France many years earlier and a college minor in the language. Susan Lee's version was slightly less than barbarous, but no less affecting, inspiring several in the audience to get up and dance. Walking Cloud kept an eye on the rose man, who gradually made his way to the bar.

"Would you like a rose?" Alsted asked Jenny.

"Sure." She smiled primly at Alsted and then at Walking Cloud.

The rose man's plastic bucket had pink, orange, and deep red. Jenny pointed to an orange rose. The rose man withdrew it, trimmed the stem with a knife and cupped it in a plastic water cylinder. Alsted paid him two dollars. The rose man looked at Walking Cloud, who said, "I'll take a red one." Walking Cloud gave him two dollars, and then gave the red rose to Anna behind the bar. She smiled.

"Thanks, Ben."

He stayed long enough to finish his beer. Then he said good night to Jenny and Alsted. He waved briefly to Anna and departed without looking again at Susan Lee, still in her French mode of another era.

Chapter Thirteen

Bloody Saturday

He awoke just before the alarm went off at 7:30. His first thought was of Susan Lee. He thought this bizarre, even the stuff of farce. If she had been providing information used in the commission of a crime, she could be charged with aiding and abetting, but not much else. If she could be persuaded to turn state's evidence, perhaps no charge would be preferred. Need to talk to McCorkle and Finegrad on this one. As he jogged around Lake of the Isles, his thoughts were on stretching his cardiovascular rhythms and wind with the work of his heart and legs going steady for over three miles. It was a cool Saturday morning, the 28th of October. When he completed his run, he jogged home where he showered again and got ready for the day. He ate a light breakfast of cereal with banana slices and one-percent milk. No sugar.

In light traffic on the way downtown, he called the office. Martridge answered.

"Has Susan Lee come in yet, Ethan?"

"Yes, sir, she has. She's working up a statement with Carol right now. Uh, Lieutenant, I got an idea about her and the red ice contact this mornin'."

"You do?"

"Yeah. We don't know the extent of her involvement, only that she's relayed at least two messages. From whom and to whom we can't prove yet. Why not take her along? We can't compel her to, but maybe it might help to break her down. Oh, we got the lip-readin' guy here, too. Charlie Wing."

"Charlie Wing again, is it?"

"Yes, sir. Charlie Wing."

"I was thinking along the same lines you were about Ms. Lee. See you in ten or less."

As he entered the squad room, Susan Lee was visible in the far corner, the back of her head dark as coal. The conversation with Carol Blumus was clandestinely recorded. No permission needed. The slightest information was valuable. Walking Cloud went into his office, followed by Mygosh.

"Good morning, Joshua."

"Morning, Ben. Carol's been with Susan Lee since she came in just after nine o'clock. She hasn't said anything useful yet. Only been talking about the guy who assaulted her last night."

"So she has no idea we're on to her, obviously. Okay, we're going to ask her to go along with us in the van. Is an extra jump seat in there?"

Mygosh looked mildly surprised.

"Yeah, there is."

"Good. Lock the doors so she can't leap out impulsively. She might be tempted if she sees someone she knows. You get to sit with her, Joshua. Ask Carol to join us after Ms. Lee signs the complaint."

Walking Cloud now went over the scenario for observing, possibly arresting, the phone contact recorded the night before. Advising his colleagues that they were taking a chance with a potential suspect in tow, he also told them as long as she stayed inside the bulletproofed van, she'd be safe. There were no questions, surprisingly.

"Okay, bring her in, Joshua."

A minute later, Susan Lee preceded Mygosh into Walking Cloud's office. She sat down in a straight-back chair. Blumus stood near the door.

"Ms. Lee, please listen to this, if you will," Walking Cloud said, pressing the c.d. recorder button.

Male Voice: "You got red or white?"

Female Voice: "Whaddya want?"

Male Voice: "Red. A bag of red."

Female Voice: "Your deal."

Male Voice: "Tomorrow, twenty-six, two-thousand."

Female Voice: "Tomorrow, twenty-six, nik, two-thousand. Got it. Deal."

Walking Cloud looked at Susan Lee, who appeared startled but said nothing.

"That was the first conversation we caught this past Monday evening, October 23rd," he told her. "Here's the second one, made last night, the 27th."

Female Voice: "Yes?"

Male Voice: "Got any red?"

Female Voice: "Affirmative."

Male Voice: "Sat, one-thousand, nik, nineteen, blue top. A bag, red eyes."

Female Voice: "Deal, one-thousand, nik, nineteen, blue top. A bag, red eyes. Deal."

Male Voice: "Deal."

Then a pair of clicks. There was barely a ripple in Susan Lee's expression.

"We haven't talked to the county attorney's people yet, Ms. Lee," advised the Lieutenant. "We have good reason to believe that this is your voice in both conversations, that you're referring both times to illegal activity."

The actress's expression now underwent a subtle change.

"What kind of illegal activity?" she asked. "Is it legal for you to be listening, recording, a private phone conversation?"

"It is if the judge says there's probable cause to suspect a criminal conspiracy. In this case, murder for hire."

Susan Lee's eyes widened. Then she frowned.

"*Murder*? How—do you know?"

Walking Cloud explained the nomenclature and what the abbreviations meant.

"Whom were you doing this for?" he asked. "Is someone or some group of people into you for something?"

"So—the police being there suddenly last night after that man grabbed me—they were there all along! You had them following me?"

"We were watching to see who came to the restaurant," explained Rails, picking up the newspaper's 'personals' page and handing it to her, "a known contact place, unbeknownst to its owners, for people making cell phone calls they think can't be traced. You were the only one. What we didn't expect was Albeen McDaniel to enter the picture a few minutes later in the parking lot."

The Lieutenant looked at his wristwatch.

"It's 9:30," he said. "We're going to check out 'nik, nineteen'— nineteenth and Nicollet, Ms. Lee—at 'one-thousand' which we assume means 10 A.M. While you're thinking about your answer, how about coming along with us? You'll be in a van. They won't be able to see you."

Susan Lee started to speak, but stopped short. A knock on the door. An Asian man about forty entered.

"This is Charlie Wing, Ms. Lee," said Walking Cloud. "In his day job, he's a probation officer with the state. He also reads lips for us from time to time. He's not deaf, but one of his parents is. Charlie, Susan Lee."

Charlie Wing and Susan Lee looked at one another and nodded.

Walking Cloud and Martridge followed the bulletproofed van with its cargo of Susan Lee, Charlie Wing, two technicians and a pair of telescopes with digital recording machines. Mygosh and Rails were in the front seat. Blumus and McDour were in a third vehicle. Unmarked police cars were alert for the vehicle with a blue top.

The parking lot was a classic scene of American flux, serving a building that housed a supermarket, a flower shop and a liquor store. The neighborhood bordered on the freeway a quarter mile north descending the hill toward downtown and was comprised mostly of older apartment buildings.

"Lieutenant," came Mygosh's voice on the intercom, "we've located a two-thousand-two Buick, Minnesota license plate B-G-T-6-0-4. Registered owner Skin Enterprises, Inc., of Minneapolis. Aietovsky's scam. Vehicle's in the southeast corner of the parking lot, down one space. A blue top. A single occupant, white male, behind the wheel. His motor's still on."

"We see him," said Walking Cloud.

McDour and Blumus had pulled into the parking lot behind the Buick. Walking Cloud looked through binoculars and recognized the man, although he didn't know his name. He was a known associate of Abe Aietovsky. The suspect was bony-faced, thin, slightly receding dark hair, a pencil-thin mustache, a thick upper torso, forty-five at most. The unmarked police van was in front of the Japanese restaurant, one door north of 19th and Nicollet. Walking Cloud and Martridge positioned their vehicle at the corner of 19th Street with a clear view of the suspect Buick. It was 9:51. The man in the Buick drew a cigarette from his shirt pocket and lit up.

"Any idea who he is?" came Rails's voice.

"Definitely one of Aietovksy's employees," said Walking Cloud. "Does Ms. Lee recognize him?"

"Negative," said Rails. "Says she's never seen him before."

The man with the pencil-thin mustache had an insidious quality the more one looked at him. But he was a follower, not a leader. Motive, probability and evidence were what Walking Cloud needed. It was 9:55. The man with the pencil-thin mustache reached into his shirt pocket and took out a cell phone.

"We got a tap on this one?" asked Walking Cloud.

"Yeah," replied Mygosh. "Sensory is picking it up. Got him on both machines, Lieutenant. We'll pipe it over."

First Voice: "Hey, I'm at the parkin' lot. This guy comin' at ten—or what?"

Second Voice: "Spozed ta be there. Still got a couple minutes. What's the problem? Cops around?"

First Voice: "Don't notice anything unusual. I can't see through walls or the back-a my head. I jus' get nervous 'bout these things in broad daylight, is all."

Second Voice: "Don't get so antsy! Ya got the down payment all ready?"

First Voice: "Yep. All set. Where's the guy, though?"

Second Voice: "Wait for him, for Chris' sake! Don't get so fuckin' jumpy! Ya got an assignment. Call back when it's done an' you're outa there. Okay?"

First Voice: "Yeah."

Now it was two minutes to ten.

"We still don't know his name," Mygosh's voice came over. "Putting a trace on the number he called. Wait a minute. Looks like he may have a visitor."

A gasp. It sounded like Susan Lee.

"What'd she say?" asked Walking Cloud. "Ask her to speak up."

A tall, clean-shaven man with long brown hair approached the driver's side of the Buick. The man with the pencil-thin mustache rolled his window partway down.

"That's Willard, the guy who just came, the one with the long hair," Susan Lee's voice came over. "All I know him by is Willard. I'm sorry. I can't—"

"Okay, Ms. Lee, that's fine," said Walking Cloud. "Charlie?"

Willard was facing the other way as he talked to the man with the pencil-thin mustache. Charlie Wing picked up their words.

"He says, 'Okay, okay, okay, get in, man. Let's talk a deal.'"

Willard went around the car and got in the passenger side. Charlie Wing's voice came over again.

"Willard says, 'Straight deal here, man. No nonsense. Who's in the bag?' The other guy says, 'It's here. Picture, name, home address. Phone numbers. All of them where her office is. Likely movements. He says, 'This mark is the mayor-a this town, man, so make it a clean hit. Ya gotta bag her by the end of next week. Here's half in cash. Twenty-five thousand. Hundreds and fifties. It's all there, man.'"

Willard was concentrating, looking down.

"Jesus, they're after the *mayor*!" exclaimed Mygosh in a low voice.

Why are they after *her*? wondered Walking Cloud. Now Charlie Wing's hurried voice.

"Willard says, 'I'm countin'! I'm countin'! Looks like it's all here. Twenty-five thou. Okay. End-a the week. Friday? Saturday?' The other guy says, 'By midnight Friday. If you bungle it, we never heard-a yuh!' Willard says, 'Gotcha. Friday midnight. Deal. Rest-a the dough when the job's done. We'll let you know. Here's a number to call. I'll expect a call from ya as soon as the job's done about when and where.' Other guy says, 'Deal.'"

"Okay," said Walking Cloud, "we have enough. Blumus, McDour, squads 119, 221 and 263, move in! We'll be right in front."

They moved in to arrest the perps. As Blumus and McDour approached from the rear on foot, the unmarked squad units moved in from three sides. Marked squad cars suddenly appeared and blocked off the area to traffic.

"This is the *police*!" announced Walking Cloud through the loudspeaker. "Both of you in the Buick with the blue top, you're under arrest! Put your hands on the dashboard! *Now*! You're *surrounded*!"

Just then, a woman carrying a grocery bag from the building screamed, distracting McDour and Blumus, who both turned their heads away from the perps for a fraction of a second. The Buick suddenly lurched back past them, smashing a police car in the front end. Willard poked a pistol out his window and fired point-blank at McDour, who went down immediately.

"Officer down!" thundered Walking Cloud as the Buick overran the sidewalk at the corner. "Officer down! Get an ambulance to this parking lot *now*!"

Walking Cloud ordered pursuit of the Buick, heading south, ripping through the front ends of two police vehicles on the way up Nicollet toward Franklin Avenue. Martridge and Walking Cloud were in the chase, two car lengths behind.

The Buick sideswiped a city bus at Nicollet and Franklin, spun around and collided with the lead squad car, disabling it, then swerved back to its original direction with a dangling right front fender and a twisted right headlight. Walking Cloud ordered all available squad units near Nicollet Avenue at points south to set up a roadblock. The Buick turned left on East 22nd and raced on to First Avenue, almost colliding with a taxi. The remaining squad car swerved around it. The Buick raced a block to Stevens Avenue and made a sharp right, knocking down a bicyclist and losing the second squad car that ran onto the corner and into a post. Now the detectives were immediately behind the Buick.

"Stay with him, Ethan!" urged Walking Cloud. The Buick went left, then right, and turned left at East 24th Street. On the right was the Minneapolis Institute of Arts. On the left was a park.

"Oh, Christ, look where he's goin'!" exclaimed Martridge as he turned onto East 24th Street where clutches of passersby stared from the sidewalk. Now a marked police car with swirling red lights came the opposite way. The Buick headed straight for it, but the police car swerved and bumped over the curve and onto the grass. The Buick turned right at Third Avenue just as Willard fired twice at the diverted police car, hitting the driver's side window.

"*Son of a bitch!*" exclaimed Walking Cloud. "*Look out!*"

A truck going south on Third Avenue got behind the Buick, forcing Martridge to stop at the curb. The truck continued on, throwing off the detectives off as the Buick sped away and then into the driveway of the Art Institute. A small phalanx of police cars came up the opposite way.

"*Goddammit!*" swore Martridge who tried to go around the truck but had to duck back when he saw a pair of bicyclists coming up the street. The detectives got to the driveway of the Institute only to find the Buick abandoned near the front door, with people of every size coming and going. The marked squad cars roared into the entrance of the driveway.

"They're *inside*, Ben!" bellowed Sergeant Delvin Wilson. This was precisely the situation Walking Cloud feared most: chasing violent and desperate perps through a heavily trafficked and enclosed area.

"Set up a perimeter around the entire block, Devlin," he said. "They have to come out somewhere!"

Three more squad cars came up behind the detectives' vehicle. People began to flee from the building. Their weapons drawn, Walking Cloud and Martridge entered through the glass doors.

"*That—way!*" a young woman pointed back, huddling two small children on the floor. To the right was an information booth. Beyond were a few short steps and the museum proper. On the left was the entrance to the Children's Theater.

"*Get down!*" Walking Cloud shouted to terrified museum patrons. He motioned uniformed officers inside. He looked up and into the open stairway going back and forth till it reached the next level. Suddenly, a man and a woman hiding behind a statue got up and bolted for the glass door exits. A cop held the door for them.

"Try and evacuate as many as you can," Walking Cloud told two cops who had come up behind him.

Screams came from an upper level. Walking Cloud and Martridge looked up to the left. Willard pointed his pistol over the railing. The detectives dived in close to the stairway as a bullet came very close, hitting the floor, ricocheting against glass somewhere, shattering it. Now three plainclothes officers, including Blumus, entered the building. She scooted a small bullhorn across the floor. The bullhorn stopped short of where it could be safely retrieved. Walking Cloud and Martridge were pinned. Blumus had her revolver pointed straight up the railing.

"SWAT's coming!" she called out. "*Go!*"

Walking Cloud raced to the stairs. Martridge grabbed the bullhorn and followed him.

"Carol, get a squad into this building from the west entrance somewhere," Walking Cloud said into his fist mike.

The perps were on the top floor. The detectives proceeded cautiously. Finally, they reached the top floor. Blumus and several uniformed cops came up behind them. In the first room of the third floor lay a number of people, none apparently injured or killed. Walking Cloud signaled for them to stay put as the cops secured the immediate area. Blumus and two other cops moved to evacuate them one by one. Walking Cloud took up the bullhorn.

"Willard, this is Lieutenant Walking Cloud of the Minneapolis Police! Throw out your weapons and surrender peaceably. You have everything to lose by not surrendering, Willard. There's no reason to hurt innocent people. They've done *nothing* to hurt you. This building is completely *surrounded*! The only way for you and your accomplice to leave here alive is to *surrender*! Do that and *no harm* will come to you. You have *my word* on it. Do you *hear* me, Willard?"

No response, except a clicking somewhere further back. With Martridge covering him, Walking Cloud moved out of the first room, past encased pottery and silken paintings. A faint crying, then more sustained sobbing, was somewhere in one of the next rooms. Now a voice in the Lieutenant's ear.

"Ben, this is Mygosh. We're comin' up through the west end-a the building. According to the floor plan, there are a helluva lotta rooms. We're on the second floor. No sign-a Willard and his pal yet."

"They're on the third floor, Joshua. I'm not sure where yet. Secure your position and hold the SWAT team in place outside the building. We're moving up here room by room east to west."

"Roger."

Walking Cloud listened to the faint crying. It sounded so futile. He held his weapon straight ahead, pointing it at the slightest movement. Martridge was a few feet behind.

"Where's that cryin' comin' from?" Martridge said in a near whisper.

Walking Cloud gestured to an unseen forward area. Blumus and several uniformed cops were following in adjacent rooms east to west. Walking Cloud and Martridge moved around what looked like ancient Chinese pottery, then past some small wall hangings and into the next room. Walking Cloud thought he saw something move. He signaled Martridge. Now they heard the crying again, more of a whimper as they got closer to another room. Walking Cloud sucked in his breath and entered, Martridge to his right. On the floor near the far wall was a young woman, it appeared—no, she was younger, a girl of perhaps fourteen. Her face looked beaten, her blouse half ripped away, her green skirt astray, blood on her knees.

"Cover me," said the Lieutenant, putting his weapon in its holster. The girl looked up at him wordlessly with a dazed expression. Without turning his head, he said into his fist mike, "Detective Blumus, get an ambulance stretcher up here. Third floor. Second room back. Then come here immediately. We need you."

"Be right there, Lieutenant," Blumus responded.

In less than a minute, Blumus was kneeling over the prostrate girl.

"Can you tell me your name? We're police officers. My name's Carol. What's *your* name?"

Tears had dampened the girl's cheeks. Her eyes and lips were puffy, and swelling up.

"He—he raped me," she said, blood oozing out of her mouth. "He hit me—and raped me. I asked him—I told him not to—"

She broke off, tried to lift her arm but it fell limply on the floor.

"I'm sorry," said Blumus. "Oh, god! Can you tell me your name? We'll help you and we'll find the man who did this to you. Can you tell me your name?"

"Ju—Julia," said the girl through her swollen mouth. "Julia White."

"Julia, alright. Thank you." Blumus turned to Walking Cloud and a uniformed female officer who had appeared. "Very severe traumatic injury. We'll need the ambulance stretcher to move her. You might tell them again."

Walking Cloud again ordered an ambulance stretcher brought up immediately.

"Lieutenant!" exclaimed Martridge. "In here! Look!"

The body of an adult male about twenty-five lay face down amidst the remnants of a shattered display case of porcelain. They moved into the room, most of it in chaos. Walking Cloud touched the young man's neck. He had been dead only a few minutes, a gunshot wound in the forehead.

"They've got a silencer," said Walking Cloud. "I didn't hear any gunshots after we got up here. Did you?"

"No, sir, I didn't."

"He just—shot him—for no reason!" came a halting female voice. It was an elderly woman in a sitting position in the corner, blood around her mouth. "Then he hit me—and told me to stay put!"

"There were two men here, weren't there?" asked Martridge, touching her face gently. She was bleeding from her nose and mouth.

"Yes, there were two of 'em. Sons of bitches! The one with the long hair shot this boy, then hit me."

"Thank you, ma'am," Martridge told her. "Here, just stay where you are. We got a stretcher comin' up for you."

A pair of uniformed cops came in and began to lift her onto a stretcher.

Walking Cloud and Martridge approached the next room. This time there were no people on the floor, no disarray. They were alert for the slightest movement, even a wisp of hair. Suddenly, there was a crash—and a scream.

Walking Cloud and Martridge raced into the room, where a middle-aged man and woman were cringing on the floor, hiding behind a marble bench. Faces from the Old Impressionist Masters—Degas, Rousseau, Monet, Cézanne—stared at them, which Walking Cloud found ironic. Two psychopaths on the loose in an art museum. Degas and Cézanne, both crotchety misanthropes, would have appreciated the absurdity. Walking Cloud pulled the bullhorn from his belt.

"Willard, this is Lieutenant Walking Cloud! You and your accomplice have done some very bad things here against innocent people! What are you trying to prove? Throw out your weapons and *surrender! Now*, Willard! There's *no way* you can escape! Give it up *now*, Willard!"

They rushed into the next room, and there were more paintings, a decapitated statue, a broken display case, and then another room until finally they saw movement in a large alcove leading into a long hallway. Now a bullet singed the wall just above Walking Cloud's head. A face from the nineteenth century looked unimpressed. Was it a Renoir or Van Gogh? Walking Cloud turned a corner and rushed to a nearby wall, in clear view of Martridge. A click. Another click. More clicks. What was that sound? Not an empty weapon, certainly. A bomb? No, but he wasn't a bomb expert. He nodded to Martridge, and they entered a large alcove. There Walking Cloud saw in a flash the right arm of the man with the pencil-thin mustache standing around a corner. Walking Cloud took aim and hit his target. The perp yelled, then turned full-face into Walking Cloud's view with a weapon raised in his other hand. The Lieutenant fired again and the perp fell backwards, a bullet wound in his chest. Was he dead? Walking Cloud and Martridge moved along the wall. The perp was dead. His weapon, now on the floor several feet from his twitching hand, had a crudely made silencer. But where was Willard?

"*Willard!*" Walking Cloud shouted. "Your buddy is *dead!* Are you gonna have to die, too, before this is over? Come out *now*,

Willard! You're *trapped! No place to go!* Throw your weapon out and put your hands on your head! Come out-a there, Willard!"

Then the clicks again, coming from the near corner of the adjacent room. A small electric fan was driving a shade flap against the broken door of a glass display case.

"*Willard, can you hear me?*" Walking Cloud shouted.

Martridge edged closer to the end of the wall and glanced down at the dead perp. He heard he sound of hurrying feet receding. The detectives turned the corner and there was Willard, fleeing with a satchel in one hand, a German-style handgun with a silencer in the other.

"*Stop, Willard!*" ordered Walking Cloud.

But Willard turned his head only fleetingly as he ran, pointing his weapon back and firing. Martridge was hit in the arm and staggered against the wall. Walking Cloud shot Willard in the thigh, causing him to fall. As Walking Cloud approached, he shouted, "*Throw the gun away! Now!*" But Willard turned it on himself, taking a bullet in the heart. His body jolted straight out as he turned on his back, his eyes straight up. Walking Cloud kicked the pistol out of his fingers.

"Is he dead?" asked Martridge, touching his own bleeding arm.

"He was his own executioner. Come on, Ethan, let's get you downstairs to an ambulance." Then into his fist mike, the Lieutenant said, "This is Walking Cloud. Both perps are dead. We're coming down. Send up two more stretchers and get these bodies to the m.e., pronto! We're gonna need their prints right away."

As Walking Cloud left the building, a police cordon held the news reporters back He approached them, anyway.

"Lieutenant, how many people were killed or injured up there?" asked Ronn Mason of Channel 4 News.

Walking Cloud sighed as he looked at the reporter and his colleagues. There was a light mist in the air.

"The two perpetrators we were pursuing from several blocks away are dead, one by his own hand. There was an innocent bystander, a young man in his twenties, killed by one of the perps. We're trying to locate next of kin. There was a minor, a young girl, beaten and raped. There was an elderly woman beaten and traumatized. They were both taken to Hennepin County General Hospital. There were also several police officers injured in this incident. No details yet. We'll have a full statement to the press later on. I'm sorry, but I can't tell you anything more at this time. Excuse me, please."

He strode past the reporters and quickly got in his unmarked car with Sergeant Wilson at the wheel.

Chapter Fourteen

The Right Thing

The high-powered AFIS computer network, or automated fingerprint identification system, tracked down the latents, or prints, taken from the two dead perps. "Willard" was in fact Roberto Albion Durangelo of North Miami, Florida, and considered a high-priced professional hit man by the FBI, who also noted that there were no outstanding warrants against him, but that he had been acquitted twice of murder charges, once in Tampa and once in New Jersey. In New York City two years earlier, there had been a mistrial in a rape case. The judge dismissed the charge. Since then, Durangelo was known to have been living and operating out of Chicago, also the hometown of Susan Lee. Walking Cloud knew Durangelo was not the same perp he'd tangled with in the hospital corridor, the one who also abducted and murdered Louis Bertram. That perp was no more than 5'10" with a lifted left shoe. Durangelo, or "Willard," was 6'3". Where was the tie-in? What more did Susan Lee know? And what about Durangelo's "client"—the man with the pencil-thin mustache? AFIS identified him as Jack Earl Winslow of Minneapolis. Local records confirmed he was born and raised on the east side of Saint Paul, a small-time hood, convictions for burglary and solicitation back in the late '70s and early '80s with workhouse time, but nothing recent. An employee of Skin Enterprises, Inc., Aietovsky's outfit.

Walking Cloud was in the squad room. Susan Lee was sitting abjectly in the reception room with Henry Merritt, an attorney in his forties. Walking Cloud was waiting for McCorkle and

Finegrad from the county attorney's office in case Susan Lee had something to say of a confessional nature. Mygosh and Rails were huddling at a computer terminal, going through fingerprint match-ups. Winchell came in and handed a file to Walking Cloud.

"Fingers had been confirmed as one of the voices talking to Susan Lee," she said. "Speaking of whom—"

"We're going to have to lean on her hard," Walking Cloud said. "Don't get juice from a lemon without squeezing somewhere."

Susan Lee was noticeably apprehensive as she and her lawyer passed through the squad room area to Interview Room #2. Observing on the other side of the one-way glass were McCorkle and Finegrad. The four detectives present all sat down across from Susan Lee and her lawyer. Walking Cloud began by explaining that "Willard" was dead and that the police needed to know exactly whom she had been working for and what her relationship was to the dead hit man. Susan Lee bit her lower lip. Clearly, she didn't want to be here. Almost a characteristic trait, noted Walking Cloud, who wondered if she had learned that in acting school.

"Ms. Lee," said Walking Cloud, "your career as an actress is not the only thing in jeopardy here. Your freedom of person is also at stake. You can kiss both your career and your freedom good-bye if you're sent to prison as an accomplice to murder. Two murders directly, several other deaths indirectly, as well as the selling of illegal drugs. On the other hand, if you cooperate, tell us what you know and testify if need be at the trial of whomever's responsible for these crimes, it's just possible the county attorney's office might see fit to regard that as a fair exchange. Your cooperation, no charges against you."

"Are you a cop or the prosecutor, Lieutenant?" Merritt snapped.

"For the sake of argument, let's say I'm both, Mr. Merritt. Your client is in pretty bad shape. Right now, we could charge her with two counts of conspiracy to murder one. We can arrest her and turn her and the evidence over to the county attorney's office right now. A grand jury wouldn't have much trouble, would they? Her career would be in shambles right there. Irretrievable. How many commercial endorsements will she get after that even if she's acquitted? Would the Guthrie take her back? I doubt it. Too much negative publicity. They don't need it, and there're lots of other aspiring actresses out there. Aren't there, Ms. Lee? The world can be a mean, rough place. So, Mr. Merritt, what do you say? If she cooperates, tells us what she knows, agrees to testify, maybe the HCA will cut a deal. And I'd be willing to put in a good word for her, *if* she cooperates."

"I can't tell you how thrilled I am at the prospect of that, Lieutenant," countered Merritt. "Let's take a break. I need to hear something more than your speculations before I'll let her say a word. Is a representative of the county attorney's office available?"

"Maybe we could produce someone," said Walking Cloud.

"Well, I suggest you produce that person," Merritt said matter-of-factly. "My client isn't under arrest yet."

"Not yet, Mr. Merritt, but we're getting very close."

"Susan, don't say anything, *not a word* to these people, till I get back in this room," said Merritt pointedly. "Understand? Susan?"

Susan Lee nodded. Walking Cloud, Mygosh and Merritt stepped outside the interview room, leaving her with Rails and Winchell.

"Let's talk in my office," said the Lieutenant, signaling McCorkle and Finegrad to join them.

"What you're offering isn't enough, Lieutenant," announced Merritt. "Oh, you're scaring the hell out her. Yeah, but what's that getting you? Your kicks?"

"Drop the sarcasm, Henry," said McCorkle. "He's doing his job. You know that. And he's right, as you must realize. We have enough to prosecute her, but she's small fry in this. We know that. So do you. We also know she's in over her head and hardly in the driver's seat. She's probably a decent enough young woman. But someone's into her for something. We want this Pandora Killer, the murderer-rapist, in the deaths of Julie Tinkham and Lori Ruth Mueller and in the murder of Louis Bertram, who I believe was a tennis partner of yours. Wasn't he?"

"Yes, and a good friend," allowed Merritt.

"All right, technically she's culpable in two counts of aiding and abetting, two counts of conspiracy to facilitate, and two counts of aggravated solicitation. Six felonies. Good for thirty, possibly thirty-five years, minimum."

Merritt smirked.

"Come now, Reggie. I didn't graduate from law school yesterday. And I've seen you bluff before. You're overdoing it, as usual. My client's testimony for full immunity—or no deal and we can go to trial."

McCorkle pressed his lips together, wondering what in fact this witness could provide, if anything. What if she knew very little, or nothing at all? Well, she knows something, obviously. McCorkle was Quinn's agent. And Quinn was preparing to run for governor. The last thing he wanted was a useless witness with immunity in a high-profile trial. Too much at stake.

"If you need to talk to Quinn, call him, Reggie," suggested Merritt with a tinge of sarcasm. "We can wait. It *is* Saturday."

"No, that's not necessary," McCorkle said almost wearily. "Alright, full immunity for full cooperation, including testimony as long as we need her, *if* she passes a lie detector test first."

Merritt had won his point. The s.o.b. may be bluffing, thought McCorkle, but he's also a crack defense lawyer. There's a lot more at stake here than Susan Lee and her acting career.

Jenny Schell mused about the previous evening with Will Alsted. Although she had been tempted to invite him to stay the night, he hadn't even made an overture in that direction. Instead, he kissed her again on the lips after she showed him her apartment. It was then that he asked her out for the next evening. He just happened to have tickets to the Guthrie Theater for *King*

Lear. Her daughter being with her father for the weekend and with no other commitment, Jenny said Yes. Perhaps this will be the night, she thought wistfully. Now it was after 3 PM. The day was fleeing by and she still had a couple errands and laundry to do.

Two hours later, Jenny completed her errands and had folded her laundry. Will would be picking her up at 7, so there was a little time to relax. She turned on the 5 o'clock news. The first image she saw was of Channel 4's Ronn Mason in front of the entrance to the Minneapolis Institute of Arts. She turned up the volume and watched the report of the melee, the first she'd heard of it. She saw a tired-looking Walking Cloud finish making a statement, then walk away and get into a car. She didn't catch the reason two men had been pursued by the police. Walking Cloud's explanation was, if anything, elliptical. Who were the men? What was their offense? Another man had been killed and a young girl raped. Was that it? Ronn Mason stood in front of the Art Institute, chatting with the in-studio anchor:

> Don, since Lieutenant Walking Cloud made that statement this morning, a police department spokesperson has told us that the police had been monitoring a murder-for-hire scheme allegedly being concocted in a supermarket parking lot a few blocks away.

Jenny switched to Channel 5, and there was Rhonda Reele also doing a standup in front of the Art Institute. Jenny marveled at the dangerous life Walking Cloud led. She also thought of Julie Tinkham and how her own description of the pitted-faced blond man was at odds with the fact that Julie's killer was probably also the murderer of the other young woman a day or so later, a rapist-murderer who had left smudges on both victims' faces. Walking Cloud had told her, in effect, that the pitted-faced blond man might not have been the killer. But then who was? The only other person in the elevator was the olive-complexioned woman carrying shopping bags. The olive-complexioned woman who also had big teeth. Jenny thought she remembered the olive-complexioned woman carrying a walking stick, too.

She remembered Julie's face, her pleasant manner—so competent, so lucky to be well educated, young and beautiful, and not afraid of anything. Julie had seen nothing wrong with the pitted-faced blond man. Jenny looked at again at the t.v., but now a commercial about facial creams with Jennifer Aniston hawking youth, forever youth, for older women. Jenny's attention drifted. The face of the olive-complexioned women came before her again. Yes, she was a fairly big woman. Probably 5'8". Maybe even taller. Jenny hadn't paid her any particular attention. But they had been standing right next to each other.

She started flipping through channels with her remote control. She turned to Channel 29, a tertiary outlet that featured mostly reruns and old movies interrupted by commercials. A still shot from *Some Like It Hot* with Jack Lemmon and Tony Curtis appeared on the screen. The movie was featured this evening. Cross dressers. Again, the face of the olive-complexioned woman came before her. No, she thought, this is too weird. Silly. It couldn't possibly be. She turned the t.v. off and went into the bathroom to wash her face. She'd had a good night's sleep and wasn't that tired, but then she thought a half-hour nap wouldn't hurt at all. She also knew it might help her think more clearly about this business which seemed so far-fetched. She set her radio alarm for 6 PM and lay down on her waterbed for an impromptu snooze.

Susan Lee didn't want to take a polygraph exam. But her lawyer took her to Peter's Grill a few blocks away for a chat. When they returned ninety minutes later, Walking Cloud thought both lawyer and client looked as if something had been decided. Merritt looked at Walking Cloud, and then at McCorkle and Finegrad, and gave a thumbs-up.

The Lieutenant had prepared a series of question to be included in the polygraph exam.

"I assume you'll be observing this, Lieutenant," said Merritt.

"If you don't mind. McCorkle and Finegrad would also like to watch."

Merritt nodded grimly.

Q#1: "Is your name Susan Lee?"

A: "Yes."

Q#2: "Are you currently employed as an actress at the Guthrie Theater?"

A: "Yes."

Q#3: "Do you aspire to a career in theater and film?"

A: "Yes."

Q#4: "Have you ever knowingly participated in or listened to a scheme to kill another person?"

A: "No."

Q#5: "Were you ever told what the words 'red, white and blue eyes' mean?"

A: "No."

Q#6: "Have you ever knowingly participated in a felonious act?"

A: "No."

Q#7: "Were you aware that the man you knew as 'Willard' was actually a professional hit man, a killer for hire, named Roberto Albion Durangelo?"

A: (*gasps*) "No."

Q#8: "Do you feel any remorse that because of your answering your cell phone at the Black Forest Inn and then delivering messages received, there have probably been at least three deaths?"

A: (*aghast*) "Yes!"

The test was completed a few minutes later. Observing along with Walking Cloud and the two prosecutors were Mygosh, Rails, Blumus and Winchell. The polygraph examiner, a potbellied man named Tom Hill, freed Susan Lee from the machine's trappings. She glanced at him uncertainly.

"Well, how did I do?"

"Oh, you seemed to be holding up," he answered indifferently.

"No, I mean, did I pass the test?"

"Well, I'll have to study the graph and then we'll all find out."

A few minutes later—nearly twenty, in fact—it was determined that Susan Lee was telling the truth to every question. Examiner Hill opined that her nervousness caused the needle waves to jump a bit at leading questions. Both prosecutors were also in the Lieutenant's office where Hill went over the results.

"If she's lying or fudging about any of these questions," Walking Cloud said, "your machine didn't pick it up. Is that it?"

"Lieutenant, this young lady may not be as pure as the driven snow, but she wasn't lying at any point on this test. Look here, the curve moves a little bit only when she receives information in a question—what we call a leading question. But when she responds, there's no significant variation of the needle's path. She passed it going away!"

Walking Cloud thanked Hill as he departed. McCorkle sighed.

"Just what kind of a witness she'll be in court depends on how much she actually knows," he said. "Let's bring her in with her lawyer and get her statement."

Susan Lee was relieved to learn she had passed the polygraph examination. Walking Cloud reminded her that she was now obligated to tell what she knew in exchange for immunity. She agreed.

"I have today off," she said. "No rehearsals, no performances. Let's get it over with. I want to do the right thing."

Henry Merritt raised his eyebrows. He was listening carefully. His client explained that she knew "Willard" in Chicago, that she met him through her older sister, Maya, who had shocked their family some years earlier by working as a call girl for visiting businessmen, first in Old Town before moving over to the more fashionable North Shore area. Although Maya was the renegade in an otherwise successful Korean-American family, she was also vulnerable to the likes and dislikes, indeed the volatile caprice, of "Willard"—who frequently traveled to other cities, such as

Minneapolis-Saint Paul, Miami, New Orleans, Los Angeles and various points in Latin and South America. When he learned Susan Lee had landed a role at the Guthrie, he made contact with her and implied that her sister's well-being in Chicago depended on her cooperation in taking and relaying messages. She refused money he offered, she said, and was never told what the nomenclature and abbreviations meant.

"Weren't you curious about why he couldn't do this himself?" Finegrad asked.

"Yes, but I didn't want to get on his bad side. In Chicago, I knew he had beaten up my sister more than once. I saw her after one of those beatings. She had a swollen eye—it was almost *closed*!—and other marks on her face and arms. No telling where else! She's also done drugs. When he withheld cocaine from her a couple times, she'd call me and was *screaming*! It was—it's been *horrible*! I was really afraid of 'Willard'! He had her dependent on him for drugs. What's his real name again?"

"Roberto Albion Durangelo," said Walking Cloud. "Your sister's name is Maya Lee?"

"Yes."

Walking Cloud typed the name into the AFIS network on a keyboard. In a few seconds, the haggard face of Maya Lee appeared on the screen in color, along with her latents, her arrest record dating back to 2004, and her last known address in Chicago.

"Oh, my god!" cried Susan Lee when she looked at the monitor. She buried her face in her hands.

"So, Ms. Lee," said Walking Cloud after a five-second pause, "you're saying his hook into you was your sister, implying she'd meet up with a bad end unless you cooperated?"

"*Yes*! Essentially. There was the implied threat that he'd do something to me, too."

"Well, he was extremely vicious," agreed Walking Cloud. "He demonstrated that today. Did he have any other contacts in the theater world here in the Twin Cities that you know of?"

Susan Lee seemed surprised by the question. Walking Cloud studied her closely. He let the image of her sister remain on the monitor screen.

"He knows—he knew—at least a couple people at the Guthrie. He was at a cast party we had for the opening of *Lear* in early summer. I'm an understudy in it. This was my first conversation with him here, when he said he had something he wanted me to do. I told him I wasn't interested. But then he took me aside and told me what was what. I realized—I *thought*—I didn't have any choice. I was also afraid for my sister. He implied strongly that he could arrange to have her tortured or killed just by making a call."

"You'll have to provide the names of those people you think Durangelo knew. Are there any actors, male actors, who have a short left leg? Put another way, do any of the male actors there wear an elevated left shoe?"

"I—I don't know," she said, as if trying to remember. "I haven't noticed that. How tall?"

"Five-nine, five-ten. A trim build. No more than forty, forty-five at most."

"That may fit several men at the Guthrie. Most actors—in the theater, at least—tend to be slim or at least they keep their weight down. An elevated shoe?"

"Yes, the left leg. About half an inch. He's also a master make-up artist and very adept in the use of disguise."

Susan Lee frowned. A look of strain crossed her face.

"I'm sorry. I really—had no idea."

"We believe you, Ms. Lee," said Walking Cloud. "We would like you to do a couple things for us, in addition to the names of Durangelo's—Willard's—friends at the Guthrie, providing Mr. Merritt agrees, of course."

Merritt and his client exchanged glances.

"Go ahead," said the lawyer.

Walking Cloud handed her composite images of Pandora Killer from the computer, then a group of four variations, based on his memory of Krewler's would-be killer. He explained that they represented variations of disguises the perp used, also that an elevated left shoe would likely be used. He gave her his card with his home number as well as those of his colleagues working on the case.

She wrote down a couple names.

"These are the only people whose names I knew who I've seen talking with him. There may be more, two or three others. But I don't know their names, a stagehand or a lighting technician."

"Could you find out those names? Anyone you remember who may have talked to any length with Durangelo."

"Sure, I'll try."

She flashed a brief, if tremulous, smile. Then she and Henry Merritt left. It was late afternoon.

Chapter Fifteen

Frances Comes Out

Arthur Boyood always admired those who had been trained and successful in theater, in film, in make-believe of almost any sort. His own attempts at acting had met with minimal success. Because his left leg was a half-inch shorter than the other, he always felt this was part of why he was never cast in roles he knew he could perform well. He had taken part in college productions and during his graduate school years when he was supposed to be studying French and Italian. When he left graduate school, his intended career as an actor was also sidelined. Having to work odd jobs made him bitter, an acridity he knew he had to control. And control meant taking his medication regularly, without fail. He had suffered from an episode of manic depression, said the psychiatrist who interviewed him after an interrupted suicide attempt four years earlier. However, the medication did not subdue his sexual desires, what he knew the psychiatrist would call "fantasies." In fact, when the subject of women came up, Boyood glossed over it, saying he'd had a girlfriend once, but the relationship ended because they drifted apart. This, of course, wasn't the truth, but what did it matter now? At 36, he knew he was a nice-looking man with good manners. He was balding a little, but that didn't detract much, if at all. Why then did women talk to him but then reject his advances? Someone had to pay for these slights. And someone already had. Then another someone paid, too. There was also that idiotic, well-dressed fool in the car he'd stopped after escaping the hospital dragnet. Anyway, that privileged, well-dressed bastard paid for having money and obvious success and just for being in the way, of course. Boyood learned afterward that the man whom he had just pleasurably forced to undress down to his skivvies before he shot him dead was a lawyer from Edina. The son of a bitch deserved a cruder death. With part of the $423 cash from the lawyer's wallet, Boyood bought more make-up supplies, the same kind the Guthrie Theater ordered for its performers.

The Guthrie was where he'd found employment lately. He had been hired as a part-time stagehand at first. The money was reasonably good, more than he ever made as a teaching assistant. Over time his shifts increased. And then recently, he was permitted to work as an extra in *King Lear*, an opportunity he relished. Now he was treated with a semblance of proper respect, although he was still not an Equity member, therefore a disposable member of the cast. But he got to hobnob with the actors and actresses, some of whom were from points East or West, and some local because they'd been in the area so long. It was in the Dram Shop, the booze bar in the inner recesses of the theater, that Boyood first encountered a man called Willard, whose principal status with the Guthrie crowd seemed to be as a discreet supplier of cocaine to one of the directors whose show was about over and also to a chubby-faced Romanian dramaturg. Willard also talked to Susan Lee, a Korean-American actress from Chicago, although she didn't seem the type to use drugs. Nonetheless, Boyood had seen Willard talk to her very seriously once or twice.

Once Boyood happened to be sitting on a bench outside near the theater. He was reading a novel, Lawrence Durrell's *Tunc*, when suddenly a voice came at him from the side. Boyood looked up. It was Willard. Very quickly, it seemed, Willard had elicited from Boyood his frustrations—and the reasons for his anger.

"You're a stagehand?"

"Yeah, it's grind work, but it's the theater. Now I'm an extra, too."

"What do ya do to those people keeping ya down like this? Isn't it about time to do something about it?"

"You mean, get even?"

"Your words. Don't they deserve it?"

"Yeah, they do. The goddamn bastards! I'd like to—to—"

"To what, man? Go ahead and say it. It's just between us."

"I'd like to see them all *die*! I *really would*!"

"And every pretty chick who's ever turned ya down, then laughed at ya behind your back. What would ya like to do to the next pretty chick ya see?"

"I'd like to humiliate her, then—"

"Yeah, then what?"

"Then send her back to the hell she came from!"

This conversation had so roused Boyood that before he realized it, he wanted to go out and actually kill. Who would he kill, though?

"Take out the next good looker ya see, my friend. That's what. Ya wanna know how to do it?"

Willard advised Boyood to think it over some more, and if he were really serious, to give him a call and they could meet again. Any time. Here, write this number down. Just call, but not after 11 PM.

"Good hit man's gotta get his rest, ya know," Willard said.

"Yeah, sure! I'll call you," Boyood replied eagerly.

Willard's grin was friendly, thought Boyood, and totally sincere. This guy was on the level. Boyood was mesmerized with the idea of causing someone to die. He went back to his attic apartment up in Kenwood. It was here that his world transfigured itself. He liked to experiment alone at first. Then gradually he thought of "parading." Various facial make-up disguises, gleaned and expanded from a textbook he'd had since college, were his first attempts. Since landing the stagehand job, Boyood tried wigs, and then clothes, particularly women's clothes, which he stored in a locked wardrobe in his apartment. He kept his wigs, eyeliner, facial creams and other material in a locked cedar chest next to the wardrobe. He distrusted the landlady, who had a key to his apartment. And there was also the fear of being burglarized. Not that Boyood was shy about his secret life. He just didn't want it invaded. It was just before his chance meeting with Willard that he began his outings. First, he shaved very close wherever it might matter. Then he dressed down, being careful not to overdo it on the make-up or the women's clothes. He was slim enough, he knew, to be taken for a tall woman. He wore a black wig with long hair, a pinkish facial with a modest eyeliner and mascara, a plain blue dress with a red belt, earrings and stylish, but not like a coquette. He also wore eyeglasses, along with low-heeled dark shoes and stuffing in the left heel. As he left his apartment, he took pains that his neighbors not recognize him. Ridicule, he reminded himself, was worse than death. He wanted respect and recognition for his superior talent. Being someone else, even a woman for a short time, was an unbelievable thrill. To think that people passing him on the street saw him not as Arthur Boyood but as a woman was beyond the wildest applause.

By the time he called Willard the day after their encounter, Boyood had already had three outings as a transvestite. He didn't know what it meant, but he felt more and more powerful. An unbelievable high. If he couldn't be someone else on stage because of the casting directors' stupidity, then he could be someone else in real life as he walked among people in the streets, in public buildings, or any place where one might be noticed. He thought back to his first phone call to Willard. They met again at the same bench a stone's throw from the theater.

"Ya wanna take command-a the situation, Arthur?"

"Yeah, I do! What can I do?"

"Ya gotta walk before ya run, right? No crawlin', though. I think ya already done enough-a that. Tell ya what to do first. Ya listening, Arthur?"

"Of course, Willard! What should I do?"

Over the next week, residents of south Minneapolis reported a number of pet killings to the police. A German shepherd was found poisoned with its throat cut. A white cat was found on Harriet Avenue South decapitated, its head hanging by the ears from a tree. Two blocks east, a cocker spaniel was found slashed to death. In his search for power, Boyood killed seven animals in seven days, his assignment from Willard. He was ecstatic when Willard complimented him on finishing the task, a report about the animal deaths being a feature one night on Channel 4's 10 PM news. There was also a small article about it in one of the daily newspapers.

Their third meeting was in a corner of the Dram Shop after a preview of *King Lear*. Willard had attended the performance. It was mildly crowded in the Dram. Willard spoke low.

"Time for graduation, Arthur. Ya know, ya did more than I expected. Hell, I didn't know ya, man. But ya came through. Ya did! Hangin' that cat's head in a tree! That was *outrageous*!"

Willard chuckled, slapping Boyood lightly on the arm.

"Ya thought of a name in this new role ya been carvin' out for yourself? Ya gotta have a name, even if it's only a secret name, Arthur. In the meantime, tell me. Ya gotta secret life or somethin'? Ya wanna tell me about it? I think I know, but tell me in your own way. I'm listenin'."

Boyood felt an unusual camaraderie with Willard. He wasn't sure why. Maybe it was that Willard knew his inner soul, his inner rage, and sympathized. Boyood also knew Willard could be trusted. So he confided that, yes, he did have a secret life.

"I like to go parading. To dress up! In drag! I go so no one recognizes me. But I dress in style. And I look so fine! I really get into character. I *do*!"

Willard didn't smile. Nor did he sneer. He looked solemnly at Boyood.

"And when you're paradin', who are ya? Do ya have a name for your new self, Arthur?"

Boyood hadn't thought about it yet. Willard persisted.

"When you're out in drag and if someone were to speak to ya, even ask your name, what would ya say?"

"I'd say—Frances. Yes, I'm Frances!"

At this, Willard's eyebrow lifted slightly, but he betrayed no other reaction. He was so respectful, thought Boyood.

"Perhaps Frances can get control for ya, Arthur. She's gotta be your instrument for retribution against those bastards who've laughed at ya, who've turned ya down. Turned ya down *flat*, Arthur! Then gone on their merry way as if it didn't matter one bit. Think of the prettiest chick you've ever seen. Maybe Frances can spot her. That young dame who's got it all. Success just by snappin' her ass the right way. The kind-a girl who got straight 'A's' in school, maybe was a cheerleader, prob'ly the prettiest one with the nicest legs 'n tits. The president of her college sorority. Then she got into Equity, not by her deservin' it, at least not ahead-a *you*, Arthur. But she got into Equity by *sleepin'* her way in! An' you're out in the cold. Now Frances—maybe she can make the bitch accountable! She can find that undeservin' cunt an' do what needs to be done, man. *Off* the slut! Right, Arthur?"

Boyood looked at Willard. In a few words, this kind man had seen into all his frustrations. In his thirty-six years, no one had ever said so much to him. Frances might well provide the needed relief and finally get some justice for all the wrongs he had endured. But these wrongs, these injustices, were real. Someone had to pay.

"Ya graduate now, my friend. Frances will help ya. Listen to her, Arthur. After a couple incidents-a this, you'll be ready for some free-lance work I got in mind. Do Frances's appearance a little different each time. Ya want her to look like an ordinary person, but different each time. So let your imagination take over. That's the assignment. Okay?"

"I gotcha. I've gotta think about this now. How to do it."

They shook hands. Willard got up and went over to the Romanian dramaturg, who had come in with a pair of young women. Boyood finished his beer, quietly slipped out of the theater, and took the bus home.

After Frances raped and killed Julie Tinkham, Boyood decided not to read about it or watch stories about it on t.v. It would only preoccupy him and go to his head. So he decided to wait. Then Willard contacted him the next day and told him he had something for him to do for money. They met at their bench, but this time they got in Willard's car and drove to Loring Park on the other side of Hennepin Avenue from the Walker Art Center. They walked slowly around the park.

"There's a guy in Hennepin County General Hospital in the cardiac ward. Name's here on the piece-a paper. Here, read it."

He held the piece of paper before Boyood as they strolled.

"Martin Krewler."

"Right. Martin Krewler. Memorize that name. Now here are some plastic latent gloves, so your fingerprints won't be picked up. Wash them in hot water before you put them on. Then put them on with your fingertips one at a time. This is a job for *you*, Arthur, not Frances. Ya can get into the hospital by usin' the orderly's outfit and i.d. I got for ya here."

Willard handed him a plastic Macy's shopping bag. Boyood saw that Willard's hands were also in thin plastic gloves. He'd not noticed this earlier.

"Put some make-up on to change your appearance. Carry another costume along. Make it simple so it doesn't take up much room on your person. I also suggest ya carry this an' use it only when ya have to."

Willard now gave him a small package wrapped in plastic. It was an automatic pistol in a shoulder holster with rounds of ammunition and a silencer.

"Ya know how to use a weapon with a silencer?"

"Yes, in fact I'm a very *good* marksman! I used to go hunting with my father. But aren't silencers illegal? I thought they were. Well, it doesn't matter."

Willard uttered something unintelligible, then handed him a thin envelope.

"It's your first hit, Arthur. Here's a down payment. The rest after your mark is dead. All right. I'll be in touch."

With that, the two men went their separate ways from the middle of Loring Park. Within six hours, Lori Ruth Mueller would be hospitalized with fatal injuries after being raped, choked and beaten. And Krewler, in the same hospital for a "coronary incident" while jogging around Lake Harriet, would suffer an attempt on his life.

Chapter Sixteen

A Night At The Theater

Jenny Schell was pleased when Will Alsted told her that after the show they'd go back to the Dram Shop to meet people involved with the production, among them the Romanian dramaturg who had issued the invitation. Jenny wondered whether to confide in Alsted about the olive-complexioned woman. She realized she should have called Detective Blumus earlier about her suddenly realized suspicions. But instead she had spent the time after her nap taking a shower and getting ready. Now she thought again about the olive-complexioned woman as they drove onto the freeway, heading for the exit near the Guthrie Theater.

"You heard about the car chase and shootout at the Art Institute this afternoon?" she asked.

"Oh yes! I saw Walking Cloud on t.v. again, but I didn't catch the whole story. Did you?"

She promptly filled him in on what she knew.

"That man has a dangerous life, doesn't he?" Alsted replied.

"He really does."

Alsted parked the car in the lot provided by the theater. They joined others walking the same direction.

In *King Lear*, Boyood was a Knight, a Messenger, an Attendant, a Soldier and finally an Officer. He was proud of these non-speaking roles and of the various costumes made just for him. He tried to put out of his mind the failure of his first murder-for-hire. The odd thing was that even after escaping Walking Cloud's dragnet, shooting the cop's tire, thereby causing the vehicle to overturn and explode, and then killing the well-dressed lawyer, Boyood had heard nothing—*zero!*—from Willard. Where was he? Boyood hoped his friend wasn't too upset at the failed hit. In fact, Willard might be impressed that Boyood had escaped so cleverly. He did the best he could. He recalled the fight with Walking Cloud, the escape to the Men's Room on the second floor where he quickly altered his appearance, garnered a wheelchair, threw together the likeness of a stuffed dummy and made his way to the 6th Street exit and outside where the melee resulting in the abduction of the lawyer with his car took place. Incredible, marveled Boyood, that he had done all that! And here he was again, back at the Guthrie and another performance of *Lear*, in which his very minor non-speaking roles permitted him insight and imaginary status into the world of professional make-believe.

Tonight, a pretty girl named Susan Lee was taking the part of Regan, Lear's middle daughter, because of the illness of the actress who had the role. Boyood spotted Susan Lee in full costume in the hallway offstage. She went into the Actors' Lounge and began to fix herself a cup of tea. Boyood wondered if she knew what had happened to Willard. He had seen them talking. But as with other Equity members he hadn't met formally, he was too shy to approach her. He also remembered that her conversations with Willard never looked happy. An inquiry about him might upset her. Besides, the show would begin in less than twenty minutes. It might throw her performance off. She was an understudy, in her first night as Regan. Boyood was proud of being so considerate of another artist.

When they got to the theater lobby, Jenny told Alsted she had to make a quick call. She went to the side and opened her cell phone. She looked in her purse for Carol Blumus's card. She found it and called her number. No answer. She called the direct line of Homicide Division. Winchell answered. A female cop answered, but it wasn't Carol.

"Have you called her cell phone?" suggested Winchell.

"Yes, but no answer. Is Lieutenant Walking Cloud there?"

"No, he's gone, too. Is there anything I can help you with? I'm a homicide detective, if that matters."

"No, no thanks."

She looked in her little book for Walking Cloud's home number, and there it was! For some reason, she felt nervous as she waited for him to answer.

"Hello, this is Walking Cloud."

The voice was unmistakable.

"Lieutenant, I'm sorry to bother you off-duty. This is Jenny Schell. I'm calling you on a hunch, really. It sounds crazy, but let me explain."

She told him about her reconsideration of the olive-complexioned woman in the elevator, that she might actually have been a male in disguise.

"It *does* make sense, Ms. Schell. Where are you now? I hear voices in the background."

"Will and I are at the Guthrie. We're about to see *King Lear*. But I had to call you."

"I'm glad you did! I'll be there in fifteen minutes. Wait in the inner lobby until you absolutely have to go in. I'll be right there."

That Walking Cloud was a man of action she knew very well. She went back to the inner lobby and found Alsted. She told him what had transpired.

"I know you think I might be crazy, Will. Walking Cloud is coming here right away. I'm not sure why, either. I hope you don't mind."

Alsted had a serious grin.

"I would have done the same thing, Jenny. How can I help?"

"Let's just wait for him to get there. He said to wait. I don't know why."

Alsted chuckled.

"Jenny, you amaze me. You think this—person could actually be the murderer of that young woman?"

"It was a strange-looking woman with an olive-complexion," she emphasized. "It's crazy, but it occurred to me when—I saw an ad on t.v. Never mind. I know it sounds crazy, but there's no other explanation."

Walking Cloud came alone. He handed Jenny and Alsted a copy of the juxtaposed likenesses of the perp he'd tangled with at the hospital. He then said something to the young man at the door, who merely nodded and pointed to the ticket office. Walking Cloud knocked on the door and went inside. He came out with a small folding chair.

"I'll need a seat next to you," he said, holding it up. "The management has kindly provided one." Then gesturing to the printout, he said, "These are four variations of what our killer could possibly look like without any make-up or costume. Study them carefully, both of you."

On the printout were four computer-simulated likenesses of a round male face, unremarkable but malleable with the right make-up. Jenny noticed the height range from 5'8" to 5'10" with an elevated left shoe. She remembered the peculiar smile, a face not unlike the late Charles Laughton in drag and the large teeth within that smile.

Walking Cloud conferred with the general manager, a stern-looking man named Jennings, who said clearly, "Lieutenant, I trust whatever you're up to won't interrupt or disturb our show tonight. After what happened at the Art Institute today, I'm very worried about your presence here."

"That was legitimate police business, Mr. Jennings, and so is this! You understand? We may have a serial killer on the premises."

Jennings frowned and shrugged. Detective Winchell rushed into the lobby with several men in plain clothes, all wearing badges, their faces serious, determined. Walking Cloud spoke with them briefly while a dozen uniformed officers came into the lobby. The theater doors were about to close. Walking Cloud went in with Jenny and Alsted.

"I'll be seated to your right, Ms. Schell," the Lieutenant said. "I know you're on the aisle."

Walking Cloud waited until she and Alsted were seated before unfolding his little chair.

"You both get a good look at those pictures?" he asked.

"Yes," said Alsted.

"We did," affirmed Jenny.

The program distributed at the door had an insert stating that Susan Lee would perform the role of Regan for the evening's performance. Walking Cloud spoke low into his fist mike: "Attention, police officers, this is Walking Cloud. Susan Lee, who was in our office this afternoon, is on stage tonight as Regan. Step lightly backstage, offstage." Of all the theaters in the community, the Guthrie was the only one declining to cooperate with a police request for personnel records and answers as to who might fit the perp's profile. Something about a "witch hunt." Walking Cloud watched the opening flourish, the entry of Lear with his train, including his three daughters. With miniature binoculars, he also scanned the male actors for any resemblance to Pandora Killer's profile. He saw none for sure. Then the flourish and the King exited with his train.

Boyood was among the train. Offstage now, he went into the hallway next to Lear's dressing room. A man and a woman in plain clothes with police badges stood next to the water faucet. Boyood shared a dressing room with three other extras downstairs. He retreated there, the dialogue and flourishes of the show coming over the intercom. He wanted to check on his weapon, which he'd brought to the theater for the first time. He fitted it with its silencer into the holster, inside his costume. Then he returned upstairs. The two plainclothes cops were nosing around. Boyood knew he'd seen them before, although neither, he sensed, appeared to take any notice of him. Boyood did not know why cops should be here, but since they were, where was Walking Cloud? This was his doing. The bastard! Why didn't he just let up? And what was the connection with Susan Lee? Boyood wondered where she was when she wasn't on stage.

Ah, but now the short colloquy between Goneril and Oswald in Scene III, then the next scene and Boyood was standing fast while Lear and the Fool traded gibes. Then Boyood was offstage again. He watched Susan Lee, who looked solemn, perhaps absorbing herself into character before appearing early in Act II in Gloster's castle. Boyood couldn't see the audience from the wings. He was now an Attendant for a scene with Cornwall and Regan. Finally the scene with Edmund was over. Cornwall and Regan and the extras left the stage, leaving Kent in the stocks to lament with Gloster. On stage, Boyood was within an arm's reach of Susan Lee. Offstage, he was now even closer.

As the next scene with Kent and Oswald grew increasingly voluble, Boyood became aware that Susan Lee might be looking for him. When he turned in her direction, she had already shifted her gaze. It was dark in the offstage wings. Then they were all on again. Boyood roved his eyes, trying to scan the audience for Walking Cloud. All he saw were blurred faces. Walking Cloud must be out there somewhere.

Jenny Schell looked from scene to scene for a face resembling the computerized etchings, even a face that could be transformed into the olive-complexioned woman. She looked at each actor in turn. Instinctively, she sensed her ability to recognize the real life villain in this drama was lacking. A call for the stocks came from Cornwall to punish Kent for his impertinence. Now Jenny realized the actress playing Regan was the singer the night before at the bar.

"I remember her!" she whispered to Walking Cloud.

"Yes, but she's not the one," he whispered back, pointing to the computerized likeness. "It's a male looking something like *this*. Keep looking."

Walking Cloud scanned the various male actors through his binoculars. He studied every face, including the extras. He looked at their feet. He realized it was getting close to Intermission.

For Boyood, these moments with Lear querying and inveighing about finding his man Kent in the stocks were an opportunity offstage to focus on Susan Lee and decide whether or not she had been looking at him. He reminded himself not to get paranoid. Again he was on stage as a servant with Regan, Cornwall and Gloster. Perhaps now he could spot Walking Cloud. He'd only left him a single note so far. No, he hadn't left it. *Frances* had.

Walking Cloud marveled at the power of Richard Gainswell, the actor playing Lear, the ennoblement of his anger and fatherly disappointment while the approaching storm was heard in the distance. Yet the Lieutenant saw no one who might bear a close enough resemblance to the perp. Jenny Schell touched his arm and asked to use the binoculars.

"Look at them all," he whispered, "including the extras, the non-speaking actors."

Jenny nodded, including Gainswell as Lear denouncing the objections of Goneril and Regan about housing his whole train of men, his dismay rivaling the thunder and lightning gradually becoming louder:

... You think I'll weep;
No, I'll not weep:—
I have full cause of weeping, but this heart
Shall break into a hundred thousand flaws
Or ere I'll weep.—Oh, fool, I shall go mad!

The King left the stage with the Fool, Gloster and Kent. Quickly now, a very short scene with Gloster, Cornwall, Goneril and Regan—and then they all departed. It was Intermission.

"I'm sorry, but I couldn't see all of them," Jenny said.

Walking Cloud allowed a faint grin, knowing she may have been impressed, as he was, by Gainswell's power as an actor. Walking Cloud got up and went into the lobby, over to an alcove near a door. He spoke into his fist mike: "This is Walking Cloud. Those of you in the offstage areas, keep alert! If you spot a likely, do not attempt to arrest him till I can get back there. Make no arrest at all *unless* he attempts to leave the building. Now let me hear where you are. Go."

Voices came into his ear. Six detectives were roaming the backstage and offstage areas. Four more were in the audience and two uniformed cops were at all doorways. John Pingally, the theater's artistic director, now presented himself to the Lieutenant in the theater lobby. Jennings introduced him to the Lieutenant.

"Lieutenant," said Pingally, "this is an unheard-of intrusion into a professional theater! Police at every corner! Detectives backstage roaming around! What the hell do you want?"

"We want a serial killer who may be a member of your cast or one of your other employees, Mr. Pingally. You refused to cooperate earlier, so now we're doing it the hard way."

Walking Cloud handed him a copy of the four juxtaposed likenesses of the perp.

"Is there anyone here who resembles this suspect? Note the particulars about height and weight. He's also a master make-up artist."

Pingally stared at the printout, and again at Walking Cloud.

"I'm not the director of this production. I don't know all the cast members. But I'll take it back to the director and—"

"Wait a minute. I'll do the questioning. No offense intended. Send someone else to get the director."

Pingally stared at Walking Cloud, who said, "Well, go on, man! There isn't much time!"

"I know where he might be," volunteered Jennings, who hurried away to the backstage door.

"You're insulting my intelligence, sir," complained Pingally. "I don't like your attitude at all!"

"Well, I'm sorry, but so far you haven't been very cooperative," Walking Cloud said evenly. "Like I said, we're just gonna have to do this the hard way."

Susan Lee was in the actors' lounge talking with Gainswell and Sharon Morley, who played Goneril. Boyood edged into the room.

"It's this Pandora Killer," she said in a lowered voice. "Look at this profile they gave me!"

She withdrew a piece of paper from her sleeve.

"The police think he's working *here!*"

Her eyes were ablaze. Boyood picked up a magazine and pretended to leaf through it. Now two strangers with badges came into the room. Susan Lee, Gainswell and other Equity actors looked at them with disdain.

"Find your murderer yet?" Gainswell shot forth with no attempt to hide his contempt.

The two detectives were visibly surprised.

"We're looking, sir," said one of them in an even tone. "Just go about your business. We'll try not to get in the way."

"What's your name, Detective?" asked Gainswell in a superior tone.

"I'm Sergeant Mygsoh, homicide division. This is Detective Rails. We're not here to interfere in your business. We're here to catch a murderer, as you know."

Gainswelll appeared suddenly mollified. Susan Lee said nothing. Now a female voice over the intercom: "Ten minutes to Act Three, cast. Ten minutes."

"Excuse me," said Gainswell, who nodded grimly to the detectives as he walked past them, glancing for an odd second at Boyood and Tom, another extra, who sat across from each other. Tom looked up at Susan Lee as she started to leave.

"May I see that?" he asked. "Just for a couple seconds. I thought—"

"Sure," she said, raising an eyebrow slightly, waiting while Tom examined the four likenesses. He showed the printout to Boyood, who leaned over cautiously, not wanting Susan Lee to pay the slightest attention to him. He tried not to smirk. The nose was too narrow, the lips too thin, the eyes in all four pictures were too close together. Then he saw that the shorter left leg was duly noted.

"This is Pandora Killer?" wondered Tom as he handed it back.

"Supposedly," she said, and left the room. Was she disgusted by the whole business? Boyood wasn't sure what she was like, although she did have that Equity attitude. An attitude Boyood disliked, a status he envied.

"Three minutes to Act Three, cast. Places, please. Three minutes to Act Three. Places, please."

Next were the Heath scenes with Lear and the storm raging, Alsted told Jenny. "The actor playing Lear—what's his name—Richard Gainswell?—he has such range in the role! Such power!"

"He has incredible power," agreed Walking Cloud, now a couple feet away with Pingally as they awaited the play's director. "He's not from this area, is he, Mr. Pingally? Richard Gainswell we're speaking of now."

Pingally had an uncomfortable look on his super-refined face, his goatee almost pointed in distress.

"He's—from New York. A native of Kansas, I believe."

Pingally's attention was suddenly diverted.

"Ah, here's Clive Garden now," he said in an instructive tone as a slender, weed-faced man with a full head of silver hair and a solemn expression accompanied Jennings through the lobby.

The Lieutenant showed the printout to Garden, who raised his eyebrows and let them settle into a frown. Unlike Pingally, he displayed no petulance. He stared at the likenesses, and glanced at his watch.

"Less than two minutes to Act Three," he muttered. "It's possible, Lieutenant. There are perhaps a dozen people here who might fit this description, except for the shorter leg. I don't know anyone with that. But it's not impossible to conceal it with an internal lift in the shoe."

"Thank you, Mr. Garden. That's what I wanted to know. I'll need a list of your personnel. Please check off the likelies, if you would. Mr. Pingally, are you listening?"

"Yes, I am, Lieutenant," replied Pingally. "We'll get the list to you right away. I'll bring it to you. Should be about twenty minutes or so. Are you going to see the rest of the play?"

The principal Heath scene was beginning, the sounds of a storm and the voice of Kent:

Who's there, besides foul weather?

Boyood went down to his dressing room. He looked into the mirror and comforted himself that the printout drawings could well have been of Santa Claus. He listened to the banter of the other extras. A stagehand came in to change clothes on the other side of the room. They were all talking about the cops in the theater. Boyood nodded agreeably when Tom looked his way.

"It's really amazing," said Boyood quietly.

The same detectives who had been in the actors' lounge upstairs now stood in the doorway. Tom looked up at them from his make-up table.

"Gentlemen, are you looking for someone—or something?"

"Any-a you seen an actor or someone who works around here who has one leg, the left leg, shorter than the other?" Detective Mygosh asked.

Boyood shook his head. So did the two others.

"Nope," said the stagehand, "would-a noticed someone like that by now. Sorry."

"We have to prepare for the next scene, if you don't mind, gentlemen," Tom said almost brusquely.

His tone of voice worked. The detectives disappeared after scouring the lower extremities of all three extras. He waited a few seconds while putting on a cape, then said, "Jesus, what damn nerve these cops have! I can't believe it!"

Boyood said nothing. But he brooded about how Walking Cloud and his detectives found out about his shorter leg as he went up the stairs to the main level. As he neared the final step, the door opened and two plainclothes cops appeared, the man and woman he'd seen earlier. The female cop was young and fairly pretty, even in her sternness. Her partner, a ruddy-faced man in his mid-thirties with a chunky body but flat stomach, also looked serious. They both gazed at Boyood as he attempted to pass by them to the door. The male detective touched his arm.

"Excuse me, sir, do you know where Susan Lee's dressing room is? She's playing Regan tonight."

"Yes, I do," Boyood said. "She's down on the next level at the far end of the hallway on the right."

Boyood felt his heart leap. The detectives appeared to be satisfied. Or were they? Their expressions were impenetrable.

"Thank you," said the male detective, unsmiling as he and his partner went down the stairs.

In the actors' lounge, to Boyood's surprise, there was Susan Lee. Over the intercom, the Heath scene resumed with storm clouds and Lear's foraging voice, then the Fool and Kent and Edgar in dialogue. Boyood sat on a half-divan across from the square-faced, oddly handsome Mark Tell, a New York actor in his early thirties, a graduate of Juilliard, everything that Boyood himself had been denied. Tell wore a stylishly thin mustache, which looked bizarre as he sniffed, or seemed to, at seeing Boyood sitting across from him. He got up and left without a word. Across the room, Susan Lee was being massaged on her neck and shoulders by Sharon Morley, who as Goneril was authoritative but offstage full of Equity hauteur. Weren't they all? thought Boyood as he watched the actresses bond with each other.

"Sisters have to take care of one another," said Sharon Morley as she expertly rubbed Susan Lee's lower neck and shoulders. Now Susan had a rapturous smile.

"Oh, yes! Thank you, dear. This feels *so good*—after a hellish day—with those fucking cops! Oh, thank you, Sharon. Yes, *right there*! Oh, *yes!*"

Boyood was transfixed. Why did she talk to the police? And where was Willard? It must have something to do with their conversations, always uneasy from Boyood's observation. Drugs. It must be drugs. But he didn't know, of course. The two women now sat up, straightening their costumes. Time for the bloody scene in Gloster's castle. They both looked at Tom, who had rushed breathlessly into the lounge.

"Hey, Arthur, how do I look? Okay?" he nearly bellowed. Boyood almost jumped at the sound of his own name. Tom spun around like a ridiculous fairy princess. Susan Lee and Sharon

Morley appeared startled by this display of panache on the part of a mere extra. Boyood gazed amenably at Tom, hoping no one else in the room noticed. But not so, he feared, now aware of Susan Lee looking at him as she was urged out of the room by Sharon Morley. Tom smiled like a fool, clearly pleased. Susan Lee stopped short, still looking in Boyood's direction.

"You're Arthur?" she said.

"Yes," said Boyood, sensing her sudden recognition of him was connected to Willard. To his astonishment, she took a step toward him with a half-smile.

"Susie, we gotta go!" implored Sharon Morley, tugging at her.

Susan Lee's eyes were fixed on Boyood.

"After the show tonight, I need to talk with you for a minute. Okay?"

"Sure."

She disappeared into the hallway with Sharon Morley.

"Hey, she likes you, maybe, Arthur?" parried Tom.

Boyood gave Tom a blank stare, although he would have liked to strike him in the kneecaps with a sledgehammer. But he checked himself.

"No more than anyone else," he said calmly.

Tom's expression showed that he really didn't care.

For the next scene, Boyood was a Servant. On stage, he had to pay close attention to the Equity actors, but was glancing out into the audience to spot Walking Cloud. Suddenly, the scene was over. Boyood now began to get tired, especially in his left leg. He thought he saw Susan Lee look in his direction.

Walking Cloud kept looking through his tiny binoculars. He began to wonder if instead of an actor, Pandora Killer might be an offstage employee, perhaps a make-up technician or in the costume department. Just what happened the other night at the hospital proved convincingly that quick changes were within his range. This Shakespeare production offered practical camouflage. Walking Cloud gave the binoculars again to Jenny, who in turn handed them to Alsted. Now Lear, dressed up with flowers, hurriedly left the stage, followed by several non-speaking servants.

"Do you see something?" whispered Walking Cloud.

Alsted lowered the binoculars, still staring at the stage occupied by only three actors, none of whom had a limp.

"I thought I did," he murmured, handing the binoculars back, "but now I'm not sure."

Pingally appeared, handing the Lieutenant the *Lear* personnel list. Walking Cloud put it in his pocket. The play was almost over. Alsted gestured for the binoculars again. He looked through them again and pointed at the stage as he gave the binoculars back.

"The third actor in the center back," he whispered. "He seems to be favoring his left leg."

"Which one?" asked Walking Cloud.

But the start of light music drowned out the answer.

"*Shhhh!*" came a warning behind them.

Walking Cloud scoured the faces of the extras again. A note from Alsted read: "He's 4th from the left." But there was movement among the cast as Cordelia and Lear exchanged dialogue. A voice came into the Lieutenant's ear: "Ben, Mygosh here. We got several possibilities on this list-a Guthrie employees. You comin' out soon?"

"Roger, Joshua. Get a rehearsal room clear. I'll be here till the end of the show. Stand by."

Finally, the penultimate action. Boyood's left leg throbbed. Albany thrust a letter at Edmund, mortally wounded on the ground. Insights and veiled regrets came from the dying man. Albany was informed that his wife, Regan, was dead and that Goneril had poisoned herself. The bodies were brought on stage. Susan Lee looked convincingly dead to Boyood, except for the slightly perceptible pulse in her neck. At Albany's command, the dying Edmund was carried away. Lear entered, carrying the dead Cordelia, followed by Edgar and the others. The King's sorrow was overwhelming. Lear laid his youngest daughter on the ground and lamented her tenderly, then died himself. It was left to Albany to sum up the tragedy in a single, memorable quatrain:

The weight of this sad time we must obey;
Speak what we feel, not what we ought to say.
The oldest hath borne most: we that are young
Shall never live so much nor live so long.

The surviving characters departed. The stage lights darkened. The applause began, the cue for the entire cast, beginning with the extras, to take bows. Although this had been rehearsed, Boyood was suddenly apprehensive.

As the extras came out on stage, Walking Cloud looked closely. There were no limps, no favored gaits or strained expressions. The pecking order of Equity actors took bows. Finally, it was Gainswell's turn. He basked in what became a standing ovation. He seemed surprised and motioned his fellow cast members forward. Through it all, Walking Cloud looked carefully, but saw nothing significant. He turned to Jenny and Alsted.

"Can you both wait in the lobby? It shouldn't be too long."

"Sure," agreed Jenny. "We'll wait."

Chapter Seventeen

Where Is He?

Boyood intended to go to his dressing room downstairs, but remembered that Susan Lee wanted to speak to him. It had to do with the absent Willard, he was sure. Could it wait? As he walked into the offstage hallway behind Mark Tell, he saw detectives and uniformed officers starting to usher people—all the cast members!—to the right and down the hall. Now Pingally and Clive Garden appeared and began speaking earnestly to the detectives. Boyood froze. Others went past them, only to be stopped by the cops who were joined by a darker-complexioned man whom Boyood recognized instantly.

"Oh, shit, it's Walking Cloud!" muttered Susan Lee. "What's he up to now?"

Sharon Morley approached. Boyood realized they might be noticed if they stood there much longer.

"I'm not sure," he said. He realized Walking Cloud had ordered a lockdown of the backstage area.

"Come on, Susie, let's just get this over with," urged Sharon Morley.

They saw Walking Cloud conversing with several people, including Clive Garden, who was speaking intensely.

"Look, we'll have the meeting in Rehearsal Room B down the hall, Lieutenant, as soon as everyone changes into street clothes. Is that acceptable?"

"We need everyone there who's involved with this production, Mr. Garden," Walking Cloud said. "No exceptions."

"And that's what you'll get. Just allow them to change out of costume. Your people are already guarding the exits."

The word was passed to gather in Rehearsal Room B. No one was supposed to be able to leave or enter, but now Walking Cloud saw Mike Quinn and his wife come through.

"Lieutenant, you remember my wife, Felicia?"

Walking Cloud acknowledged her politely, but focused on Quinn.

"Pandora Killer is somewhere in the building, but we couldn't spot him on stage. Not for sure, anyway. We have at least one possible."

Quinn's expression showed that he expected good things to happen.

"You saved the taxpayers considerable expense by taking out those hit men this afternoon, Lieutenant. Don't worry about the art lover crowd. We'd better get out of your way and let you proceed."

"No, stick around, Mike. We'd like to make this arrest as seamless as possible. Then you'll have your defendant."

"Who's that talking with Walking Cloud?" wondered Susan Lee. "He looks familiar."

"Mike Quinn," said Sharon Morley with disgust. "The local county attorney. I saw him on t.v. the other night. He's also running for governor. A showboat!"

"Oh, really?" She looked at both Sharon Morley and Boyood. "Come on, let's go the other way downstairs. Back around the stage."

Walking Cloud caught a flicker of movement when three figures retreated from the other side of the stage doorway. Other actors and theater personnel had been going past them into the hallway. Rails also saw them.

"Looks like they got other ideas, Lieutenant."

Walking Cloud turned to Garden.

"Who were the two cast members with Susan Lee over there, Mr. Garden? They turned around rather than come through here."

Garden lifted his eyebrows and shrugged.

"I didn't see them, Lieutenant. Look, I mean no offense, but there *are* some people who just don't like the idea of police invading a theater, especially during a performance. Don't you understand why?"

Garden's manner and voice were civil, but he was exasperated.

"We have a job to do, Mr. Garden," said Walking Cloud neutrally. "I'm sorry, but you know why we're here." He turned to Mygosh and Rails. "Find out where they're going and—'"

"Wait, Lieutenant," interrupted Garden. "Please. They're *my* cast members. *I'll* find out where they're going. *May* I?"

Instinctively, Walking Cloud was wary of advice from interested parties in murder investigations, but also knew the delicacy involved.

"Go ahead, Mr. Garden, but Sergeant Mygosh and Detective Rails will go with you. Tell your actors to be up in Rehearsal Room B in seventeen minutes and not to be late."

Garden frowned, but made no further complaint.

Boyood followed the two women past the moving backstage set. The stage curtain, now closed, had not obscured the thrust stage from the audience. The curtain was no more than ten yards on the right. Boyood was excited. Less than an hour earlier, neither of these Equity actresses would have spoken to him beyond *obligato*, the peremptory gesture. Now here he was moving with them.

"Arthur," declared Susan Lee as they descended the stairwell, "let's trade phone numbers in my dressing room. We can't talk in this building, obviously."

"Fine," Boyood replied. As soon as they stepped into the hallway, they found the same cops he'd spoken to earlier in the opposite stairwell. He remembered they had asked about Susan Lee's dressing room.

"Got it," said the female cop into her phone. "We just found her, Lieutenant."

"Miss Lee?" said the male cop.

"Yes, I'm Susan Lee," replied the actress with an unmistakable glare. "What do you want?"

"There's a meeting of all personnel involved with the *King Lear* production in fifteen minutes up in Rehearsal Room B. Lieutenant Walking Cloud asked us to tell you."

Susan Lee looked puzzled, although Boyood had expected as much. Sharon Morley was poker-faced.

"Thank you," Susan Lee answered. "We'll be there. Now, if you please—"

The detectives went on down the hallway, although Boyood knew they would stay in the vicinity.

When the cops were nearly out of earshot, Susan Lee said in a near-whisper, "Arthur, wait, I'll walk you down to your dressing room. You're down there, right?"

"Yes."

Just as they were about to go toward Boyood's dressing room, the blue stairwell door behind them opened.

"Susan!" exclaimed Clive Garden, flanked by two male detectives Boyood recognized. "Where are you going? There's a meeting upstairs—"

"In Rehearsal Room B," she said wearily. "I know. I'll be there, Clive. I just need to talk to Arthur for a few seconds. Okay?"

"Of course," said Garden, "but you have to change out of costume first. Please hurry."

Sharon Morley retreated into the next dressing room and shut the door. Garden and the two male detectives huddled near the blue stairwell door. Susan Lee and Boyood went down the hallway, aware of the other detectives down at the other end. She handed him her cell phone and asked for his. They'd trade phone numbers that way.

"Arthur, as soon as we get out of here, call me," she said in a very low voice. "Keep calling until you get me. Understand?"

"You're going home?"

"Yeah, I guess so."

"Okay."

Boyood opened his dressing-room door to discover Tom and the others, including two stagehands, abuzz about the cops and the impending meeting upstairs.

"Arthur, where have you been?" wondered Tom. "You know about the meeting in a few minutes, don't you?"

Boyood said Yes, then slipped as unobtrusively as he could over to his corner. He carefully removed his outer top, not wanting to reveal his weapon.

Walking Cloud listened to his earpiece as Mygosh explained what had taken place. Susan Lee was now in her dressing room. Who were the two cast members with her, by the way? Sharon Morley, who played Goneril, and an unidentified male extra she was seen speaking to in low, inaudible voice down the hallway. Susan Lee probably had good reason to have a confidante among the other cast members. But an extra? Garden now returned with Mygosh and Rails.

"Now what, Lieutenant?" the director asked.

Walking Cloud remembered that Jenny Schell and Alsted were waiting in the lobby. He sent Rails to fetch them.

"What happens now is when everybody gets in that room and I'll take it from there. Okay, Mr. Garden?"

Garden had a look of resignation.

"Alright, but most of these people are very tired, Lieutenant. This is a difficult and strenuous play to do every night. I hope you won't take up much of their time. They all need to go home and get a good night's sleep."

"I understand that."

He then introduced Garden to the Hennepin County Attorney and his wife. Garden looked even more worried. The cast members, among others, began appearing in the hallway and were directed to Rehearsal Room B. Mygosh checked off their names at the door.

When Jenny Schell and Alsted came backstage, Walking Cloud said merely that he'd like her to look among the actors for anyone who might, with sufficient make-up, resemble the olive-complexioned woman.

"Also," he told them, "be alert for a limp, the slightest listing of the left leg."

Now two police photographers arrived, a suggestion of Detective Winchell.

Boyood knew Walking Cloud would try to trick him into making a mistake, even the smallest one. When Tom's attention was elsewhere, Boyood checked the internal lift taped to his bare left heel. Over his feet he pulled on black socks and then the street shoes he always wore to the theater. His .44 magnum pistol was strapped tightly on his left side under his armpit. A couple spare clips were zipped into a large inside pocket of his floppy jacket. All this he managed in the dressing room while the others were diverted with gossip and silly jokes. He also knew that if he could escape Walking Cloud's detection in Rehearsal Room B, it would be because Frances needed to go out, be on her own, and maybe settle a score or two. He also had to call Susan Lee, a pretty girl. Now he was ready to go upstairs.

"Hey, Arthur, how're you and Susan Lee gettin' along?" Tom effused impishly.

"Why do you ask?" Boyood parried.

"Jus' checkin', man!" guffawed Tom, the stagehands in near-laughter. "I think she likes you, Arthur! The question is, what will she *do* for yuh?"

Boyood realized he hated Tom and all his dilettantish foppery.

"You might think of better things to talk about, Tom. But if you can't, just leave me out of it. Okay?"

His gaze met Tom's, and the latter seemed to relent, perhaps disappointed that he hadn't sufficiently provoked Boyood.

"Uh, sure, Arthur. Sure."

With that, Boyood left the room, taking care not to slam the door. Then he heard the unmistakable sounds of high-pitched laughter. Ridicule, he reminded himself again, was something he could not abide. But getting back at Tom was not his immediate concern.

Walking Cloud was aware that Quinn wanted to be seen by the media in a favorable light. Quinn had appeared with his wife in the midst of a police dragnet for a psychopathic killer of resourceful means. After the perp was arrested, Quinn could present himself to the public as a gubernatorial candidate tough on crime, no holds barred. Walking Cloud waited with his cops and with the Quinns as the various theater personnel went down the hall. When Boyood appeared at the doorway, no one seemed to take any special notice.

"Your name, sir?" asked Mygosh.

"Boyood, Arthur. I'm an extra."

"Thank you. Please take a seat. It shouldn't be too long."

Boyood found a chair in the back of the room and sat down. He watched the police photographer set up a camera on a tripod with a white sheet background. Now a disconcerted Gainswell appeared. The actor stared at the detective with the clipboard.

"What is this?" Gainswell was heard to say.

"Your name, sir?" said Mygosh blandly. "I need to know your name so I can check you off."

Suddenly Garden came up behind Gainswell, looking worried.

"Are we all under arrest—or what?" wondered Gainswell loudly.

"No, sir," replied Mygosh. "No one's under arrest yet."

"*No*? No one's under arrest? Then why are the police here in such numbers? Why is a *police photographer* here? What—"

"*Please*, Richard!" implored Garden. "We have to cooperate with them. They say a serial killer is loose somewhere in the theater complex."

By now, most of the cast and crew, except for the technical people still working behind the stage, had come to the room. In the hallway, Walking Cloud heard the voices of Gainswell and Garden. He knew if someone proved disruptive, there was little they could do to force cooperation. The lockdown was still in effect.

"I don't care, Clive," retorted Gainswell. "I'm not about to be photographed by the police, at least not willingly. Unless I'm under arrest! *Am* I?"

"No, sir, no one is, as I just told you," said Mygosh. "You're Richard Gainswell? Just take a seat."

"Come on, Richard," urged Garden. "Let's do as he says."

Boyood watched as a surly Gainswell was coaxed to a chair. Now at the doorway appeared a serene but alert-looking Susan Lee in fashionable street clothes, followed by Sharon Morley. Both actresses spoke briefly with Mygosh and sat down next to Gainswell, who was whispering intensely with Garden.

As he surveyed the room, Boyood saw a pert-faced little brunette sitting with a tweedy-faced, bespectacled man with a mustache. Then he heard the loud whisperings of Gainswell. Everyone else had submitted with varying degrees of meekness. It was true that Gainswell's role was the most demanding. So his irritation was understandable, more than just Equity hauteur.

Jenny cautiously looked around the room. She and Alsted were in the far back corner. She tired to remember details of the olive-complexioned woman. What of her colors, her clothes? Jenny thought she couldn't remember, but the impressions were a kind of mauve mixed with yellow and green and brown. Was she wearing a hat? Jenny couldn't remember. She scanned the myriad gathering of faces again. Several young men came into the room. Jenny guessed they were extras or stagehands. None resembled the size of the olive-complexioned woman, but then with make-up, padding, coloring here and there, could it be possible? No one in this room seemed to be.

Tom sat down in front of Boyood, two seats up. A perfect aim, Boyood thought. Now Walking Cloud's profile filled the doorway. He was impressive-looking, but hardly smart enough to capture Frances or Pandora Killer. In fact, Pandora Killer had once smacked him to the floor with a mop handle.

"Good evening. I'm Lieutenant Walking Cloud of the Minneapolis Police, homicide division. We have strong evidence that a triple murderer is and has been in this theater tonight—"

Suddenly it was dark! A power failure could not have been more detrimental from the police perspective. Boyood remembered exactly where Tom was sitting. It was tempting.

"Everyone remain where you are!" Walking Cloud commanded.

"*Shit!*" came a voice recognizable as Gainswell's. "*Why* do we have to stay here, Lieutenant? I understand we're not under arrest. I'd like to *leave now!*"

"Stay where you are, Mr. Gainswell," shouted Walking Cloud, "or you'll be arrested for interfering in police business."

"For exercising my rights as a citizen? *Bullshit*, Lieutenant! I'm leaving right *now*! I encourage everyone else to leave *now, too!*"

A door opened. Someone near the front lit a match. Someone, then two or three more, moved toward the door. The match went out. Then a slight sound Walking Cloud knew instantly was a pistol with a silencer. One shot. Something fell to the floor. A woman's scream. A man shouted "Stay calm, everyone!" Two or three more people moved toward the door. His weapon drawn, Walking Cloud realized that several people had left the room.

"*Get down, everyone!*" he shouted. "*Get down*! Someone has a *gun* with a *silencer!*"

Another scream. Someone with a flashlight entered the room. It was a uniformed officer, followed by another, both with weapons drawn. After what had seemed an eternity, though it had been less than five minutes, a generator in a distant room groaned—and the lights were back on! Another scream—it was from Felicia Quinn—at the revealed sight of a dead body with a bullet wound in the temple. In the corner near the door, Mygosh was getting off the floor, his nose and lips bleeding. Walking Cloud ordered the two uniformed officers to look for escaping theater personnel. In fact, about a third of the room, including Gainswell, Garden, and Susan Lee, had fled.

Now they were looking for a quadruple murderer. A frightened young man, a stagehand, by the name of Will Schneider identified the fresh corpse as Tom Egglesman, an extra. Who might have shot him, and why? asked Walking Cloud. Schneider looked even more frightened and said he had no idea.

Mygosh recovered his clipboard. Names were checked off again. Uniformed police and detectives seemed to swarm into the room. The new crime scene was chaotic, at first. Gradually, the Lieutenant was able to pare matters down. Seven actors, three actresses, two male extras and the director were gone, bolted in the dark, all but one unaware that a murder had taken place as they fled. Gainswell's hysterics exacerbated an already tense situation and the power failure colluded with someone's rage at Tom Egglesman. What had the dead man done to provoke his own death? Someone must know something. Will Schneider seemed scared when Walking Cloud questioned him briefly. Schneider asked to use the bathroom. Walking Cloud told him to return immediately and nodded at Rails to make sure he did.

Quinn and his wife approached the Lieutenant.

"Did either of you see anything when the lights were off?" Walking Cloud asked, realizing they, like everyone else, wanted to leave.

"I'm afraid not," said Quinn without his usual self-puffery.

"I didn't, either," said Felicia Quinn, looking shaken and nervous.

"Anyone who might have done this? Did you see—"

"No, nothing," reiterated Quinn, grasping his wife around the shoulders. "You know, Lieutenant, what I regret when I see something like this is that there's no death penalty in this state."

"My god, I can't believe this," said Jenny Schell as a blue sheet was placed over the dead man.

"*Jesus*! I didn't see anything or anyone when it happened, Lieutenant," said Alsted. "Did you, Jenny?"

Jenny wasn't so sure she hadn't seen anything. She had looked at every face that entered the room, some more memorable than others. She had tried to place the veneer of the olive-complexioned woman on each face. A pair of faces flitted before her again. One was indeed a woman, an older woman whom she now saw standing a few feet away, looking speechless and horrified. The other face, she thought, was of a man in his thirties, slightly balding, slender. But he had no limp. In fact, he seemed to float as he walked and looked very calm, as if a violent thought had never possessed him. So at first she dismissed him as a possible. Gainswell was now gone, as were others, including the Asian actress who'd sung at the Loring the night before.

"Ms. Schell?" asked the Lieutenant. "Did you hear me?"

"Oh, I'm sorry," she said.

"Did you see or notice anything before or after the lights went out?"

The face of the calm-looking man in his thirties seemed a remote possibility, but where had he been sitting? Why was he gone?

"There was one person," she said slowly.

Chapter Eighteen

Get Him!

Gainswell was furious and clever, observed Boyood. Susan Lee, Sharon Morley, Mark Tell and several others, including a dithery Clive Garden, had snuck out the Stage Door exit. No police guards were there, as Gainswell predicted. The power failure had apparently confused them. Yet police officers were roaming around outside, some talking to each other casually, oblivious of what had just happened in Rehearsal Room B. Squad cars with twirling red lights were parked here and there, although no police cordon had been set up.

"Arthur, call me as soon as you can," Susan Lee repeated as Gainswell unlocked the door of his convertible for her and Sharon Morley.

"I will," said Boyood.

He was elated. Slipping through Walking Cloud's trap had been a breeze, thanks to Gainswell's histrionics and the power failure. It was sheer impulse that he had risen to join Gainswell's call to leave—and then in the pure dark, surrounded by a scream, he submitted to the delightful impulse to kill Tom, pumping one bullet into his head. A thump, more like a tick, and he knew he'd hit his mark. Then he saw Gainswell's profile moving toward the detective who might try to block their leaving. Boyood stepped around Gainswell and struck the cop in the forehead with the butt of his .44 magnum, then chopping him in the face as he fell. Boyood was proud of his physical prowess, solving a problem so quickly.

"Which one was he, Ms. Schell?"

Jenny remembered his face.

"He was—about thirty-four—I'd guess. Trim. Average male height, I think. Receding hair. Kind of a soft face. He sat—down—right over there. I think he did, anyway."

She pointed to the back of the room.

"Anyone here know who she's talking about?" Walking Cloud asked those left in the room. Half now were police officers. "Is there a group photo of the cast anywhere?"

Pingally said he had one in his office. Minutes later, Jenny was scanning a cast photo in which the actors were facing the camera. All but one, that is. She studied each face. Then she frowned.

"I don't see him here. At least if he is, I don't recognize him."

"Then he's missing from the cast photo?" wondered Mygosh. "Or is he a tech person, not in the cast?"

Pingally shrugged. "I don't know. Clive Garden would know, of course. But he's not here, is he?"

"Is the stagehand here who identified this victim?" Walking Cloud asked. "Will Schneider?"

"Uh, huh," said Rails, who motioned Schneider from across the room. Walking Cloud showed him the cast photograph.

"Mr. Schneider, this lady has a description of a possible suspect in this death. Please listen to her."

Schneider nodded gravely. His thin face shook a little bit as Jenny spoke, perspiration on his forehead. His blue eyes were aghast, as if he knew the person she was describing. In short, congruent sentences, Jenny drew a picture of the trim, slightly balding man in his thirties. Then she took the group photograph from Walking Cloud's fingers.

"He's not in this picture. At least I don't see him here. Do you?"

Schneider shook his head as he looked at the photograph.

"I don't know why he's not there," he said, pausing. "I'm sure it's—Arthur Boyood. He's an Extra. A carpenter, too. He's also worked with us—I mean, the stagehands—although since he got his Extra part in this production, it's been—well, he's behaved as if he's too good for us. He and Tom didn't get along very well."

"Tom?"

"Tom Egglesman," said Schneider, gesturing at the corpse under the blue sheet as a medic crew entered the room with a body bag.

"Does this Boyood have one leg shorter than the other—the left leg?" asked Rails.

"Not—not that I ever noticed," replied Schneider. "But that doesn't mean he doesn't."

Pingally reported that Boyood had a street address on his personnel form. His phone was not listed. But Pingally was reluctant to give out the address.

"This is a murder suspect, quite possibly," Walking Cloud told him.

"I don't make the rules, Lieutenant."

Walking Cloud glared at him. "Do you want it known that you on behalf of the Guthrie have been uncooperative after murder right here in the theater premises?"

Pingally looked confused and frightened. His shoulders sagged, and then he handed the sheet with Boyood's address to the Lieutenant.

"Where is Susan Lee staying?" Walking Cloud pressed further. "Do you have her cell number? She's *not* a suspect, but I need to talk with her."

Pingally looked up the information and wrote it down. Walking Cloud then tried her number but she didn't answer. He left a voice mail message: "Ms. Lee, this is Lieutenant Walking Cloud. Call me back immediately when you get this message!"

"You know about Willard, don't you, Arthur?"

"No, what happened to him? I was expecting to see him."

"He's dead! The police killed him in a shoot-out at the Minneapolis Art Institute this afternoon after listening to him on a wiretap. He was talking about killing someone for money."

"Jesus—"

"Willard wasn't his real name, Arthur. He had a Hispanic name. Roberto Durangelo. He was a *monster*! I knew him in Chicago. He was a professional *killer*! He told me you were his friend, but I'll bet you didn't know that about him, did you?"

A pause. Boyood did know that, but he didn't care.

"No, I didn't. I'm—shocked. He's really *dead*?"

"Yes, he's dead! Thank God. He was an evil man, Arthur! The things he'd do to women, make them do, were *disgusting*."

Suddenly, the sound of her voice began to grate. He wanted her to shut up.

"So what happens now?" he asked in an almost frivolous turn of mood. "You think Walking Cloud will come looking for you 'cause we all left?"

"I don't know. He seems pretty determined to catch his bad guy. Richard's just down the hall from me here. I heard him say he was going to bed. Long day."

"And you? What are you going to do now?"

"I'm wide awake! I should be tired, but I'm not."

Minutes later, Susan Lee left the building where she and the other out-of-town actors were staying. She had readily agreed to Boyood's invitation to meet for a drink. But where? he wondered. The Loring Pasta Bar in Dinkytown, she replied. A minute after she left in her car, two police vehicles arrived at the door of her building. Walking Cloud, Mygosh, Rails and Winchell were accompanied by Pingally, who was also staying there and had a key. In the hallway, they encountered Gainswell, who was tending his laundry.

"Lieutenant Walking Cloud!" the actor exclaimed wearily.

"Mr. Gainswell," said the Lieutenant, "you disobeyed a lawful police order back there and I have a good mind to arrest you. But I'll settle for less. Where is Susan Lee's apartment?"

Gainswell looked too tired to argue.

"At the end of the hall on the left," he said. "One-oh-five. But she's not there. She went out, I think. She asked me and a couple other people to go with her, but I said No. Mark Tell and Sharon may have gone with her."

"Where did she go? Did she say?"

"The Loring Pasta Bar. I think it's in Dinkytown—near the University? Said she was meeting Arthur what's-his-face there. He's an extra—"

"Yes, we know!" said Walking Cloud.

"Pandora Killer," said Rails. "Fits the profile, Lieutenant. We might check on Boyood first. You got his address, right. It's 1900 Lincoln, the third floor, apartment 6."

"How soon did she say she was meeting him at the Loring?" Walking Cloud asked Gainswell.

"Something about midnight, I think."

Walking Cloud looked at his watch. "It's eleven-twenty."

Boyood told Susan Lee, a pretty girl, that he'd dress up, maybe even wear a disguise. She giggled, but said to come as he was. There wasn't that much time left, anyway. But then Boyood realized that Frances might not want to "parade" at the Loring Pasta Bar. He shaved again, washed up a bit, changed clothes, donned a new wig he'd recently purchased and put an earring on his left earlobe. He left his building and walked down the street to wait for the #6 bus taking him to Dinkytown across the river. The night was electric with possibility. He had a date, if a short date, with an Equity actress, a pretty girl who had no idea who he really was or his true connection to Willard. Now he heard a siren. Two police cars interrupted the traffic flow on Hennepin at Vineland and came across from Oak Grove Street. Then an unmarked car sped through with a silent red light and went south up the hill. Boyood recognized Walking Cloud in the front seat. He smiled at the circling directions the cops must be going in trying to find him.

Rails was driving. Mygosh, Winchell and Peterson were in the back seat.

"1900 Lincoln," said Mygosh, looking at a Hudson street map. "That's an East-West street coming up next, Bill. Turn right."

"Gotcha," said Rails, turning right at Lincoln as the two marked squad cars followed.

At 1900 Lincoln, they found an older, three-story building on the corner. A light was on in the third-floor unit. Sergeant Delvin Wilson and Quinn got out of one of the squad cars.

"Find out where the other exits are from the third floor," Walking Cloud ordered. "We want him alive, Delvin."

"Right-o!" said Wilson.

The front entrance was locked. A knock on the door brought no response, at first. The landlady was suspicious. Her white hair seemed to stiffen when Walking Cloud displayed his shield i.d.

"No, I don't know whether he's home or not," she said. "I don't keep track of my tenants. He's quiet, is all I care about. And he pays rent on time. What else he does isn't my concern."

She produced a key ring.

"Don't you have to show me something—like a search warrant?"

"Here you go!" said Winchell, who handed her a folded piece of paper. "The judge issued it this evening. I filled in your address. It's legit."

The woman looked at the search warrant with a frown.

"All right, I'll let you in. This way."

Boyood's apartment was rectangular, neatly kept and roomy. The detectives all wore plastic gloves. So did Quinn. Walking Cloud noted the locks on an old trunk and a clothes cabinet.

"You have your lock-pick?" Walking Cloud asked Rails.

When the wardrobe and trunk locks were opened, the contents were surprising.

"My, my, my!" exclaimed Mygosh, holding up a hanger with a red dress. "This guy's a queen, looks like!"

Walking Cloud examined a blond wig, then a reddish brown one. More digging around and a large paper bag was discovered. Inside were plastic gloves. Winchell handed them to the Lieutenant.

"Amazing stuff here," said Walking Cloud, turning to Quinn. "See this, Mike? The reason no prints have been found at any of these murders. This guy's very thorough. Bill, get the lab in here to dust this place. Set up a perimeter outside in case we miss him at the Loring Pasta Bar."

The detectives scanned the posters and pictures on the wall. Rails found a photograph showing a homely, slightly balding man in his thirties with an older man and a sad-faced woman in her fifties standing in front of a wooded area. On the back of the photo, the words were in thick blue script:

Arthur Boyood, Margaret Boyood and Wm Boyood Spring, 2006

"Here's our guy!" said Walking Cloud. "Picture's a while back, but it's *him*. Everyone, take a good long look at the guy on the left. Doesn't look much like the perp at the hospital."

Walking Cloud remembered the fake orderly in the hallway as he swung the mop handle, then as he pushed the wheelchair with the dummy, and as he stopped traffic and commandeered a vehicle.

"Lieutenant, look-a here," said Mygosh, leaning over an open plastic box. "Looks like a make-up kit. Colored tints. Creams. Eyelash pencils."

"Yeah, get the lab to compare 'em with the substance found on those two female victims, Joshua. What about shoes? Find any shoes?"

Winchell found a pair of black shoes under the bed. The left one was elevated in the heel.

"See if there're any more pairs," said Walking Cloud, checking his watch. "Alright, bag 'em up. Make an inventory of what you take out of here. It's 11:45. Let's get to the Loring Pasta Bar."

On the small stage were Dan Newton on accordion and others on guitar, bass fiddle and drums. Old style ballads were the fête of the evening, the room dimly lit by bowl candles. People were dancing slowly in an area on the side of the large room's dining area. Walking Cloud had instructed his officers to create as little disturbance as possible.

Boyood had anticipated the police. He spotted Susan Lee sitting with Mark Tell and Sharon Morley at a front table. As she looked up, Susan Lee stared in disbelief and then smiled, her mouth open and beautiful white teeth projecting sex in Boyood's starved eyes. A pretty girl she certainly was!

"Arthur!" she gasped. "My god! You do look different! What—"

"A new look is all," he answered, realizing Tell and Sharon Morley were staring at him.

"Changes your appearance completely," observed Tell.

"Shall we dance?" he asked Susan Lee.

She smiled, this time a warm, incredulous glow.

They joined the small crowd of dancers. Gradually, he moved her to the side near the entrance of the larger room. She was soft to the touch and responsive to his lead. He kept alert, wondering if the police were on to him for killing Tom, or would they wander continuously in a daze? He saw the interested stares of Tell and Sharon Morley. They were talking amusedly.

"You're a very good dancer, Susan," he heard himself say.

"Of course I am. Dance was part of my training. You're not so bad yourself. In fact—"

Her sentence was cut off by the end of the song and spontaneous applause. She seemed happy. He noticed a flicker in her expression as she looked at him.

"What?" he asked.

"Don't look now, but I just saw Walking Cloud and his pals come up to the bar over there. Oh God, he's everywhere! *What* does he want?"

"No telling," said Boyood. At the front door, he saw the detectives he first encountered in the theater stairwell. While they appeared to have seen Susan Lee, they did not focus on him.

"Would you like to go into the bar?" he asked.

"Sure."

They threaded through people at the doorway. Winchell and Peterson approached the outer edge of the dance floor.

Walking Cloud noticed Susan Lee, but her companion didn't resemble Boyood in the photograph. The actress was essential to finding Boyood. He nodded to Winchell and Peterson to keep watch on her. He spoke into his fist mike.

"Beth, Dick, follow her wherever she goes. She's gotta be the bait. Remember, we want Boyood alive."

"Roger, Lieutenant," came Winchell's voice in his ear.

Walking Cloud watched as Susan Lee and her dance partner made their way to the bar area in the next room. As he and Mygosh and Rails began to make their way around the bar, Walking Cloud felt a pull on his elbow. It was Quinn.

"Lieutenant, do you expect to find him in this zoo? It's unbelievable here!"

"You recognize anyone here from the Guthrie?" Walking Cloud answered. "Let me know if you do."

Quinn raised his eyebrows and said, "I just saw two people over there who were in that back room at the theater." He pointed toward the front tables.

Walking Cloud propelled the surprised Quinn in front of him to lead the way. Then he recognized two faces from the Guthrie, though he couldn't remember their names. Mark Tell and Sharon Morley looked up with resignation as he approached. Tell stood up and introduced himself and Sharon Morley.

"Where is Arthur Boyood?" Walking Cloud asked. "Have you seen him here tonight?"

Neither Tell nor Sharon Morley looked surprised by the question.

"Is that his last name?" said Tell. "I never knew. I think he just slipped into the other room with Susan. He's wearing a brown toupee. Looks completely different."

A puzzled look overcame Tell's features.

"You're not looking for him because he's your *killer?*"

"Stay here, Mister Tell," Walking Cloud said. "Neither of you leave this table. You never saw us here, if he comes back. Understand?"

The dining room was crowded. Walking Cloud spoke into his fist mike.

"The man who left the dance area with Susan Lee might be our perp, Beth and Dick. Where are they now?"

"We've lost sight of 'em!" came Winchell's frantic voice.

"Beth, you and Dick get into the bar! You hear me?"

"Roger, Lieutenant."

Drawing his weapon would incite a stampede. Walking Cloud spotted Winchell and Peterson at the edge of the bar. Winchell spoke into her fist mike.

"He's right here, Lieutenant! See him? He's standing at the bar facing us. Susan Lee's next to him sipping a drink."

As Winchell and Peterson drifted through the crowd, Walking Cloud took stock of the situation. Standing next to the actress, who suddenly looked up and stared directly at Walking Cloud, was a nondescript, trim man with a blue corduroy sports jacket, dark slacks and a brown toupee. He looked unusually normal, nothing out of the ordinary. Boyood saw Walking Cloud before Susan Lee nudged him. He had one hand on his piece and with the other put his glass of mineral water on the counter.

"Come with me, Susan," he said quietly. "*Now!*"

She looked at him in disbelief. He took her by the arm and they bolted back into the dining room leading across to the side exit. There were two or three people moving near a bathroom door, and two more figures waiting at the exit.

"*Arthur Boyood!*" came Walking Cloud's voice through a small bullhorn. "Put down your weapon and *surrender!* No harm will come to you!"

Boyood's weapon was drawn. Panic screams and shouting erupted. He looked again at the two figures at the exit. He'd seen them when he and Susan Lee were dancing. They had now pulled their weapons against him. He fired at their knees, striking them both. They went down, dropping their weapons.

"My god!" cried Susan Lee. "Arthur! What are you—"

"Shut up!" he barked. "Let's go!"

As they ran toward the side door, Boyood scooped up the weapons of both fallen detectives. When he saw Walking Cloud peer around the corner, Boyood fired one shot that missed. Clutching Susan Lee by the arm, he bolted out the door.

"*Where are you taking me?*" she yelled.

"*Shut up!*" he snapped.

Suddenly, Gainswell got out of the nearest parked car in front of the Shaung Cheng restaurant across the narrow alleyway.

"What the—" the actor exclaimed.

"Get *back* in your car, King Lear!" Boyood commanded. "Walking Cloud's on the warpath."

He shoved Gainswell back to his driver's door and told him to open it. A police car with swirling red lights and an unbearable siren came around the corner from University Avenue. Boyood fired one shot at the front tire, causing the vehicle to pitch on its left, swerve and smash into two parked cars a few spaces ahead of Gainswell's vehicle. Boyood turned again and fired at the Loring Pasta Bar side door where two figures, then a third, emerged. One of them fell to the sidewalk.

"*Hold your fire!*" shouted one of them. Boyood got in the back seat of Gainswell's convertible with the top up. Gainswell got behind the wheel. Susan Lee, frightened and gasping for breath, was also in the front seat.

"*Drive! Go up to Hennepin and across the river to downtown!*" shouted Boyood as Gainswell inserted the ignition key.

They drove past the smashed police car and the two other vehicles in flames. Then an explosion shot up, engulfing the three machines in flames in front of the old Varsity movie theater.

"My god!" said Gainswell incredulously, turning left on Hennepin. "So *you're* the one they've been looking for! You really *are* a killer!"

"*Shut up, King Lear!*" shouted Boyood, putting his weapon to the back of Gainswell's head. "I *don't* need your superior Equity attitude. *Stuff it!*"

"All right!" conceded the actor.

"Go straight across the bridge!" Boyood ordered. Gainswell nodded.

"Surprised to see you come to the Loring," Boyood sneered. "*Wait!* Keep going through downtown all the way to Thirteenth. Ya hear me, *King Lear!*"

"I heard you," replied Gainswell with steady nerves. "Where can you go, Arthur? What good are we to you as hostages? Tell me, did you really kill all those people, rape those women?"

"Shut *up,* Lear!" shouted an enraged Boyood. "Just keep driving and *shut up!*"

"My name isn't Lear, by the way," rejoined Gainswell mildly. "It's Richard. Remember? And in reply to what you said before, I was curious about whether you really might be the mad killer they were looking for. It seemed a more compelling story that staying put and doing my laundry. I don't know why."

"A lot of highfalutin Equity *bullshit!*" snarled Boyood.

Rails had been hit in the groin. He was on the sidewalk. Winchell and Peterson were felled by bullet wounds in the knees, enough to keep them out of action for a good while. Walking Cloud waited till the first ambulance arrived. The attendants rushed out and bent over Rails. Sergeant Williams got out of a squad car with three other uniformed cops. Another ambulance sped up behind the one into which Rails was being loaded. A third ambulance, followed by a fire truck, approached the burning vehicles.

"Two officers burning up alive there!" shouted a young cop running from the scene.

Another of Pandora Killer's signature marks: cripple if you can't kill for sure. This was the second time he'd shot the tires of a squad car, causing it to smash, ignite, and kill the cops inside.

"Come on!" he said to Mygosh and Quinn. They ran around the corner to his car. Mygosh took the wheel. Walking Cloud called in an all-points alert, describing Gainswell's car, a green convertible with the white top up and New York license plates.

"Where to, Ben?" wondered Mygosh in a determined voice.

"I don't know. Go to Hennepin and downtown. They couldn't have gone very far."

They went through downtown all the way to Thirteenth. A coffeehouse was on the northeast corner. Inside, an older black woman was looking out the window. She rose immediately, waved both hands, and rushed out to the corner.

"See that woman, Joshua?" Walking Cloud said. "Let's see what she wants."

Mygosh turned right and pulled over.

"What can we do for you, ma'am?" he asked.

"You're the cops, aren't you?"

"You guessed it. Did you see a green convertible with a white top go by here in the last few minutes?"

"That's why I signaled you. I saw 'em! A guy in the back seat holdin' a gun to the head-a the driver. I seen it! They drove up, turned here on Thirteenth and went on down there and turned left. I came out and looked where they went. They all white folks."

"Thanks," said Mygosh, handing her a business card. "You better go inside now. If you see 'em again, call this number. Sergeant Mygosh. That's me. Or Lieutenant Walking Cloud, sitting next to me here. Take a look at him."

The woman looked at Walking Cloud, then for a second at Quinn in the back.

"Okay, I'll go back in. I'm Mrs. Preston. Lavonna Preston."

"Alright, Mrs. Preston. Be careful now."

Mygosh drove on.

"Good thing we had the red light on," he said.

"I ask again, Arthur. What good are we as hostages? The police know who you are. Your life is completely exposed now. The Guthrie won't take you back. You killed someone there. Remember?"

Boyood realized he was in a sudden tailspin, a deep depression. It was a sharp fall from the elixir of the past hour. Where could he go? His world was destroyed.

"Arthur, would you like to go somewhere and talk this over?" Gainswell suggested. "I mean, what's the point of driving around this time of night?"

"There was a coffeehouse back there," volunteered Susan Lee. "Right when we turned off Hennepin. How about that, Arthur?"

"Arthur, I'm going to turn left here and head back toward that coffeehouse," said Gainswell. "Is that okay?"

They were trying to weaken his resolve. What else could he do? Where would he go? He didn't have that much money and it would run out soon enough.

"Yeah, okay."

Gainswell turned left at Hennepin. Down at the end of the block on the left, as they got closer, Boyood saw the coffeehouse. *Espresso Royale*, read the sign. Gainswell turned right at Thirteenth and parked across the street.

"Don't trick me now," Boyood told him. "I don't like being tricked."

Susan Lee turned and looked at him.

"He wouldn't do that to you, Arthur. Richard is right. We should talk."

"Fine. Let's talk."

Boyood put the weapon in his coat pocket and followed Gainswell and Susan Lee into the coffeehouse. At first, Boyood did not see the furtive stares of the older black woman sitting near the side window. Fatigue now began to enter his body, his brain. His thought processes began to cloud. Depression had set into his brain. His medication was failing him now. He stopped at a side table near the wall, where he couldn't be seen, he thought, from the windows.

"Can I buy you a coffee, Arthur?" asked Gainswell.

"Yeah," Boyood replied. "Black."

Gainswell said something inaudible to Susan Lee, who murmured back. She turned to sit down across from where Boyood was standing. They sat down next to a short wall. She looked at him a different way now, he realized.

He turned his attention to Gainswell, who was supposedly ordering coffee for them. But was he in fact telling the counter person to call the cops? No, perhaps he could trust Gainswell. In a matter of seconds, it seemed, things seemed okay. The young man behind the counter was pouring coffee and putting the cups on a tray. Gainswell pulled out his billfold. And in no time, the Equity actor was carrying a tray of steaming coffee cups to their table. Like the waiter he might have been if his life had been as miserable as Boyood's.

"Here's your black coffee, Arthur. A latté for Susan. A large espresso for me."

Directly behind Susan Lee, Boyood noticed, was an older black woman who looked now and then at a newspaper between glances at them. She was unimportant, he decided, despite her peekaboo stares.

"So, Arthur, let's talk about this," said Gainswell in a low voice after he sat down next to Susan Lee. "I'm not trying to pry. But we have to decide what to do. You read me?"

"I read you."

"The choice is yours, Arthur. *You've* got the gun in your pocket. We're not here because we want to be. I don't think you are, either. Are you?"

No, he wasn't, but he was too upset to speak. He wanted to be secret, masked in his intentions, in his other life, still viable in his future as an actor, even as an Equity actor! He knew he had talent. He shook his head at the question.

"Arthur," began Susan Lee in a quavering voice, "how—did you get started doing this? Killing people, I mean. Was it Willard? Was he—"

"Yes!" Boyood said abruptly, glaring at her. "How did he die? You said he died."

"In a shootout with Walking Cloud. They tried to arrest him after listening him talk about a murder-for-hire scheme. But he escaped and they chased him and trapped him in the Art Institute, where he took his own life. It was on the t.v. news. You didn't see it?"

"No. He killed himself? That explains why I didn't hear from him."

"What I don't understand," said Susan Lee, "is why you started—killing people. Didn't you realize it would come back to you, that you—"

Boyood put up his hand, as if to stop her, but she kept on.

"—that you would be the ultimate victim, Arthur, in addition to the people you—"

Then she stopped.

"My father taught me how to shoot, how to hunt," explained Boyood slowly. "He taught me survival skills. He was a Ranger in Vietnam and he knew about guns and stuff. But—"

"But what, Arthur?" pushed Gainswell softly.

"He didn't love me. When it really came down to it, he treated me like I was a *failure*. And my mother—she didn't care about me. They both resented me."

"Where are they now?" wondered Gainswell.

"He died last year. Heart attack. Working out at his health club. Sixty years old. My mother moved back to Duluth after that. She's living with her spinster sister, my aunt Georgia. She just left me here. I've got nobody now."

"You realize you can't run," said Gainswell. "You can't run from this. Nothing but more tragedy will happen if you try that. And—you don't want that, do you?"

"No, I—guess not."

Boyood looked transfixed at Gainswell. The actor had an irritating habit of being right too much of the time. Boyood had no arguments and no energy left to counter what he said.

"So your options aren't very many," said Gainswell.

Boyood put his hand to his forehead. He had a headache now. He was tired. Normally, he would have been in bed by now, tucked away in his attic apartment on Lincoln Avenue. When he looked again, past Gainswell and Susan Lee, he saw that the older black woman was gone.

Mygosh pulled his cell phone from his pocket.

"Sergeant Mygosh, homicide."

Mygosh listened for a few seconds, then turned to Walking Cloud.

"It's that old black gal we just talked to outside the coffeehouse. She says the perp's inside there with a man and a woman, talking and drinking coffee. She's now half a block north-a there on Hennepin calling on her cell phone. *God!*"

They turned around immediately. Walking Cloud ordered eight marked squad units to approach the coffeehouse from different directions but to keep half a block away. Two plainclothes officers from robbery, Sergeant Judy Abrams and Detective Tom Petrie, were ordered to meet Lavonna Preston half a block north of the coffeehouse on Hennepin.

"Roger, Lieutenant, we're about to talk to her now," came a female voice.

Walking Cloud saw an unmarked car with a dead red light on top pull over to talk to someone on the sidewalk.

"We see you, Judy," said Walking Cloud. "Put her in the back of your vehicle for safety until we have the perp in custody."

Walking Cloud glanced at Mygosh.

"You want this collar, Joshua?"

"I'd love it!"

Walking Cloud watched as Mygosh, with Abrams and Petrie, strolled ahead of him and entered the coffeehouse. He was parked across the street on Hennepin with a clear view of the perp and his two hostages. He handed an extra pair of binoculars to Quinn. The three detectives went to the counter. Boyood's back was to the front, so he didn't see them.

"Jesus Christ, this is cuttin' close," Quinn said. "What if there's—"

"Wait a minute, Mike! Let's see what the audio picks up."

Walking Cloud turned up the volume. The sound was from Mygosh's lapel mike. Suddenly, as if on cue, Susan Lee excused herself to go to the restroom. All the while, Gainswell kept talking low-key. Walking Cloud adjusted the reception as Abrams ordered three coffees.

"Arthur, why not consider quitting this?" Gainswell suggested. "Enough people have died! Their survivors, their loved ones, *their lives* have been changed forever. Why hurt more people?"

"Loved ones?" protested Boyood. "You know no one's ever loved *me*, Mister Equity Actor! You know that?"

Suddenly, Boyood's right hand came up empty on the table as he sipped his coffee. Mygosh made his move. He raced, virtually leaped, toward the perp with his weapon drawn.

"*Don't move!*" shouted Mygosh, his pistol right at the side of Boyood's head. "Now, *slowly*, stand up. Put your hands at the back of your head. *Now*, Mister!"

Boyood slowly stood up. Abrams and Petrie had their weapons trained on him. As Mygosh reached for his left hand, Boyood turned and grabbed his wrist, hitting him flush in the face and wresting his pistol away. He threw Mygosh flat against Abrams and Petrie, knocking them both down. He kicked Abrams's weapon out of her hand and grabbed her by the hair, punching her in the face with Mygosh's weapon.

"*Shit!*" blurted the Lieutenant. He gave orders for all cars in the area to converge and set up a perimeter at Thirteenth and

Hennepin. He and Quinn got out on the far side of their vehicle. He handed Quinn a pistol.

"Know how to use this?"

"You bet I do."

"Don't fire unless your life is threatened, Mike."

Walking Cloud took up his bullhorn as Boyood ushered a wide-eyed Gainswell out the front door, followed by Susan Lee, then Petrie and Abrams, their hands handcuffed behind them. Mygosh lay unconscious back inside the coffeehouse. Boyood had Abrams by the hair.

"*Release those people, Boyood!*" ordered Walking Cloud. "*Give it up now!* You can only *lose* in the end!"

"*Fuck you!*" Boyood shouted at Walking Cloud. "*Stay away or I'll kill 'em all! Get rid of the blockade you've set up!*"

Boyood forced his captives into Gainswell's car, got in the back, still holding Abrams by her hair. Abrams and Petrie were on the floor, doubled up, handcuffed back to back. Gainswell slowly drove away.

"Arthur, *please* don't kill us!" pleaded Susan Lee. "We haven't hurt you! We haven't harmed you in *any way!*"

"Be quiet, *pretty girl!*" Boyood thundered. "*Shut up!*"

"Where to, Arthur?" asked Gainswell, abject resignation in his voice.

Walking Cloud got back in his vehicle, motioning Quinn to stay put on the street. He drove right behind the green convertible, and suddenly swerved left. His passenger door window was down. When he got close, he fired his revolver twice, shattering the window and killing Boyood, who sprawled back on the rear seat. Walking Cloud rammed the convertible. A confused Gainswell pulled to a stop, his hands to the sides of his head.

Walking Cloud opened the driver's door, carefully helping Gainswell out of the vehicle. The actor was in shock, shaking violently. Susan Lee rushed out on the other side and put her arms around Gainswell. Blues and more detectives came up to the Lieutenant.

"Call the wagon!" he told one of them, a young robbery detective.

Then he unlocked the cuffs and helped Abrams and Petrie out of the back of the convertible. Boyood lay on the back seat, his eyes and mouth open. Plastic gloves on, the Lieutenant removed Mygosh's weapon from the perp's dead hand and the .44 magnum from the holster inside his jacket.

"It's over, folks," he told Abrams and Petrie, both of whom were speechless and breathing heavily out of their mouths as they stood in the street under police lights. Within bare minutes, t.v. reporters waited not far away at a police cordon. Quinn came up and gave the .38 pistol back to the Lieutenant.

"That was the most amazing thing I've ever seen!" said Quinn. "Pandora Killer is dead. *Finally*, after four days and nights! *You did it, Ben!* You and no one else! *Congratulations!*"

"No, that's not—correct, Mike. There are a number of people dead. They paid the ultimate price. We need to get Aietovsky somehow. Then we'll all be a lot safer. Our work doesn't end here."

"Right. Well, let's go talk to the press. They're waiting."

"No, you go ahead. Make the announcement yourself. I'm a cop. You're the politician. It's your show."

For once, Quinn was without words.

"Go on, you talk to 'em," said Walking Cloud. "Tell 'em the police department will have a statement tomorrow. Pandora Killer is dead. That's the important thing. I've got some things to finish up here. I don't have to talk to 'em. You do it. You don't need me for that."

The morgue wagon backed up to Gainswell's convertible. Quinn looked in the direction of news reporters shouting his name from the yellow police cordon. Walking Cloud watched the medics remove the body and place it in a dark plastic bag.

For a few seconds, Quinn felt sick. He didn't want to talk to the press. Not alone. Not this time. But he knew he was on his own. He drew in his breath. Words ran through his brain. Time to make a statement. The citizens needed to be reassured. And he was the county attorney.